BETROTHED #10

PENELOPE SKY

HARTWICK PUBLISHING

Hartwick Publishing

Truth

CONTENTS

ONE

HEATH

THE FIRST WEEK WAS A BLUR BECAUSE I PURPOSELY blocked it out.

I felt like shit—worse than shit.

At week two, I still felt like a bag of broken bones, but there was major improvement from the week before. I could get through the night without waking up in pain. I could walk without wincing. I could carry myself like a man, make myself a sandwich without relying on Catalina to do it for me.

But I still had a long road ahead of me.

I walked into the living room a few weeks after coming home and saw Balto sitting there, his elbows on his knees as he watched the TV.

"You just come and go as you please now?" I didn't walk at my usual pace, taking my time getting from one spot to the next, feeling the ache of my broken ribs on my right side. I made jokes to Catalina about the whole thing, but I've never been in so much pain...and I would never tell her.

Balto looked up at me, his eyes narrowed. "Now you know how it feels."

I opened the cabinet and grabbed the bottle of vodka.

"Catalina isn't here, is she?"

I poured it into a glass. "No. She's out."

"Just because she's not here doesn't mean you're going to get away with that."

I looked at him over my shoulder.

He nodded. "Put it back, Heath."

"Come on. One glass—"

"Put it back, or I'll tell her."

I rolled my eyes and did as he asked. "Fucking tattletale..." I shoved everything back into the cabinet and grabbed a glass of water instead. "I'd offer you something, but if I can't drink, neither can you."

"That's fine with me."

I lowered myself to the other couch, groaning with the movement.

"How do you feel?"

"Better." I rested my cheek against my curled knuckles, looking at the TV in front of me. I was used to being shirtless all the time, but since I looked so terrible, I tried to hide it from Catalina. My face was better, starting to resemble my old features. "So, how's the office?"

"You made Vox a blood traitor?" he asked.

"Oh yeah." I dragged my fingers across my jawline, feeling the shadow of hair because I hadn't shaved in weeks. My skin burned slightly at the touch. "Forgot about that."

"Why?"

"Because I've got a lot more on my mind—"

"No. Why did you mark him as a traitor?"

"Because he organized a coup with Damien."

Balto never told me how to run the Skull Kings or lead. He bowed out and let me have the reins without question. But judging by the expression on his face, he didn't agree with that at all. "You should have killed him, Heath. That's a killable offense."

"I know. But I'd just shot one of the guys...wasn't popular at the time. I thought that would redeem me—and it did."

Balto didn't agree. "He's going to keep coming after you—"

"The reason he's difficult is because he wants the throne for himself. Now that he can't possibly have that—ever—there's not much point anymore."

"Or he's going to kill you for taking away the one thing he actually cares about."

I shrugged. "Balto, it's done. Nothing we can do about it now."

He shook his head slightly as he rubbed his palms together.

"No one has figured out it's you and not me?"

"No."

"Wow. I'm not sure if that's flattering or insulting."

He watched the TV for a while. "Your ban on slavery is unpopular, even though it seems to be transitioning as well as it possibly could. But you stopped taking money from Damien, and they're starting to ask questions. Are you going to resume that?" He turned back to me.

"No."

His eyes narrowed again.

"I'm not sure where we stand right now, but I'm not going to undo all the work I did by pissing him off again."

"And how will you explain that to the men?"

"Why do I have to explain anything at all?" I snapped.

He rubbed his palms together again. "A good leader rules with respect, not fear."

"I'm not threatening them. I just don't need to explain this."

"Do they know about Catalina?"

"Only Steel does."

"Well, if they ever figure out you made all these changes because of a woman..." He bowed his head and looked at the floor. "That'll be bad news. They pull the throne out from underneath you."

"Not gonna happen. I've always kept Catalina a secret."

"But are you going to continue to be the Skull King?" Balto asked. "Now that you got what you want with her, how is that going to work?"

"It's going to work exactly the way it did before."

"But you were a secret before. Now this is real, right?"

I shrugged. "Honestly, she and I haven't talked about it, but yes, I assume so."

"Where is she?" He looked over his shoulder, as if she was standing right behind him.

"With Damien, actually."

He faced forward again and nodded. "I'm just saying...you can't have both."

"I don't see why not."

"Because your woman will always be in danger."

"Not if I never admit she exists."

He got that annoyed look on his face, the same look he'd worn since we were kids, like he was frustrated with my simplicity. "You'll see what I mean..."

"Not every relationship is the same, Balto. Your retirement was the right decision for you and Cassini. But Catalina and I are different."

He turned to me, his blue eyes still. "What if she asked you to step down?"

"Today? This very moment?"

"Just in general."

I hadn't really thought about it. Our future had been so hazy since the beginning. Even now, I wasn't entirely sure where we stood. She wouldn't have rescued me unless she wanted to be with me, but I wasn't sure if she'd changed her mind about marriage. "Depends."

"On?"

"If it was going to last forever, I guess I would."

That seemed to be the answer Balto wanted, so he dropped the conversation. "I'll keep this up as long as you need. Take your time getting better."

"I'll be as good as new in a couple weeks, so don't worry, it won't be long. I'm sure Cassini is worried sick."

He didn't answer.

"I appreciate you doing this for me." I didn't say sappy bullshit often, so a thank-you was all I could extend.

"I know you do." He turned his gaze back to me, playful. "Asshole."

I grinned. "You liked my note?"

"Who writes two sentences when they're about to die?" he asked incredulously.

I shrugged. "What? You expect me to write you a love letter?"

He snapped his fingers as if he'd realized something. "I just remembered you can't read or write—that makes sense."

I rolled my eyes at the taunt. "I'll get you for that...eventually."

"I'll believe it when I see it."

———

CATALINA WAS GONE for a long time.

So long, I almost called her.

But I suspected that conversation with her brother was intense, and the last thing she needed was my call making her phone light up and vibrate on the table while they tried to talk. Yeah, he was a dick for what he did to me, especially since I made it clear it was never a fair fight, but I didn't want to weaken her relationship with her brother.

I understood how important he was to her.

Because Balto was so important to me.

My relationship with my brother was a little different because we were both men, and also, twins. We shared a connection that was a step above typical sibling love because our brains were the same, our souls were the same. Looking at your brother and seeing yourself was a unique experience. Not too many people could say the same. We'd swapped places all our lives to either trick people or to get something we wanted. I was terrible at interviews, so when we were young, he helped me get my first job by interviewing in my place. I was better at math than he was, so I'd taken a test for him a couple times.

If I ever lost him...I would lose myself.

It was past ten when Catalina walked inside.

I rose from the couch and turned off the TV. "Hey, baby."

"Hey." She set her purse on the counter and immediately went for a bottle of wine. She poured a glass, her lipstick marking the cup. Her eyes were down, like she was trying to hide the puffiness of her cheeks, the redness in her eyes.

I came toward her slowly, wishing I could enjoy that wine with her, lick it off her, all kinds of things. With one hand on the kitchen island, I watched her, watched her try to hide her feelings from me. "Didn't go well?"

"It was just...a long conversation." She drank from her glass again, her eyes still averted.

I grabbed the glass by the stem and pulled it away. "Look at me."

She sighed like that was the last thing she wanted.

My fingers moved under her chin, and I lifted her gaze, forcing her to look at me. "Talk to me." My hand slid to her cheek so my thumb could feel her soft skin, move across the single freckle close to her nose.

She closed her eyes at my touch, turning into my hand so she could kiss my palm.

My thumb traced her bottom lip, getting so lost in her exquisite beauty that I forgot what we were talking about for a second. Instead of her tears being a turn-off, she looked more beautiful with wet eyes, puffy cheeks. There was something about her sadness that turned me on—even though I never wanted her to be sad.

"He said he wouldn't hurt you again..."

"That sounds like good news to me."

"Yeah...but I had to beg."

I'd love to have seen that, see her beg for me.

"He's disappointed in me. He's angry. But...at least it's over."

"It'll get better. Give it time."

She averted her gaze again.

"Baby."

She turned back to me, knowing I would force her if she didn't.

"Something else you aren't telling me?"

Her eyes shifted back and forth as she looked into mine, taking a long time to answer. "No. It was just a lot of arguing... It was exhausting. I don't really want to talk about it anymore."

"Alright." My hand slid to her neck, my fingers wrapping around her slender throat. "Hungry? I can make you something to eat?"

"I should be making you something to eat," she said with a light chuckle.

"Come on, I'm not that weak anymore." I dropped my hand from her neck and opened the fridge. "Balto brought this over. Cassini made it." I placed it on the counter and pulled off the lid. "Not as good as what you make me, but it's good enough."

She looked into the pan, seeing slices of chicken breast with wine sauce and mushrooms on a bed of fettuccine. She constantly controlled the calories that she pushed into her mouth, so she was always hungry, and when her eyes narrowed slightly on the pan, it was obvious she was hungry now. "Ugh, that looks way better than anything I make."

I grabbed a plate and shoveled the food onto the dish. "I disagree."

She gave me an incredulous look. "The best thing I can make is mac and cheese."

I put it in the microwave and leaned against the counter as I waited for it to be ready. "And it's damn good mac and cheese."

She rolled her eyes but did it playfully. "You're just saying that."

"When a woman cooks for a man, it's innately sexual, innately possessive. I will never like a woman's cooking more than yours, even if it is better, because you're my woman and she's not. So yes, I'd rather have your mac and cheese than eat someone else's Wagyu steak, alright?"

A soft smile came over her face. "That makes sense, actually."

The microwave beeped, and I pulled the dish out and set it on the counter. It was steaming hot, still fresh because Cassini must have made it earlier that afternoon. I placed a fork on top then watched her.

She spun the fork in her noodles. "You're just going to watch me?"

"I watch you all the time." I leaned against the counter, ignoring the pain of my ribs, the burn in my aching muscles. I missed being myself, standing tall, making jokes...just being me. And I liked that she was more herself again, finally dropping her guilt and relaxing around me. She always had her wall up, as if she didn't deserve to be with me after what she did. She did some bad things...I did some bad things. We were even as far as I was concerned.

"True." She took a bite, chewing the fettuccine, one cheek popping out because it was a lot for her small mouth.

I loved watching her no matter what she did, because she made everything sexy, even brushing her teeth. And anytime something was in her mouth, I imagined my dick replacing the object, and then it turned into a porno in my mind.

She continued to eat, taking breaks and drinking her wine. "You should sit down. You shouldn't be on your feet so much."

"I'm tired of sitting."

"I don't care what you're tired of." She turned bossy, flashing me her irritated look. "And it's late. You should be in bed."

"Ooh...I like it when you boss me around." No one else could do it, especially not as good as she could.

"Then why don't you listen?"

I shrugged. "Because then you keep doing it."

She grabbed her fork again. "You sound like a child."

"That's funny. Cassini says the same thing."

She raised her arm to slap me playfully but quickly lowered her hand when she stopped herself. "Just get in bed, alright?"

"Will you join me?"

"Why wouldn't I?"

"Wasn't sure if your conversation with Damien changed anything."

She turned back to her food. "No."

I had a hunch that she was lying, but I let it go. "Alright." I moved into her side and wrapped my arm around her waist, my face moving into her hairline. She smelled the way I remembered, like a beautiful summer day—fresh-cut grass, new flowers, sunshine. I kissed her skin, savoring the touch of her against me, treasuring this moment, because just weeks ago, I thought I would never see her again.

She stilled at my touch, affected by my kiss the way I was, like it brought her to life in the exact same way. She stopped eating, even stopped breathing. She subtly turned her cheek my way.

I pulled away and looked down into her face, seeing the single most beautiful woman in the world, the woman I would lay down my life for in a heartbeat, the woman I would sacrifice everything for...because there was nothing more important.

The connection we used to have was still there, as if everything that had just happened never happened at all. She looked at me the way she used to, like I was the tinder to her fire, the dynamite to her explosion, the sunlight to her flower petals.

I LAY in bed and watched her undress.

She pulled the sweater over her head, her back to me. Then her arms reached behind her back and unclasped the black bra before she placed it on my dresser. She bent over and pushed off her jeans, giving me an incredible view of her ass.

I'd been thinking about that ass every single day.

Her bag was on the dresser, so she pulled out her little shorts and soft cotton tank. She put everything on, her silhouette so sexy in the dark. She held her small frame with such strength, deepened the arch in her back as she stood straight, stretching.

It was practically foreplay for me.

She moved to the nightstand and put her phone on silent before she took a drink of her water. Her makeup was gone because she'd washed it off when she brushed her teeth. Then she pulled back the sheets and finally joined me.

Man, I could not wait to fuck her again.

My body was still too weak to do it right, to hold myself on top of her without wincing. And I didn't want to do it half-assed, a compromised version to accommodate my injury. I wanted to be the man she remembered, the man I still was.

So, I had to be patient.

She turned on her side and faced me, so small in my bed. She pulled the covers to her shoulders then stared at me, her hair pushed behind her ear so it wouldn't be in her face and tickle her nose. She closed her eyes.

I stared at her, watched her eyelashes spread down her cheeks, watched her lips soften as she relaxed. When she didn't touch me, she kept her knees to her chest and she took up almost no space, like a dog at the end of the bed.

"Come here."

She opened her eyes.

My hand reached for her wrist and gave her a gentle tug. "Closer."

"I don't want to hurt you…"

"You're hurting me more by staying over there."

She must have wanted to be close to me too, because she shifted toward me, coming as close as she could without actually touching me. She brought the pillow with her, leaving her face just inches from mine.

It wasn't exactly what I wanted—but some of her was better than none of her.

My hand grabbed hers and held it on my chest, on my left pec where my heart was. The weight didn't hurt me since that was one of the few places where I didn't ache. I interlocked our fingers and stared at her.

She watched me too, looked into my face with her beautiful green eyes, eyes so gentle that she could never hurt anyone who didn't deserve it.

Her beauty was more powerful than all the pain killers I took. She took away my pain just by looking at me, just by loving me. She brought me peace, brought the stars to my ceiling, brought the summer meadow right into my bedroom. "I love you." There was no specific moment that those feelings had dawned on me, that she'd said something that suddenly made me feel that way. It had just happened, and when it did, the feeling was infinite, like I'd always felt that way, even before I met her. I couldn't remember what my life was like before she walked into it, even though it had only been a few months ago that I was fucking whores and picking up strangers at bars. It was like...when your life suddenly became so complete that you didn't want to remember what it was like to be incomplete.

Her fingers lightly pressed into mine, as if she was saying it back with her affection instead of her words. Her eyes lit up slightly, like she still wasn't used to hearing me say those words, and she wasn't used to saying them back. "I love you too."

TWO
CATALINA

I decided not to tell him the truth.

There was no point when I wasn't sure what I was going to do about it.

My heart wanted to stay, wanted to be with the man who made me feel things no one else ever would. But I was also a smart girl, and I knew this high wouldn't be enough to keep myself happy forever. Someday, I would want more.

Heath could never give that to me.

It was selfish to ask my father and brother to like someone they had every right to loathe.

So, I chose not to think about it, chose not to dwell on it, to live in the moment...until that moment was gone.

I walked upstairs and looked through the glass doors, seeing Heath work with the physical therapist who came to his place to help him. His ribs were broken and wrapped tight, and they would heal on their own in time, but he needed to keep moving if he wanted to keep his strength, to minimize the pain.

Heath dropped onto the bench and sat there, taking a break because the pain was too much. With his head bowed, he breathed hard, like he'd picked up a monster truck tire over his head just seconds ago.

The therapist held the resistance bands and waited, giving him a moment to pull himself together.

I felt wrong watching him struggle. I knew he wouldn't want me to see him like that, not at his full capacity, so I turned away and headed back downstairs. I looked out the large floor-to-ceiling windows and tried to clear my throat, to drain the water that formed in my eyes. Seeing him in pain was unbearable. I tried to focus on his progress rather than his pain, because he was doing so well. Just had to be patient.

My phone lit up with a text message from Anna. *Hey, I stopped by your apartment to say hello. You aren't home?*

I guess that meant Damien didn't discuss me with her much. *I'm at Heath's.*

Well, you want to meet for lunch?

I looked up the stairs like I expected Heath to be standing there, but I knew he would be occupied for the next hour. He didn't need me right now. *Sure. Where do you want to go?*

WE SHARED an appetizer while we waited for the food to come out. We also shared a bottle of wine, even though she had to go back to work when this was over.

"Sofia is gone." She answered my question about the hotel. "She went on maternity leave a week ago and had the baby. He's healthy and super cute."

"Aww, that's great," I said. "What's his name?"

"Demetri."

"Demetri Lombardi," I said. "Sounds like a king or something."

"Well, Sofia and Hades love him like he is," she said with a chuckle. "I'm happy for them, but I do miss having her in the office."

"Do you think she'll come back? She's got two kids now."

"I think so. Her mother lives with them, so she watches the kids while Sofia's at work. She likes working."

"I used to have a crush on Hades when we were younger."

"Really?" she asked before she took a drink from her wine.

"Yeah, but this was like..." He'd been in my life a long time, since I was young, because they were so much older than me. "When I was eighteen, nineteen, so a long time ago. Now I just see him as another brother, sorta."

"Don't tell Damien I said this, but Hades is hot. And definitely don't tell Sofia I said that."

I laughed. "Your secret is safe with me. But I'm sure she already suspects every woman thinks that." I definitely knew every time Heath went *anywhere*, every woman was staring at him, wanting to rip off his clothes. "So, how are you guys?"

She didn't talk about the rift between Damien and me, trying to stay positive so it wouldn't bring me down. "We're fine.

He's been a little distracted lately, but he's getting better with every passing day. What about you?"

I didn't answer because the waiter brought our food. After setting it down, he walked away. I grabbed my silverware and started to eat my salad. "Honestly, I haven't been all that great. I've been staying at Heath's to help him... He was in such bad shape." That was all I could say about it.

Anna had pity in her eyes, but she was also quiet, like she didn't know what to say. She was loyal to Damien, and she also had a strong attachment to my father. Her feelings were obviously conflicted. "Is he doing better now?"

"Much," I said quietly. "He's not the kind of man to let anything defeat him, so he's working hard to heal."

"That's good." She pushed her salad around with her fork.

I could feel it beginning already, feel the awkwardness that descended on the table when we discussed the man I was sleeping with, the man who had been unanimously ostracized by my family, even Anna, who wasn't actually married to my brother yet.

"So...you're going to stay with him, then?" She stabbed her fork into her food, bits of egg, bacon, and cheese, before placing it into her mouth. There was a melancholy tone to her voice, as if what she asked was forbidden.

"I...I don't know what I'm doing." I tried not to think about the decision I would have to face since I was falling more in love with him every second I was by his side. He looked at me in a way no one else ever had, like he saw me all the way down to the bone.

She stopped eating, giving me all of her attention. "Yeah... I can't imagine."

"This is the man I love. But I know everything Damien said is right. It's not the kind of relationship that I want forever."

"Then be with him until it burns out. You're young."

"I've thought of that, but I'm afraid it'll just get harder and harder to leave."

"Yeah..."

I pushed aside a big chunk of tomato then went straight for the cheese crumble. "I don't understand why this is happening to me. I don't know why I have to love a man who's not right for me." Why did the gypsy give me that reading? This was bound to happen whether I visited her or not, but why did it have to happen at all?

"I'm sorry, Cat. Did you tell him about all this?"

I shook my head. "No. If I do, he'll try to talk me out of it, and I'll be stuck. I need to think it over for a while, then make a clean break if I decide to."

"Honestly, it sounds like you've already made up your mind."

I looked at her. "Yeah?"

"It sounds like you're going to leave him...eventually."

I dropped my gaze, my heart breaking at the thought. What we had was real, true, and I didn't want to live my life without that man beside me. But I didn't want to lose my family either, lose the future I'd pictured in my head since I was young. My father wouldn't be around much longer, and Damien would be the only family I had left.

WHEN I GOT HOME, Heath had already showered after his workout. He wore sweatpants without a shirt, standing in the kitchen while he put together a sandwich for lunch. His ribs were no longer wrapped and there were still blotches of discoloration on his skin, but he wasn't the punching bag he used to be. His firm muscles were visible again, his fair skin beautiful now that some of it had healed.

He tore a few pieces of lettuce and placed it on top. "You want a sandwich?"

"No, I already ate." He didn't ask me where I'd been even though he knew I'd left the house. I moved into him, seeing the strong muscles of his back.

He turned to me, his arm circling my waist as he pulled me in. His face looked down into mine, and he stared at me like he was waiting for permission. His mouth wasn't cut up anymore, and the swelling had gone down. He had even healed enough to shave.

We hadn't kissed yet. He'd been too injured for that kind of affection. But now he looked at me like he wanted to, like he wanted to embrace me the way he used to. He tugged me a little closer, his large hand spreading across my entire back.

I rose on my tiptoes, my eyes open and locked on to his, and I kissed him.

He kissed me back, watching me with his possessive gaze.

Just like always, I felt it. Felt that powerful spark between our lips. My hand moved to his arm, and I felt his muscles, felt the powerful frame that was still strong under those bruises. I closed my eyes as I let my lips linger against his.

His other hand moved into my hair, sliding until he cupped the back of my head. He kissed me again, moaning between our breaths like he'd never had a kiss so good, even though we were barely moving our lips. It was our chemistry, our connection, that lit us on fire.

He pulled away and placed his forehead against mine, his eyes closed. "I can't wait to make love to you."

My hand cupped his cheek, looking up into the face of the most beautiful man I'd ever seen. The second we were apart, I was cold as ice, but when we were together, I melted all over again...became a slave to this powerful man. "You're doing it right now."

I PACKED my bag on the edge of the bed and zipped it up.

Heath entered the bedroom but stopped when he noticed what I was doing. He leaned against the frame of the door, crossing his arms over his chest, like he intended to block my path so I could never leave.

"I have to work tonight...and tomorrow."

He stared at me coldly, like he didn't accept that answer.

I pulled the strap over my shoulder. "You'll be fine without me."

"I never needed you to begin with. It was just an excuse to have you here." His voice was quiet, but it contained a natural amplification, like the depth of his voice made it more potent.

I moved around the bed and headed toward the door. "I can't stay here all the time."

"Why not?"

A sigh escaped my lips. "I'll be back in a few days." I approached the doorway and waited for him to move.

He stared at me defiantly, like he wasn't going to go anywhere. But then he dropped his arms and stepped aside.

I moved down the hallway and started to descend the stairs.

He was close behind me, his bare feet loud against the hardwood floor.

I didn't want him to take the stairs when he was still recovering, so I turned around to say goodbye.

He wore a slightly sad expression in his eyes, like it was hard to watch me go. He never asked me if I wanted to be with him or if my stance on our relationship had changed. He just assumed we were together again.

But that was a fair assumption to make.

His arm circled my waist, and he pulled me close, his lips near mine. "It's hard for me to let you go...when I just got you back."

My hands gently rested against his chest, my eyes on his mouth. "It's not for long."

"It's an eternity to me." He pressed his lips to my forehead, letting his warm mouth linger as he embraced me. "I'll be back to normal soon. I'll be the man you fell in love with. I'll be the man who protects you, the man who can lift you with a single arm and throw you over my shoulder."

I pulled back so I could look him in the eye. "Babe, I don't think less of you." My attraction to him hadn't changed. He was still the most desirable man on the planet, even with his scars.

He sighed quietly, as if he thought less of himself.

"I know that's your entire identity, but there's more to you than that. And all those things are still there."

"Yeah?" he whispered.

"Yeah. Like your arrogance, your sarcasm..."

He smiled slightly, immediately feeling better when I teased him.

"The way you look at me...the way you kiss me..."

His arm tightened on my back.

"And I'll never forget the way you looked in that cage. You've come so far, survived when anyone else would have died. Look at you now, and it's only been a few weeks. I don't think less of you... I think more of you."

I WORKED OVER THE WEEKEND, back to the stage after telling everyone I was sick with the flu—again. But no one seemed annoyed by my absence, especially not my understudy, who finally got to take the stage for a few nights.

When the performances were over, I went home to my apartment—alone.

I wanted some time away from Heath because I'd been at his side since I'd seen him in the cage. We'd been inseparable, and I'd barely had the opportunity to process what had happened.

Damien texted me. *Want to come over for dinner?*

Maybe Anna had told him how miserable I was, and he felt bad for me. Or maybe the invitation was completely unrelated. Or maybe he was proving how my life would be if I stayed with Heath—that the man I loved would never be included. *Just the three of us?*

Hades and Sofia are coming too. Hades is also bringing his brother Ash. And Dad.

I didn't know Hades had a brother. *That's quite the dinner party.* It made me feel worse that I couldn't bring Heath, because if I'd wanted to bring anyone else, the answer would have been yes.

Well, it's a special occasion...

I read his text a couple times, growing suspicious of his meaning. *Is that supposed to mean what I think it means...?* I didn't want to spell it out in case Anna got a glimpse of his screen or his messages popped up on his iPad.

Yes.

I cupped my mouth with my hand as I understood exactly what was about to happen. *I'll be there in 15 mins.*

WE GATHERED in the dining room, our loud voices bouncing off the vaulted ceiling and becoming even louder when they echoed back at us. The empty bottles of wine were quickly replaced, and Hades had Andrew in his arm, while Sofia took care of Demetri, who managed to sleep through most of the dinner.

"Your babies are so cute," I said. "Are you guys going to have more?"

"No," Hades answered. "Two is enough." He moved Andrew to the other arm when he started to get fussy.

His brother Ash was beside him, similar in appearance and just as quiet. He seemed to be older than Hades, but not by much. My father clearly took a liking to him because he kept talking to him.

Ash was nice enough to pretend to be interested.

Damien clinked his spoon against his wineglass to get our attention. "Hey, shut up for a second." He rose to his feet.

"Yeah, that's a great way to get us to be quiet," I said sarcastically.

Anna smiled up at him, clearly having no idea what was about to happen next.

I knew Anna didn't have a family and she'd adopted us as her own—so it was the perfect way to ask.

"Everyone here is like family to me," Damien said, turning his gaze on Anna. "But there's someone here who shouldn't be like family. She should be family..."

When Anna started to understand what was happening, her expression completely changed, a mixture of shock, joy, and love.

"She should have my last name. She should be the mother of my children. And she should be the person I grow old with." He set the glass down and fell to one knee, pulling out a ring from his pocket. He held it between his fingertips as he looked her in the eye. "Will you be my wife, Annabella?"

She covered her mouth and gasped when she saw the enormous rock he presented to her, the ring I'd convinced Damien to get instead of the modest one he'd originally picked out, and her reaction was purely genuine.

You're welcome, Damien.

"Oh my god...yes."

He smiled before he slipped the ring onto her finger.

We all clapped and shouted, getting even louder as we celebrated.

Dad seemed to be the happiest, staring at his son with joy in his eyes, like he'd wanted this moment longer than anyone else...and he was thinking of my mother at the same time.

I wanted my father to look at me the same way when it was my turn, and if I married Heath...that would never happen.

———

"GIRL, THAT RING." Sofia grabbed Anna's wrist and turned her hand. "Jesus, that is the size of a boulder."

"I know," Anna said. "My hand is already sore."

"It's stunning," I said, so happy she liked it. "You love it?"

"It's gorgeous," Anna said, examining her own hand like she couldn't stop staring at it.

I wanted to tell her I'd helped my brother pick it out, but I didn't want to make it about me, so I kept my mouth shut.

Dad came over and wrapped his arm around her shoulders. "Now, I have two girls, equally beautiful."

"I disagree with that," Damien said from the other side of the room.

"If my wife were here, she would love you," he said. "Absolutely love you."

"Thank you, Richard," Anna said quietly.

"Dad, she is here," I said. "She's always here."

He gave me an affectionate look before he placed his hand on my shoulder. "Come with me for a second..."

"I already had a piece of cake, Dad," I said, assuming he was directing me to the dessert table.

"No." He guided me right to Ash. "I was getting to know this nice young man, and he's a delight to talk to."

Ash turned to me, his eyes serious but the corner of his lip slightly raised, like he knew exactly what my father was trying to do and found it amusing.

I found it a bit horrifying.

"He plays the guitar," Dad said. "Why don't you two...?" He pointed at us both before he ditched me—then grabbed another slice of cake from the table.

I watched him go with a sigh before I turned back to Ash. "He's already had one piece of cake, which was too much. Now he's going for a second, and he knows better."

Ash held his glass of champagne at his side, filling out his clothes the same way Hades did. "It's a special night. Let him celebrate."

"I know, I just want him to live for all the special nights."

He slid his hand into his pocket and looked at the floor for a moment, like he didn't know what to say. "I'm flattered your father likes me enough to force his daughter into a very uncomfortable situation."

I chuckled, liking his sense of humor. "Don't be too flattered. I think he's trying to marry me off fast now that my brother has settled down."

"This is new for me. Not a lot of people are pushing me to marry their friends and sisters."

"Why?" I blurted, finding him even more attractive than his brother.

He shrugged. "I'm not really marriage material. Maybe your father should have asked me that first."

"I'm surprised he didn't pull out a list of questions from his pocket."

Now it was his turn to chuckle. "I don't think you need help finding a man anyway. And I don't need help finding a woman."

He was definitely more arrogant than his brother, or just more honest. "Actually, I'm seeing someone." We'd never established if we were in a relationship, and it would be smart to get out of it before it really turned into something. But when I was faced with a possible suitor, Heath was the only man I could think of. I felt obligated to state that he existed...because I was committed to him.

"Oh? Your father doesn't like him?"

"No. Doesn't know about him."

"Does Damien know?"

"Yes, he's not a fan."

"Now I understand," he said as he gave a slight nod. "Damien doesn't seem to like anyone, so I guess that doesn't surprise me."

Well, this time, it was actually legitimate. "Thanks for putting up with my father. He sees a handsome man and immediately tries to play matchmaker."

He grinned. "I am handsome, aren't I?"

I chuckled before I took a drink of my wine. "I used to have a crush on Hades when I was young, and you look very similar."

"I bet you would have had a crush on me instead if we'd met."

I shrugged. "Maybe I would have liked you both."

"Two men...that's a lot for one woman to handle."

I smiled. "Not for me."

———

AT THE END of the night, we said goodbye at the door. Sofia and Hades carried their kids to the car and went home. Ash shook hands with everyone before he walked to his car at the curb outside. I was the last one to leave, giving Anna a hug.

"Now, I get a sister. I've always wanted a sister instead of a brother."

She laughed as she hugged me back. "I know you don't mean that, but thank you. And thank you for being so kind to me since the beginning. The instant we met, you were so easy to talk to... You made me feel welcome. I really appreciate that." She pulled away and gave me a slight smile.

"Well, I tend to like everyone unless they give me a reason not to."

Damien stood there, watching us. My father had already gone to bed because he was wiped out after all the festivities. He had a distinct joy for life, but it made him burn out quickly. Damien came to me next, being a gentleman by walking me to my car outside since it was late in the evening. "Good call on the ring."

"Told you," I said when we were out of earshot. "If you gave her that candy ring, she probably would have said no. And if she didn't, she should have."

"It wasn't that bad, but you're right. She seems to really love it."

"Damn right, she does."

He stopped when he reached my car. "Saw you talking to Ash."

"Yeah, I talked to everyone there." I expected my father to push me onto somebody, but not my brother.

He didn't say anything more about it, just stared at me with his hands in his pockets. He didn't mention Heath just as he said he wouldn't, but his gaze showed his disappointment perfectly.

"I hope you didn't invite him just for my sake."

"No. Ash and I have become good friends over the years. I was surprised Dad took such a liking to him."

"Because Dad likes everybody." I rolled my eyes.

"Not everyone." The meaning of that statement was unmistakable.

I brushed it off. "Well, congratulations. I'm really happy for you."

"Thank you. And thank you for being so good to her."

"Of course," I said. "Even if I didn't like her, I would be nice to her—for you." There was no double meaning to my words, but after I said them, I realized they could be interpreted in a different way. "You know what I mean..."

He didn't say anything.

It would be easy for me to dislike Anna because she'd been married to the same man—twice. That relationship caused a lot of turmoil for my brother, put my family in jeopardy, even briefly held my own life in the balance. But that wasn't how I judged people. I saw them for who they were, not their baggage. But maybe that kindness put me in the situation I was in now...

"Good night, Cat." Damien turned away and headed back to the house.

I watched him walk away, already feeling the change in our relationship, feeling the change in everything. "Goodnight..."

THREE
HEATH

My ability to read people so well was one of the main reasons behind my success.

Along with my brute force, intelligence, and savage sarcasm.

And since I knew my woman so well, I could read her like she was under a microscope. There was definitely a barrier around her, a bit of distance that was still in place between us. I felt it diminish when we were together, when our eyes were locked and the love flowed between our hearts. But then it returned, subtly.

I decided to let her work it out on her own, not to question her in case it spooked her.

But she'd gone home for the weekend, and now it was Tuesday, and I hadn't heard from her. No text. No phone call. Nothing.

I was too proud to chase after someone who didn't want to be chased, but my patience was my weakness because I didn't have any. If I had it my way, I'd burn her apartment to the ground and move her ass into my place.

But that wasn't going to work on a woman like her.

She'd kick my ass.

And I'd enjoy every second of it.

When my patience had officially expired, I caved and texted her. *Baby.* That was all I said, that single word packed with an entire essay.

She texted back right away, those three little dots appearing. *Sorry. Just been busy.*

I didn't like that excuse. *Remember what happened last time you were too busy for me.* I didn't mean to threaten her, but threatening people was my entire life, and it just came out. I was frustrated she wasn't there with me, that she wasn't at least sleeping with me before she took off to take care of things.

The three dots didn't show up in the message box.

Good. She better think about what I said.

The three dots appeared minutes later. *I'll be there soon.*

That's what I thought.

SHE WALKED in the door with her bag over her shoulder. Her makeup was gone, like she'd been at home doing nothing except drinking wine in front of the TV. Her hand moved through her hair as she set the bag on the kitchen island.

I didn't rise from my seat on the couch. I leaned forward with my elbows on my knees, my gaze down on the table. I didn't look at her as I spoke. "Don't play games with me." After a few heartbeats, I lifted my gaze and stared at her. In the last four days, I'd improved, the bruises fading further, the physical therapy helping. I was shirtless in my sweatpants, watching the game as I drank water even though I craved something better.

She stood in front of the counter, slowly crossing her arms over her chest like she was uncomfortable. She was in jeans and a sweater, looking constrained by all the clothes she wore. "I'm not playing games—"

"Then why haven't I seen you in four days?" I rose to my feet and slowly came toward her, able to hold my frame perfectly straight now that my body had healed enough. My shoulders were squared, my back was rigid, and my ribs didn't ache so much. "Why haven't I heard from you?" I didn't want to be a man who demanded all of her attention, but my intuition was never wrong. There was something wrong, something off.

She didn't step back as I came closer. "I worked all weekend, and then my brother got engaged—"

"That's not the answer I'm looking for." I stopped in front of her, staring down at this beautiful woman with full lips, eyes like gems, and the sexiest little freckle. "Don't waste my time. Don't insult me either." After she'd saved my life, I'd made a lot of assumptions, but every assumption was reasonable. "You're either with me, or you aren't with me. Leave and don't come back...or stay. Choose—and stick to it." I didn't want her to choose the option I despised, but I also didn't want to be with a woman who didn't want to be with me. I deserved better than that.

She dropped her gaze to the floor.

"When you have a conversation with me, you look at me." My hand moved under her chin and forced her gaze up, being aggressive rather than gentle. I was treating her like one of my men rather than the woman I loved, but sometimes it was hard to keep the two separate. I released her.

This time, she didn't look away. "Everything happened so quickly. We never really had a chance to talk—"

"Then talk." I didn't like where this conversation was going —at all.

She was quiet for a long time, like she didn't want to be honest with me, didn't want to say these things to me. "I saved you because I love you. I saw you, and I just...acted. I was so angry with you for what you did, but my love triumphed my hatred, and I got you out of there...and I don't regret it."

I held my breath as I stared at her, actually afraid. Afraid that she would hurt me worse than she did last time.

"And I love you...so much." She closed her eyes and her voice escaped as a whisper, like saying the words out loud consumed every drop of emotion her body could create. When she looked at me, a film of moisture was on the surface of her eyes. "There's no one else I want to be with. You're the man I want...forever."

I still didn't breathe because I knew that wasn't the end of the conversation.

"But...I talked to Damien."

I hated that motherfucker even more. I didn't care about the destruction he'd inflicted on my body. Taking his sister away, the woman I loved, was a million times more painful than some broken ribs.

"I asked him to drop his crusade. He agreed."

I finally released the air I was holding because my lungs couldn't handle the stress anymore.

"But he told me he would never accept you, he would never approve of you, and neither would my father. You'll never be a part of our lives, a part of our family. So, for every holiday, every major event, it'll just be me...and not you. So, this has no future... We can never have a future."

"Things change, Catalina."

"Yes, but not this." Her tears grew so large in size that they streaked down her cheeks.

"Hades and Damien didn't speak for a long time. But they figured it out—"

"Totally different—"

"It's not different. Damien made a lot of mistakes that caused terrible things to happen to Hades's wife. He's not so fucking innocent. He makes mistakes too. Time changes perspectives. Look how your perspective on me has changed. It takes time—a lot of time."

Her arms tightened over her chest. "He's not going to change his perspective—"

"Don't give up on me." I couldn't lose her. I did it once, and it was unbearable. I'd handed myself over to Damien because I was so delirious. "Give me a chance. I can change his mind—eventually."

She shook her head slightly.

"Baby, please." The idea of obtaining Damien's forgiveness sounded like a ton of effort and a pain in the ass, but I would work hard to make it happen—because she was worth it. "You told me you aren't looking for a husband for a few years anyway. You've got time. Give that time to me."

"I've thought about that too...but the longer I stay, the harder it'll be to leave. And I can already see how things are different with my family. I can feel the awkwardness that wasn't there before, even with Anna. You've been ostracized by my family, and now they treat me differently because of it. I don't want to lose my family."

"You'll never lose them, baby."

"But it's not the same anymore. I can't imagine you asking my father's permission to marry me and him saying yes—"

Now I took a deep breath, feeling the pain in my lungs because I'd sucked in the air so fast. "You think about marrying me?"

She was quiet for a while. "No. I just mean hypothetically—"

"Don't lie to me. Can you really walk away from the man you want to marry?"

She looked away.

"What did I say about looking at me?" I snapped.

She turned back to me, her nostrils flaring in annoyance.

"Don't walk away from me. Not yet." I wanted to chain her to my bed so she couldn't leave. I wanted to take her away, start over somewhere new, just so we could be together. But she would never truly be happy—because she needed both of us.

She was quiet for a long time, breathing hard. "I want a husband who calls Damien a friend. That's so important to me because my father won't be around after another decade, and he'll be all I have left—"

"Balto is all I have left too. I understand how you feel."

She rubbed her arms like she was cold. "I want our kids to play together. I want us to be close. But if Damien refuses to acknowledge your existence, I'll have to go over there alone with our kids and you can't come and it's just... I don't want that. I want the four of us to be a family. I just can't see that happening with you."

"Right now, no. But in time, yes. I can make that happen."

She shook her head like my suggestion was ridiculous. "The gypsy told me I would only love one man...and he would be an enemy to my family."

"But she didn't say there was no hope. She didn't say things can't change. She only told you one truth about your life—the rest is up for grabs. Look, I'm a man who can make shit happen. At least let me try."

"If I get out now, it'll be much easier than if I wait—"

"Let. Me. Try." I raised my voice because my temper was starting to rise. "I lost you once, and I can't do it again. I won't fucking do it again." I started to breathe hard, my body aching because of all the exertion I was putting forth. "All that shit with Damien just happened weeks ago. Of course he's still angry. Fuck, I'm still angry. Let him cool off. Let the dust settle. Then, let's try."

She ran her fingers through her hair, clearly flustered by the risk she was taking. "Even if you're successful, there's still my father—"

"I'll win him over too."

"I-I don't know about that." She shook her head. "And I need his blessing, even if he's gone. I just can't be with a man my father doesn't approve of—"

"I've seen him with you, Catalina. That man is not bitter, cold, or selfish. He loves you so much, and there's nothing he wouldn't give you—if it made you happy. All you'd have to do is talk to him, and I'm sure he would be responsive."

"And then Damien would talk him out of it again. His son's opinion matters to him—"

"Then let me work on Damien." I raised my hand to silence her. "I'm just asking for some time. I let your brother beat me nearly to death. I'm clearly willing to do anything to make this happen. Anything at all. So please...let me fucking try."

She sighed quietly, closing her eyes for a few seconds as she considered the offer. She was still at odds with her feelings, still afraid to give me any chance because it would hurt her so much if it didn't work out.

"We're supposed to be together, Catalina."

Her eyes focused on my face. "You said you didn't believe in fate and stuff like that."

"I don't," I whispered. "But I believe in this." I moved closer to her, touching my forehead to hers, reminding her of the blinding feeling we shared so easily, so organically. "I believe in us."

Her arms rested on mine, her fingers lightly pressing into my flesh. She stared at my lips for a few seconds before she closed her eyes, like she could hear the unison of our two heartbeats, feel the tightness of our souls as they wrapped together into a knot. "Alright..."

I SAT ON THE COUCH, my back against the cushion with my knees apart, my bare feet on the rug. My hands were still at my sides, my hard cock against my stomach as I stared at Catalina in front of me.

Her sweater was somewhere on the rug, her bra on the coffee table, and after she got her jeans off, her thumbs slipped under the lace of her panties before she pulled them down. Her pussy was perfectly groomed, her little nub visible between the slit at the apex of her thighs. She pushed them down over her strong thighs, and when she released the fabric, they fell the rest of the way to the floor. She stepped out of them then came close.

I could barely fucking breathe.

The living room was dark because the TV was off, the windows were open to the view of the city, the lit-up cathedral in the distance, and it was so quiet that I could hear every sound, from her slow breathing to the stretch of the fabric of the couch once her knees landed on the cushion.

It'd been so goddamn long.

My cock hadn't been anywhere else, not even in my hand. My body wanted sex, but my heart wanted this spiritual connection, to feel her in a way no one else ever had, to feel our breaths sync, our heartbeats race even though we hardly moved.

Her hands went to the back of the couch as she guided herself down, careful not to grab me or cause my injuries to flare up. She planted her feet on either side of me on the couch, holding herself up like the fit athlete she was.

My hands went to her strong cheeks, and I gripped them hard, feeling the muscles that turned me on.

She brought her face close to mine, holding herself without even touching me, her lips ready to consume mine.

My fingers kneaded her flesh, touching that sexy ass in my hands. I pulled her a little closer, wanting to feel her tits rest against my chest, feel those hard nipples drag against me. I breathed against her mouth, excited like a boy rather than prepared like a man.

Her lips landed against mine, her mouth softer than her silky legs, softer than her rose-petal cheeks. It started off so gentle, like she was getting used to my kiss all over again.

I closed my eyes and fell hard, fell more in love with her at the simple touch.

I'd wondered if she'd been with anyone else, late at night when my thoughts haunted me. It wasn't just jealousy that drove me crazy, but possessiveness, because she was still mine according to my heart. I didn't care where she'd been, how many guys had had the honor to fuck her, but now that she was mine, I wanted to be her one and only...and her last.

One hand spanned across her ass, while the other moved into her hair, stroking the silky curtain that trailed down her back. My fingers cupped her face, my thumb brushing over the corner of her mouth as I kissed her. My dick oozed from the tip and dripped down my length to my balls just from her kiss.

She grabbed my base and guided me straight before she lowered herself, her lips wrapping around me in the sexiest embrace, coating me with her wetness, squeezing me with her tightness.

I looked her in the eye as I watched her take me, watched her handle that big dick like a pro.

She lowered herself farther, sliding down my length, going slow because her body wasn't used to me anymore. Her breathing became more labored the farther she went, like the discomfort was brand-new.

I struggled at just the contact, struggled at the feeling of our combined bodies, of the way she loved me and I loved her. My hands went back to her ass so I could support her a bit, my arms aching with the exertion.

She grabbed both of my wrists, her shoulders back and her tits pushed forward. She pulled my arms away, showing me that she didn't need my help at all, that she didn't want me to hurt myself by trying to lift her body. She placed my hands on her narrow waist, my thumbs stretching across her stomach to her belly button—where her skull diamond still was.

I wondered if she'd ever removed it.

She started to move up and down, holding on to the couch for balance, her body so fit that she could do all the work and not even struggle.

Every time she pushed her tight pussy down to my base, I released a moan, getting louder and louder with each movement. My fingers gripped her stomach, digging into her flesh and feeling her abs underneath.

I closed my eyes because I couldn't fight it, couldn't fight the urge to fill that pussy because it was mine. "Baby, I'm sorry..." I came loudly, falling apart within the first few strokes, letting go like I'd never fucked a woman before. My cock twitched hard inside her, and I pumped so much of my seed into her that it instantly started to drip, like there simply wasn't enough room to hold it all. My feet pushed against the floor, and I felt the heat spread through my skin, making me hot and sweaty even though I'd barely lifted a finger.

She watched me with intent eyes, like it was a turn-on rather than a disappointment.

I whispered through my heavy breathing. "My last time...was you." I had been too depressed to jerk off when she left me. I didn't even feel aroused because the liquor watered down all my desire. The last time was the way I'd come just now.

She started to move again, sliding through the white come that dripped down my dick. It was added lubricant, not that we needed it. "I like feeling your come inside me..." She continued to ride my semi-hard dick, bringing it back to stiff hardness with a few strokes. She moved up and down, her ass and thighs tight as she lowered and raised herself nice and slow, her fingers sliding into the back of my hair as she breathed in my face, enjoyed the potent desire between our bodies.

I got lost in those green eyes, got lost in the spiritual connection between our bodies, traveled through the clouds and the stars as she took me somewhere out of this world. I understood exactly what Balto felt, why it was so easy for him to give up his entire way of life for a single person.

Because she was his new way of life.

Catalina continued to rise to the top of my dick, her wetness kissing the crown of my head, and then push down, my shaft stretching her again before she rose and started over.

I already wanted to come again. "Baby...I love you." I'd never before said how I felt when I felt it because our feelings had been classified from our own minds. But now I felt it, and I wanted to say it every time I felt it, unafraid to feel the most powerful emotion created. It was stronger than hate, stronger than jealousy, stronger than greed...stronger than all known forces combined. Power always remained in the person who cared less, who had nothing to lose, and I had forsaken all that control because it didn't matter anymore.

She continued to rise and fall, her back arched, her tits dragging against me, her lips slightly parted, so perfect. "I love you..."

I WAS dead asleep when the phone started to ring on my nightstand.

Catalina groaned and turned over, pulling the sheets over her head like that would block out the sound.

I grabbed the device, saw Balto's name on the screen with squinted eyes, and took the call because it was important. He wouldn't call me at this time of night unless it was urgent. In fact, he hardly ever called me unless it was urgent. "Yeah?" I sat up then rose from the bed, leaving the bedroom so I wouldn't wake Catalina.

He got right to the point. "Cassini needs you to take her to the hospital." Despite the words he spoke, his voice was controlled. "She's having pain with the baby."

My heart started to pound. "Of course. But—"

"I'm too far away, Heath. I'm in the middle of collections in the north. I can't get to her. And it would take too long for us to swap."

I felt like shit. Felt worse than I had at the bottom of that cage. "I'll take care of it...and I'm sorry."

Click.

I went back into the bedroom and got dressed.

Catalina woke up at the sound of my movements. "What are you doing...? Are you leaving?"

I quickly pulled a long-sleeved shirt over my head and got my jeans on, invincible to the pain it caused me. "I can't explain right now. I have to go."

She got out of bed, wearing nothing but her panties. "What's wrong?"

"I have to help Cassini." I grabbed all the stuff off my night-stand and headed down the hallway.

She followed me. "I don't understand. What's wrong? Let me come with you—"

"I don't have time to wait." I took the stairs to the garage. "She needs me to get her to the hospital. Something is wrong with the baby. And Balto is working—in my fucking place—so he can't do it." I despised myself for doing this to him, for taking care of his wife when it should be him.

"Oh no…"

I hit the button on the wall so the garage door opened. "I have to go."

"Alright."

───────

I GRABBED Cassini and got her to the hospital. I did exactly what Balto would do, bossing people around and making threats until she saw a doctor right away—cutting through everyone in line because I didn't give a shit about anyone else.

When she was in the room, the doctor did a few tests, including watching the baby on the ultrasound machine.

She was scared—and in pain.

I held her hand and whispered to her. "Everything is going to be alright, Cassini. I'm sure he's fine." I interlocked our fingers, looking into her tear-stained face as I felt my self-loathing grow. I shouldn't be the one comforting her right now.

"I'm scared," she whispered. "He's my baby…"

"I know." I squeezed her hand. "But he'll be alright." I lied to her, lied to her to calm her down.

When the doctor was finally done, he delivered the news. "Your son is fine. You're just experiencing some early contractions, but they're temporary and will pass. Most women don't even feel them."

"He's going to be okay?" she asked, squeezing my hand hard. "He's fine?"

"Yes. Everything looks normal." He shut down the ultrasound. "I'll give you two a minute."

When the doctor left, she broke down in sobs. "Oh my god..." Both of her hands went to her stomach as she faced the ceiling, her eyes closed, tears dripping from the corners of her eyes to her ears.

My hand rested on her arm. "He's alright, Cassini."

"I know... I was just so scared."

I rubbed her gently. "I know. But this is Balto's son. You know he's a beast."

She smiled slightly, still crying.

"The doctor said he'll give you something to stop the pain for the next few days. How about I drop you off at home then wait at the pharmacy until it's ready?"

She wiped her tears away and ignored what I said. "Can you call him?"

I knew he was in the middle of something, so a phone call probably wasn't practical. I pulled out my phone and texted him. *Cassini is okay, so is the baby. Everything is fine. I'm going to take her home now.*

He didn't text back, but he'd probably look at that message as soon as possible and feel relieved.

"I texted him, probably shouldn't call him right now."

She nodded, still lying on the bed. "I wish he were here..."

I bowed my head in shame, closing my eyes. "I'm so sorry."

She grabbed my hand again. "It's okay, Heath. Thank you for taking care of me."

"Of course. I'm always here for you." I would die for her, because that was the kind of loyalty that was shared between Balto and me. He would do the same for me if I had a wife. I squeezed her hand. "And I'll go back to work so Balto can be home with you."

She didn't argue with that, not hiding the fact that she hated Balto impersonating me.

"I'm sorry I even allowed him to."

She still didn't say anything.

I felt terrible.

"I don't want it to happen again, Heath," she whispered. "You're the one who chose to be the Skull King. Balto chose to leave. Don't put us in that situation ever again."

Balto had offered, and I never would have asked. But I didn't tell her that. "I promise."

"Then take me home."

I got to my feet and helped her off the bed and to the floor.

"Could you do something else for me?"

I tucked her arm through mine so I could support her as I walked her out of the hospital. "Anything."

"Maybe some ice cream? Balto never has sweets in the house—"

"I'll get you anything you want." I smiled at her. "Let's get you home, and I'll grab the medication and everything else."

"Okay, thank you."

I GOT her into the house before I returned to my truck and drove to the pharmacy. I was about to open the door when Balto called.

I answered right away. "I just dropped her off at home. I'm grabbing her medication at the pharmacy."

He must have been alone because he was candid. "What did the doctor say?"

"Something about early contractions—but they are normal. I guess all women have them, but most don't feel them. I'm grabbing the medication the doctor prescribed to make her more comfortable until they pass. She also asked me to get her some ice cream."

He didn't chuckle at the last thing I said. "My son is fine?"

"Yes."

"And my wife?"

"A little shaken up, but she's okay."

He sighed into the phone, showing all of his emotion in just that simple pause.

"I'll return tomorrow. You've done enough."

He was quiet for a long time. "I want to help you, Heath. But my wife and son come first—"

"You don't need to explain yourself, Balto. I understand. I shouldn't have let you take my place to begin with."

"Are you sure you're strong enough?"

It didn't matter if I was in a wheelchair. "Yes. Finish up what you're doing, and go home to your wife."

He sighed again. "I should have been there..."

I closed my eyes. "I know...but you'll be there for everything else."

"Yeah."

We sat in silence for a long time, like Balto just wanted the comfort of my presence.

"What kind of ice cream does she like—"

"Chocolate. But she'll eat anything."

I smiled slightly. "Alright. Let me get that to her. When you get home, she'll be pain-free and fed—and really happy to see you."

WHEN I GOT HOME, it was sunrise.

Catalina sat in the living room, like she'd been waiting for me for the last few hours. The second I reached the top of the stairs, she jumped to her feet and came to me, wearing one of my shirts. "Is everything okay?"

"Yeah. Cassini and the baby are fine. She was having pregnancy pain, but it was normal."

"Oh, that's a relief. And Balto?"

"He'll be home any minute."

She nodded. "Good thing you could take her to the hospital and everything."

That wasn't something to celebrate. "It should have been Balto. If it weren't for me, it would have been him." I sighed quietly. "I'm going back to work tomorrow."

"Are you sure that's a good idea?"

"I'm much better than I used to be. No one will know."

"But...I'm still worried."

"I can't let Balto keep working." I walked past her and headed to the bedroom. "I shouldn't have allowed it in the first place. I'll lie low for a while. In a few weeks, I'll be as good as new anyway." I walked into the bedroom and stripped off my clothes.

She stood there and watched me, her eyes scanning over my bruises. "Couldn't you take a vacation or something?"

I chuckled. "No such thing as vacation time, baby."

"Well, could you quit?"

When I was in my boxers, I moved to the bed. "Yes. But I don't want to." I sat on the edge.

She looked at me with her arms crossed over her chest. She'd never expressed any dislike for my career choice, but our relationship had always been a fling. Now that we talked about the future we wanted to have, she probably felt differently about it. But she didn't say that now. "Why not?"

"I worked hard for the position. I'm not going to hand it over to someone else."

"So, you enjoy it, then?"

I nodded. "Yes."

She dropped her arms and moved to the other side of the bed.

With my back to her, I addressed the thoughts I assumed she had. "But if you ever asked me to leave...I would."

Her body made the mattress dip, but then she went still, like those words affected her.

Balto made a hard decision when he picked domesticated life over the blood-pumping excitement of the Underground. But he knew he couldn't have both, couldn't keep his family safe if he continued to be the king. So, he made his decision—and didn't regret it. I hadn't thought that far down the line, but I knew I would do anything to keep this woman, so if it came down to it, I would do it...in a heartbeat.

FOUR

CATALINA

Even though she'd just gotten engaged a week ago, Anna was eager to get a wedding dress.

I met her in the dining room at Damien's house so we could have lunch before we left.

"What do you think about this?" She pushed an open magazine toward me.

I didn't look at the picture. "I don't think it matters what I think." I pressed my fingers to the paper and pushed it back. "You don't need my opinion."

She pushed it back again. "But I need you to tell me how gorgeous I would look in it."

I smiled then looked down at the gown she wanted me to see. "Wow, it's beautiful. Very elegant. I think it'd look great on you."

"Would you wear it?"

I pushed the magazine back before I drank my coffee. "I'm not the one getting married. You are."

"I know, but I'm curious."

"Personally?" I asked. "I'd probably go for something sluttier. That's just how I am. Probably low cut in the front to highlight my cleavage, you know, barely appropriate for a church. Something really tight, like a mermaid dress."

She smiled. "I can totally see it."

My father came into the room and joined us. "What are you ladies up to?"

"Picking out a wedding dress," I answered.

"Ooh, let me see." He pulled the open magazine toward him. "Very nice."

Anna smiled, finding my father adorable.

He was a bit adorable.

"We were just leaving to try a couple on," I said. "We don't have a wedding date, but we've got to get this dress, apparently."

"Well, I don't think Damien and I are going to do anything big," Anna said. "Something small. Just you guys. Casual."

"Do you think I could tag along?" My father was usually anxious for lunch every single day, and it was the first time food didn't seem to be his priority. If he wanted to tag along, he'd have to skip the meal.

Anna looked surprised by the question. "Of course..."

"I know it's not traditional," my father said. "But my wife would be there if she were still alive, so I thought I'd step in for her."

My father was the sweetest man on the planet.

"I would be honored," Anna said, placing her hand on his.

"Does that mean you're going to help me pick out a dress too, Dad?" I asked playfully.

"Definitely," he answered. "Wouldn't miss it."

I wanted to keep smiling, but that was hard to do. When I pictured the man I was most interested in marrying, I couldn't imagine my family being supportive, couldn't imagine my father being thrilled enough to join me in picking out a dress. And the thought made me sad.

***

ANNA CAME out of the dressing room in a long-sleeved gown made of thin lace. The dress narrowed around her waist then flared out again, elegant and perfect for a winter wedding. "What do you think?"

"It's nice," I said, reacting neutrally to everything so she could pick what she really wanted without being swayed by my opinion.

"Is this the 1800s?" my father asked. "It looks like my grandmother's wedding dress. You're too beautiful to wear something that covers so much of your nice skin."

She chuckled. "Alright, I'll try another. Cat, could you help me?"

I walked with her into the dressing room then started to unfasten the miles of buttons down her back. "Don't listen to my dad. If you like it, get it."

"No, he's right. It's hard to pick out a dress Damien will like when he can't even see it on me."

"Well, he'll like anything you wear. I promise you that."

She looked at herself in the mirror as the dress slowly became looser and looser, relaxing off her shoulders and arms so she could eventually slip it off.

I glanced at her from time to time, thinking about the one subject that was usually on my mind. "Anna, I was wondering if you could do me a favor..."

"Sure. What is it?"

"Well, Heath and I talked."

She stiffened at the subject.

"I think I'm going to hope for the best, hope Damien changes his mind...eventually. I was wondering if—"

Anna turned around when the last button was unfastened. "Catalina, I'm going to be honest with you. I want to help you because you're my friend. I want you to be happy. But Damien is set in his ways, and I don't want to upset him. We're really happy right now, and anytime that subject comes up, he gets angry. I feel like I'm stuck in the middle, and I just...don't want to be."

She was the perfect person to meddle on my behalf because he might actually listen to her, but I understood her request, understood why she wanted to stay impartial and not stick her neck out for me. "No, I understand."

She dropped her gaze in sadness. "I'm sorry, Cat."

"I know."

"And to be honest... I'm not sure if I like you being with Heath either. I've become so fond of your father. He's so sweet. I can forget what happened with Liam because that was my ex who orchestrated all of that, but I'm not sure I can forget about what happened to your dad."

"You've never met Heath. You might feel differently if you did."

She shrugged. "Maybe. But I do agree with what Damien says, that you deserve the best. You're such an amazing person, Catalina. I just imagine you being with the perfect guy."

I pictured myself with a handsome man my family loved, but I also pictured that staleness, the nonexistent fire, the lack of excitement. "I'm not sure if perfect is what I want, Anna. I've been with a lot of guys, and he's the only I've ever loved. That's got to count for something."

Her eyes softened, like she really felt my pain. "You're going to stay with him, then?"

"For now. He said, in time, he would make Damien feel differently. I just need to be patient."

"Well, you're going to have to be really patient, because I don't see that happening for a very long time."

I SAT at my vanity backstage, taking all the pins out of my hair before letting it fall down and relax around my shoulders.

My phone lit up with a text message. *Baby*. He was short with me over text, like he wasn't obligated to say much since I was officially his, like a simple word could convey his need to see me.

Just finished a show.

And now what?

Girls want me to go out with them.

Out where?

For drinks.

He went silent, like he expected me to text more.

Want to meet me?

About time you asked.

Are you sure you're able to do that?

Baby, I'm fine.

We hadn't spoken since he went back to work the other night, but I assumed he was fine because he continued to go. *I'll let you know where we end up.*

What are you wearing?

I smiled when I heard his voice in my head. *You'll just have to see.*

I KEPT LOOKING at the door as we sat at the table together. Most of the girls found other people to talk to, but Tracy was still with me.

"Why do you keep looking at the door?" she asked. "Expecting someone?"

I never told her we'd gotten back together. She was a close friend, but I didn't confide all the details of my life. I doubted she would believe me if I did. "Heath and I got back together."

"Really?" she asked. "After that fight you guys had?"

"Yeah, he won me over."

"I think that's great news. You aren't going to find another man like that. He's Grade A, top choice beef."

"Oh, I know." That was why I was still there, why I was going against everything I believed in just to be with him. "But he is more than his looks. He's sweet, thoughtful, loyal...a lot of things."

"Sounds like you love him. I've never seen you with the same guy for so long."

Because I never had been. "I do."

She gave me a surprised look, as if she didn't expect me to admit it. "And he loves you?"

I nodded.

"I guess that's obvious just by the way he looks at you." She spun her olive around in her glass. "Man, why does his brother have to be married...?"

I chuckled. "You'll find someone, Tracy."

"Not like that," she said as she flipped her hair. "He's one in a million."

Yeah, he was.

My eyes went to the entryway when I saw a six-foot-three hunk walk inside. All eyes turned his way, cataloguing all the features that were impossible not to notice, his massive build, the way he stretched the fabric of his long-sleeved shirt over his strong pecs, his scorching blue eyes, his hard jawline sprinkled with a shadow of hair.

He headed to the bar first and ordered his drink.

I stared at his ass, liking the snug fit of his jeans.

It didn't take long for a woman to make a move, to touch him on the arm and make a pass. He didn't smile playfully, didn't say more than a few words with an annoyed expression, before he walked across the bar to me, like he already knew where I was without checking.

I felt my stomach tighten with excitement, looking at the sexiest man I'd ever seen. It was hard to believe he was the man who'd assaulted me months ago, took me captive by choking me out. Now, he was everything to me.

I got to my feet because anything less than a deep kiss wasn't good enough to greet him—according to him.

He looked me up and down subtly, liking the tightness of my red dress, his blue eyes flashing in approval. When he reached the table, he set his drink down without taking his gaze off me. Then his arm hooked around my waist, his hand flattening against the arch in my back. He looked down at me as he pulled me close, giving me a much different expression than he gave to that admirer at the bar. He held his lips there as he stared at me, like he expected me to do the rest.

I was in high heels, so it was easy for me to move into him, to plant my lips against his, to smear a drop of lipstick against the corner of his mouth. My hand slid to his chest, and I almost forgot he still had injuries under those clothes. I kept my touch gentle but my kiss hard.

He kissed me like we were alone, even though we were in public. His hand squeezed my ass as he gave me a little tongue. His deep voice whispered to me. "So sexy in that dress." He lowered himself into the chair I'd just been occupying then patted his thigh, as if he expected me to sit there.

I wasn't sure if he could handle it, but I didn't want to ask in front of Tracy, so I lowered myself across his lap, my feet dangling above the floor.

His arm hooked around my waist, and he supported me like the back of the chair, his eyes all over me like his hands in the bedroom.

Tracy stared at us, like she didn't know what to say.

I looked at my friend and tried to ignore the way Heath looked at me, with a gaze so hot, it burned my skin like a tanning bed. I grabbed my drink and sipped it, letting the fruity tang splash across my tongue along with the tequila.

Tracy continued to stare. "So...do you have any friends you could set me up with?"

Heath directed his gaze to her. "All my friends are assholes."

"Like, assholes like you or..."

He smiled slightly. "No. As in, bad assholes."

She sighed. "Oh damn." She sipped her drink until it was empty then headed to the bar to get another. "I can't watch this fine piece of man be all over you. I need to go find me a man." She walked off.

With my arm around his shoulders, I turned to him. "Thanks for chasing off my friend."

"I'm not the problem. You are."

"Me?" I asked incredulously.

"Yeah. She's jealous of you. Not me." He grabbed his glass off the table and took a drink, not showing a wince or any sign of discomfort. When he was done, he set it down and placed his hand on my thigh. "How was the show?"

"Good. Nothing new."

"Every time I watch you, it feels new." He looked at me, his fingers lightly touching the soft skin of my thigh. "In any capacity." He stared at me, his blue eyes taking in my expression like I was prey he was able to take home to his cave.

I loved the way he stared at me. I loved the way he was eager to claim me in front of everyone in the room, even though he was the more desirable one. I loved the way he needed to touch me with both hands, to make me feel worshiped in every way imaginable, with his look, his touch, and his words. "How's work been?"

"Fine." He'd never said much about his job before, so his silence wasn't that odd.

"Was it difficult to adjust?"

"Balto brought me up to speed."

"And no one figured out it was Balto for the last month?"

He shook his head. "A bit insulting, isn't it?"

"Or maybe your brother just knows you really well."

"Maybe." His fingers traced a circle around my knee over and over, his callused fingertips slightly abrasive against my softness.

"You're feeling okay?"

"Yes," he said with confidence. "I'm getting better every single day."

"Just don't want you to have a setback…"

He shook his head. "No. I'm practically brand-new at this point. I'm young and healthy—I heal fast."

"Thank god for that."

His arm tugged me a little closer, bringing my lips to his so he could kiss me as he stared into my eyes, his coarse hair rubbing against me just like his fingertips did. "Anything new with you?" He released me, talking to me like we were home alone, not in the middle of a crowded bar.

A few things had happened that I hadn't mentioned. "My brother asked Anna to marry him."

He had no reaction to that. "And did she say yes?"

"Of course she did. Why wouldn't she?"

He shrugged. "She could do better."

I knew he was joking, so all I did was narrow my eyes in response. "We went shopping for a wedding dress this afternoon."

"Did she find anything?"

"No, actually. My dad came along and was very opinionated about everything."

He grinned. "Your dad is passionate about wedding dresses?"

"He's trying to stand in for my mom, and in his defense, that's exactly how she'd act."

He chuckled. "That's kinda cute, actually."

"Yeah, he's adorable." Now that I'd forgiven Heath for what he did, I didn't always think about his actions whenever I mentioned my father. I gave Heath a clean slate, saw him as a different man.

"I'm sure he'll do the same for you."

"Yeah, and we'll scream at each other."

"You think he won't like your dress?"

"Not sure. I know I want something more scandalous, so I'm not sure how he'll feel about it."

He gave a slight nod in approval. "Yeah...that's what I want to hear."

I rolled my eyes playfully, but I felt the smile move into my lips. "Well, we chased my friends away, so I guess there's no point in sticking around."

"We didn't chase them away. They'd watch us have sex if they could."

"Whoa. What did you say?"

He grinned. "Come on, they would. I'd do it too, but I don't need to."

I rose to my feet and smoothed out my dress so my ass wouldn't hang out.

He gave it a playful spank as he stood up. "What are you wearing underneath?" He grabbed his glass and finished it off before he wiped his mouth with his thumb.

"Nosy, aren't you?"

His arm curled around my waist, and he walked me out. "Want to be prepared when we get home." He opened the door for me, and once we were outside in the cold air, he wrapped his arms tighter around me, keeping me warm in the fog. "Black thong? Red panties?" His truck was up ahead, so he fished out his keys and hit the button so the engine would start and the interior would warm up for me.

"No."

"Hmm..." He cocked an eyebrow as he opened the passenger door for me. "Pink? Purple?" He had my panties memorized pretty well, because he seemed to be thinking of pairs he'd specifically seen on his bedroom floor.

I used his hand for balance to get inside without toppling. "No."

He stood with his hand on the door, subtly frustrated that he couldn't guess correctly.

I pushed his chest so he would back up and I could grab the door handle. "I'm not wearing anything." Then I shut the door in his face.

He stood there, frozen to the spot as he stared at me through the glass. Then his eyes focused harder on my face, and his jaw turned tight like he pictured screwing me right there. His chest rose and fell with the deep breath he took, and he shook his head slightly as he walked away. His voice was audible before he moved around the truck. "Baby..."

HE USUALLY UNDRESSED me completely before he took me, but he was too anxious to be patient. He shoved my dress to my hips, left my heels on, and sank into me on the bed, his jeans gone but his shirt still covering his torso.

It was the first time he'd been on top of me since his injuries— and he seemed ready for it.

He moaned once he was fully buried within me, his fat and long cock occupying every inch of me, claiming my pussy so aggressively it hurt a little. His face rested above mine, his lips just inches away.

My hands slipped underneath his shirt, and I pulled it up as he started to rock into me, lifted it to his chest so I could feel his strength, see his display of black tattoos.

He reached one hand behind his neck and tugged it free, tossing the fabric to the side so I could enjoy him the way I liked, see his naked strength on top of me. He moved slowly inside me, rocking me with an easy pace, like just being inside me was enough. "Baby..." His forehead rested against mine as he struggled to get used to this, as he controlled himself to keep from letting go right away. Our abstinence had ruined his threshold, and now he had to start over, get used to his cock surrounded by my heat, my wetness.

I didn't care that he couldn't last. It was hot watching him struggle, watching him lose the battle with every thrust. Watching him come apart instantly the first time we were together had been a turn-on, because it proved that he'd really been alone, that he really had no exposure to pleasure at all. That my pussy was the last thing his cock had touched.

And when he came inside me, I could feel it; I could feel the heaviness, feel the heat, feel it spread with the movement of his shaft. He could always keep going with a semi-hard dick because he was big enough, and it only took him a minute to get rock-hard again.

So, it didn't bother me in the least.

He wasn't one of those boys who walked away the second he was finished. He could keep going...and going, his desire for me so great that it forced his dick to full mast within minutes.

He came with a groan, his cock pulsing inside me as he filled me with his load. He looked me in the eye as long as he could before he had to close them, his hips bucking slightly as the feeling overcame him.

I grabbed his ass and pulled him hard inside me, my head rolling back as I felt his seed fill me. The experience was still new to me, to have this kind of connection with a man, nothing keeping us apart.

When he finished, he breathed close to my face, his lips barely touching mine. His dick was still hard, still thick and defined, like nothing happened at all. Then he kept going, this time harder, like he could handle a pace that would make me come in seconds.

That was all it took—a few seconds.

I gripped the back of his neck and moaned in his face, my cunt squeezing him hard, constricting around his length like a strong grip. When he made me come, tears usually sprouted from my eyes, which was something I'd never done before him. He made me come in a different way, made me explode in a way other men never could. Even when we wore a condom, he made it happen, so it was either his size, the way he used it, or because we fell in love almost instantly.

He pounded me into the bed as he watched me, working his body hard to keep the climax going, to squeeze the juice from the lemon and make it last as long as possible. He ground his body against my clit after every thrust, pleasing me like he knew exactly where all my triggers were—and when to hit them.

I finished with tears dripping to my ears, my nails carving him like a pumpkin on Halloween.

He watched my performance without interrupting his own, and once the preliminary orgasms were out of the way, he changed, turned into the aggressive man who used to boss me around. "This pussy is mine." He increased the effect of his words with his hard thrusts, slamming his dick through my come as well as his. "Fucking mine." Sometimes he made love to me, told me he loved me, kissed me like he wanted to feel our souls wrap around each other. But sometimes, he just wanted to claim me, to remind me that I belonged to him, that he wouldn't let me go—not now, not ever.

I wasn't sure which I liked more.

HEATH MADE dinner in the kitchen, wearing only his sweatpants. He wasn't afraid of the hot oil splashing onto his naked body, because he always seemed to put just the right amount into the pan.

His fair skin had returned to its natural color, with a few scars that were mostly hidden on his tattooed skin. I suspected the ink obscured most of his injuries, so it was misleading, but he was much better, nonetheless.

I pulled the plates out of the cabinet, wearing his shirt with my panties underneath. We returned to the quiet companionship we used to share, making dinner with little conversation, just comfortable being together.

He scooped the food out of the pan then added the veggies next.

"Looks good."

"Talking about me or the food?" he teased.

"Both."

We sat at the dining table and each had a glass of wine. Now that he was off his medication, he could enjoy alcohol again, but he seemed to have gotten used to living without it because he didn't drink as much as he used to.

I watched him as I stabbed my fork into my food and took a bite. "Thank you for dinner." He always cooked for me when I stayed over, making a gourmet meal with his expensive pans and fancy cooking oil.

"Don't thank me," he said as he kept eating. "What's mine is yours."

"I do have one complaint..."

He lifted his gaze, his expression hard at my words.

"Maybe have some sweets once in a while..."

A soft smile sprinkled his lips. "I'm surprised you would ask that."

"Once in a while isn't going to hurt."

He continued to eat. "I'm glad your attitude about food has changed."

"I do eat more with you. But I also jog now, to keep it off."

"When?"

"Before I take a shower. I'm not big on exercise, but I force myself to do it."

"You don't need to," he said. "But whatever makes you happy."

I was glad I had a man who didn't care about my weight. Men I'd been with complimented my figure, but they wouldn't encourage me to eat. Heath was such a big man that it didn't matter what my size was, he would always be the bigger one of the two of us. Gave me some wiggle room. "I asked Anna to talk to Damien, but she said no." I didn't want to mention my brother to him, but he was on my mind a lot, and I felt uncomfortable hiding it from Heath. We were honest with each other, speaking our minds. "She said she didn't want to get in the middle of it."

He didn't show his annoyance at my statement. "It's too soon anyway, baby. Just leave it alone."

"Yeah, but Anna has a tight hold on him. If anyone could talk to him, it would be her."

"Still too soon. Time and distance are what we need right now."

"I guess I could ask her again some other time..."

"Baby, I told you I would fix it. Let me take care of it." He lifted his chin and looked at me instead of his food.

When he gave me that expression, I knew to back off. "Alright."

He went back to eating, either looking at his food or out the window behind me, quiet. His elbows were on the table, his broad shoulders blocking most of the view behind him. His cut arms showed the distinctions between his different muscles, something even his ink couldn't hide.

"Can I ask you something?"

"Anything," he blurted out, choosing to be transparent. He'd lied to me before, but he seemed intent on proving he would never do it again.

"You said you were open to getting married...but not having children."

He finished chewing his bite but didn't take another. He set his fork down and looked at me boldly, not avoiding my gaze at the difficult subject.

"Do you still feel that way?" I pulled the glass of wine closer to me, my fingers resting on the rim.

He didn't say anything.

"I know this is the beginning. We've barely had time to be together. But I won't waste my time and go through this unless I know you're willing. Because I have to have children. Nonnegotiable." He didn't seem like the fatherly type, with his profession and his sleeves of tattoos. He didn't seem like the kind of man that would drop them off at school in the morning then take them to soccer practice. But I would love to have a son in his likeness, with those blue eyes and light brown hair.

He was still quiet.

Not a good sign.

"I'm not sure if I'd be a good father." He held my gaze as he spoke, not directly answering the question, but at least responding to it.

"Because of what you do?"

"Among other reasons..."

"What other reasons?"

"I'm impatient. I'm authoritative. I'm selfish."

"Authoritative is a good skill to have when raising kids. The other two, we're all like that. Everyone has their reservations about being a parent. Hades didn't seem like the father type to me, but he's an amazing dad."

"What makes an amazing dad?"

"Loving your kids. It's that simple."

"Well, I love you... So I'd imagine love wouldn't be an issue." He grabbed his fork again and continued to eat.

"Are you going to answer my question or just continue to ignore it?" I asked bluntly.

He smiled slightly, aroused by my bossiness rather than irritated. "You're right, that's a long way away. I'm not in that place right now. But if that's a requirement to be with you and we made it that far...yes."

That was the answer I'd been hoping for.

"I didn't think Balto would ever be a father, and his son isn't even here yet and I can tell he's going to be great at it."

"If you can run an underground world of thieves and criminals, being a father should be a simple task in comparison."

"I can leave the Underground whenever I want. But I'd never stop being a father. I'd be a father until the day I die."

FIVE

HEATH

I took the elevator to the top floor then stepped inside.

Balto was on the couch, shirtless, wearing a hooded expression as he regarded me. "What's that?" He glanced at the flowers in my hand.

"They aren't for you." I held up the grocery bag in my hand. "And neither is this."

"So, you're bringing flowers to my wife?" He rose to his feet. "Get your own woman flowers."

Cassini came out of the kitchen, wearing jeans and a loose black top to hide her stomach. "Wow, they're beautiful." She took the lilies from my hand and smelled them. "That was thoughtful of you. Thank you." She looked down at my bag. "And there's more?"

I held up the bag and opened it. "Ice cream, cookies, brownies...since Balto runs this place like a prison."

She chuckled. "Thank you, Heath. That was very thoughtful." She took the bag into the kitchen then placed the flowers in a vase filled with water. She set it on the dining table, so they could feel the sun in the morning.

"Just wanted to see how you were doing." I felt guilty for everything, even though it had all turned out alright. I'd taken something from Balto that wasn't mine...and it was wrong.

"I'm fine," she said. "The pain stopped, and everything returned to normal." She placed her hand over her stomach as she came back to me. "And having my husband back is nice, even though he's been a little moody."

Balto stood there, quietly hostile.

I knew that hostility was directed at me. "He's always been that way, so that's nothing new."

She smiled then looked at her husband. "Aren't you going to say anything?"

"Don't need to," he answered. "My brother already knows exactly what I want to say."

"Yeah," I said, placing my fingers against my temple like I was reading his mind. "Lots of f-bombs and liberal use of the word asshole." I dropped my fingers, trying to lighten the mood with a joke.

Cassini continued to watch her husband. "Balto, let it go." She placed her palm against his shoulder and gave him a gentle squeeze. "You had to be there for your brother, and then he was there for me."

"I don't need another man to be there for my wife. I can do that by my damn self." He turned away and headed back to the living room.

That stung. "I think he's just jealous that I didn't bring him flowers."

He halted but didn't turn around. Then he kept walking again.

Cassini lowered her voice so he wouldn't hear. "He'll get over it. Don't worry about him." She moved into me and kissed me on the cheek. She squeezed my hand before she turned to the kitchen to continue preparing lunch.

Balto sat on the couch, staring at the TV and ignoring me.

I walked over to him. "I got some chocolate ice cream bars."

He stared at the screen, his hands together as his elbows rested on his knees.

I hated it when my brother was mad at me—especially when I deserved it. I moved to the armchair across from him.

He still ignored me.

"It won't happen again, alright?"

"Doesn't matter if it won't happen again." He turned back to me. "It already happened. You took my wife to the hospital when it should have been me. I'm the fucking father. I'm the fucking husband."

I bowed my head in shame.

"If you're lucky enough to have a wife and a kid someday, you'll understand how shitty that feels—when your wife needs you and you aren't there. You took that away from me. For what? So I could collect money you don't even need?"

Cassini came back out of the kitchen, probably hearing every word because Balto spoke so loudly. "Balto." She raised her voice, her hands on her hips, her attitude in full force. "We can't change the past, so just drop it. It wasn't like Heath took a vacation and asked you to fill in. He was really hurt—might have died."

Now Balto bowed his head.

"Our son is fine, Balto. Forgive your brother." She turned away and headed back into the kitchen.

He was quiet.

I lifted my head and stared at him for a while. "You have no idea how terrible I feel..."

"You don't feel worse than I do," he whispered. "Now my first memory as a father will always be that..."

"But your first memory won't matter compared to all the other memories you'll make, Balto. The first real memory is the day he's born—and you'll be there for that. I'll be there too because I'm not going to miss it for anything."

He took a quiet breath, like he was beginning to calm down.

"I understand you're angry, but I am sorry."

He finally looked at me, less hostile. "I thought I was okay with it, but then it hit me later."

"I get it."

He rubbed his palms together. "My life is different now. I don't expect you to understand."

"I do understand," I said quietly. "And if I didn't, I understood when I took Cassini to the hospital. I was scared for her because I love her, would die for her, and I love your son because he's my nephew."

He calmed down further.

"So...are we good?"

"Yes," he said. "But not because of the bribe you just brought."

It was a relief to hear him make a joke. "I don't know...you should try those cookies."

"I'm not going to have a dad bod, so no." He looked at the TV. "How's the office?"

I shrugged. "Nothing new."

"No one asked about your scars?"

"I don't work naked, so no."

He rolled his eyes at my comeback. "And Catalina?"

"She's going to stay with me, but I've got to work it out with Damien."

He chuckled. "Good luck with that. The guy almost killed you. That's real hate right there."

"Well, I love her, so I'm going to figure it out."

He shook his head slightly. "I think that's hopeless, but I wish you the best."

I had to figure it out if I wanted to keep Catalina, so I would find a way to break his shell...somehow.

"I'd just pay Bones to kill him, if I were you. She'll never know."

"But she'll lose her brother—which will leave her miserable."

"She'll get over it," he said simply.

"Well, I'd never get over losing you, so I doubt it."

He turned back to me, his eyes slightly soft.

"She asked me about having kids last night."

"Yeah?" Now our previous conversation seemed like ancient history. "What did you say?"

"I told her I would do it...someday."

"Did you mean it?" he asked.

"I was honest. Told her I wasn't interested in that right this second, but if it was important to her, I would get on board. My answer may just have been no altogether, but seeing you do it makes me realize I could do it."

"Well, I haven't actually done it yet."

"But you're excited about it. You're prepared. I never would have pictured that before you met Cassini."

He shrugged. "When you love a woman, shit changes."

"Yeah. I can see that."

"I mean, I'll never bring her flowers because that's pussy shit, but I'm there for her in other ways."

"She seemed to like them, so maybe you should give it a try."

He gave me a cold stare.

"Just saying..."

"Don't tell me how to be a husband when you barely know how to be a boyfriend."

"Boyfriend?" I asked. "I'm not a fucking boyfriend."

"Then what are you?"

"I'm her fucking man," I snapped. "I fuck her like a man, and no one else does. That's what I am."

He chuckled slightly when he got a rise out of me. "Yeah, you're definitely in love with this woman. Too bad her brother is standing in the way. Too bad you didn't meet her sooner, so a lot of this could have been avoided."

"Yeah. Fate isn't on my side."

Cassini came into the living room. "Want to stay for lunch, Heath?"

I looked at Balto, asking for his permission. "Depends."

Balto shook his head slightly before he caved. "Yeah. You can join us."

———

I WALKED UP to her door.

Last time I was here, I stood on the doorstep, listening to the TV in the background. I left the flowers and walked away, because I'd had no right to enter her apartment anymore. I should have returned her key, but I didn't want to do that because it felt too harsh, too final.

So, I put the key in the lock and opened it.

I stepped inside because I could, because I had every right to come and go as I pleased. It was an out-of-body experience, like living a dream, because her absence was still so potent in my mind.

She was on the couch watching TV, and she immediately sat up to look at me, dressed in her little shorts. She walked over to me, looking at the sunflowers in my hand that I'd brought for her, the ones I grew just for her. She stared at them awhile, her emotion so subtle, almost unnoticeable.

She lifted her gaze to look into mine for a few seconds before she took them, placed them against her nose to smell them, and she closed her eyes as she inhaled the forgotten scent of summer. Wordlessly, she grabbed a vase from underneath the sink and filled it with water before setting it on the kitchen island. Then she arranged them, making them good enough to sit in the window at a flower shop.

I watched her, feeling my heart grow for her every time I looked at her.

She walked around the kitchen island and came up to me, that look in her eyes the one I loved to see, like she wanted me with her mind, body, and soul. Her hands pressed into my chest as she stepped into me, her lips crashing hard to mine, like she wanted me then and there, didn't want to waste a second by speaking.

My arms held her close, pulling her petite frame tight to my chest, kissing her with the same urgency, our mouths breaking apart and joining again, a sexy exchange of tongues and breaths. My hand moved into her hair, and I told her I loved her without actually saying it.

She tugged on my shirt then yanked it over my head, barely pausing our kiss because just a few seconds without me was too long. She hopped up on the counter so we could be eye level, so she could undo my jeans and push them off.

"Fuck, baby." My hand dug into her hair, and I kissed her hard, lost in the combustible chemistry that lit us up like a display of fireworks. I couldn't get enough of her, couldn't get my boxers off quick enough, could get her shorts off fast enough so I could be inside her, where I belonged.

She grabbed my hips and yanked me inside her, releasing a moan so loud, it was like she'd never had me before.

I stilled too, breathing against her mouth, panting with indescribable desire.

We breathed together, paused for a long time, before we finally started to move.

I PICKED up the bag from the floor and carried it into the vault, grimacing slightly because anything heavy still made my ribs ache. But I hid my expression from the men, kept quiet, and ignored the pain.

Steel set down his bags. "What happened to you?"

I turned around, keeping a blank expression. "Meaning?"

"You're moving like you're injured. You were fine just a few days ago."

I held his expression and considered my response. "You know, boxing too hard." I rubbed my hand over my stomach, touching the opposite side of where my healing ribs were located.

Steel didn't call me out on it, but he didn't seem to believe me.

I walked away to grab the next bag.

"Still doesn't explain why you can't lift more than fifty pounds."

I stopped and turned to Ian, the only witness to the conversation. "Leave us."

Ian dropped his bag and walked off.

I shut the door behind him then turned to Steel. "If you want to say something, just say it."

He faced me, squared his shoulders like we were enemies rather than friends. "I know Balto took your place."

I guess he wasn't as stupid as the rest of them. I came toward him, getting close to his face. "Why would you say that?"

"Because I worked with Balto for years. I know his tells. You guys are completely different in every way but appearance."

"Do the other men believe this conspiracy?"

"I don't know. Never asked." He stepped back, proving his loyalty by keeping his mouth shut. "Why didn't you tell me?"

I didn't keep up the lie anymore. "I couldn't."

"What happened to you?" He turned back to me, standing in the sea of bags that still needed to be placed in the vault.

"Got hurt—bad."

He crossed his arms over his chest, his head tilted. "And why is that something to hide?"

"Because I was practically a corpse." It had been hard to look in the mirror and see the beating I'd taken without fighting back. It was difficult to see my punishment, even if I'd deserved it.

His anger started to fade. "Who did this to you?"

"It was a personal matter, so had nothing to do with our organization."

He raised both eyebrows. "Someone kicked your ass, and your response is to do nothing?"

"I deserved it," I snapped. "And this is exactly why I didn't tell you. The men would want justice for what was done to me, and if I didn't do something myself, they would question my leadership. And if Vox saw me in my weakened state, he might have taken the opportunity to replace me or finish me off. It was easier this way."

He was quiet for a long time, staring at me with his arms still crossed over his chest. "You still could have told me. I could have helped."

"I needed you to keep working. You're one of the men I trust most. I knew Balto could rely on you."

That didn't end his disappointment. "So, what happened?"

"I told you." I grabbed a bag and carried it into the vault. "It's a personal matter..." I tossed it onto the pile to be counted later before I turned back to him.

Steel didn't like that answer, but he didn't complain. "Fine." He turned away and started working again, quietly hostile, loudly disappointed.

I grabbed him by the arm and forced him to look at me. "You remember that woman I told you about?"

He nodded.

"I had to do something for her...and it cost me." I released my hand. "That's all I'll say about it."

I WALKED through the dancers backstage and spotted my woman at her vanity, looking into her mirror as she pulled all the dark pins from her hair, slowly releasing those silky strands so they came free and cascaded down her back. Everything happened in real time, but for me, it was slow motion.

I came up behind her, the sunflowers held at my stomach.

When she saw me in the reflection, her eyes focused on the flowers I'd brought for her. She stared for a while before she lifted her gaze and looked into my face.

I was in a black jacket with a shirt underneath, ignoring the dress code they tried to force me to obey. I moved to the vase on the corner of her table and dropped them inside. There was also a bottle of water there, so I removed the cap and filled the vase, letting the stems soak up the moisture to last during the week.

With a slight smile, she stared at the vase before she raised her chin to look at me. "Never pictured you as the candy and flowers kinda guy..."

"It gets me laid, so I am now." I sat on the bench beside her, my hand immediately moving to her thigh, the mirror positioned in front of us both. My body inched closer to hers until our foreheads touched. I stared at her lips, which were still painted with a bold red color.

Her hand went to the front of my shirt, and she grasped it as she lifted her mouth to kiss me. Then she whispered, her lips moving right against mine as she spoke. "I love you…"

I rubbed my nose against hers before I kissed her again. "And I you."

Her fingers released my shirt so I could rise.

I got to my feet and stepped out of the way so she could finish removing her heavy makeup. That was when I saw him.

Damien.

He stood with Anna by his side, dressed in his finest for a night at the ballet.

Catalina must have seen him in the reflection, because she released a quiet gasp, like her heart jumped into her throat.

I was frozen to the spot, caught off guard for the first time in my life, because I hadn't noticed him in the theatre. But then again, I wasn't really looking because now I wasn't living a lie anymore.

He stared at me for several heartbeats, all his rage and disappointment so obvious in his subtle reactions, the way his lips were slightly tight with an irritated scowl, the way his eyes were all about business and not pleasure.

Anna didn't know what to do, so she looked in a different direction, her hand still in Damien's. She was in a gown, her brown hair pinned back.

It must have been even more difficult for Damien to look at me when Anna was with him since I'd been the one to take her from the hospital.

Silence grew, and nothing happened.

I didn't know what to do, whether to crack a joke or keep my mouth shut. But I didn't want to make the situation worse.

Damien stepped forward, closer to his sister. As if he was being possessive of her, he placed his body between us, cutting me off from her. "Leave." He dropped Anna's hand and stared me down, like a lion defending his pride. He didn't raise his voice, but his threat was unmistakable. He wouldn't hunt me down and hurt me, but he would protect what he considered to be his.

Even though his sister was mine.

He waited for me to leave, didn't blink once as he looked at me, furious.

I didn't want to walk away. I didn't want to cave. I had every right to be there, to bring her flowers and tell her I loved her. But the confrontation told me how soft my grasp on her wrist was, how she could never really be mine until her brother stopped looking at me like that. "I love her." That was the only thing that came to mind, the only thing I could say that was still a rebuttal but not a hostile one. He must have seen the way I'd brought her flowers, the way I'd sat beside her and kissed her, the way she'd grabbed me and told me she loved me. How could he watch that and feel nothing at all? How could his hatred be so potent?

He stepped closer to me, getting so close that he blocked my view of the girls. "If you really loved her, you would leave." His eyes shifted back and forth as he looked into mine. "Not the situation. *Her.* You would leave her. You're a selfish motherfucker who would rather drive a wedge between her and her family than bow out. You would rather waste her time than let her find the man she deserves. So, no, you don't fucking love her. You never did. And you never will."

SIX
CATALINA

It was unlike Heath to back down from a fight, but he did.

He left out the back entrance.

He didn't look at me before he went. He didn't challenge my brother. He just walked away.

There was no other decision except that one, and I was glad I didn't have to talk Heath into it. The instant I noticed my brother was behind me, my lungs became so cold, they tightened and stopped me from breathing. I felt like I'd been caught red-handed stealing or having a boy in my bedroom when I was specifically told not to.

When it was just us, I stared at myself for a few seconds in the vanity before I wiped at my skin, getting rid of the ridiculous stage makeup that highlighted every single expression I made under the hot lights.

Then I rose to my feet, grabbed my bag, and faced my brother.

He still looked angry. He stared at me for a long time without speaking, like he was disgusted with me for the display of affection I'd just shown, grabbing and kissing a man he'd declared a blood enemy, an enemy who would be passed down through generations.

I had no idea how my face looked at that moment, if I appeared embarrassed by what he'd witnessed, uncomfortable that he was there, angry with him for ordering my lover away when he shouldn't have. I really had no idea.

"Annabella and I wanted to invite you to dinner." He forced out the words with effort, like it pained him to pretend that nothing had happened.

"I'm not hungry." Heath had probably been planning to take me out to dinner, to tell me how beautiful I looked onstage, to stare at me like he couldn't believe I was his. He could have joined us and done all those things, but he was exiled.

Damien seemed annoyed by my response but didn't reprimand me for it. "Then we'll take you home."

I was too numb to argue, so I didn't say anything.

Anna didn't say anything either, her eyes downcast like she thought she was prying by being there.

The three of us walked to the parking lot, and Damien drove me to my apartment. Anna stayed in the car, probably because she anticipated a fight she shouldn't witness, and my brother walked me to the door.

I unlocked the door and stepped inside. I hung my heavy coat by the door and tossed my purse onto the table against the wall. While I was happy Damien had come to see my performance, I was also annoyed he'd ruined my night. "What's the point of this, Damien?" I turned to him, the logs of my fire rekindling because there was a subtle spark there, underneath the simmering embers. "I'm going to Heath's place when you leave anyway." With my hands on my hips, I faced my brother. He never stuck his nose into my business and never tried the protective brother act, but now he was being a goddamn dictator.

All he did was stare at me.

"This is stupid. Don't you think this is stupid?" My voice rose, packed with emotional frustration.

He kept his voice calm. "I don't want to see him. I don't want to talk about him. I don't want to know he exists. Made that pretty clear."

"Well, the theatre is a public place. It's not your home or a family dinner. He shouldn't have to disappear every time you step into the room—"

"Yes, he should." His eyes started to light up like mine. "He's a smart guy. He could have figured out I was in the theatre if he paid attention."

"Well, maybe he was too busy watching me," I snapped.

My brother didn't lose his temper like I did, but his quiet rage was somehow just as potent. "I won't apologize for what I did. I won't change my behavior. Learn from your mistakes." He turned to the door.

"Learn from my mistakes?" I asked incredulously. "You really want nothing to do with him? Then you should text me and tell me when you're coming to a show. Tell me when you're stopping by my apartment."

He slowly turned back to me. "I'm your goddamn family. I don't have to do that."

"You can't have it both ways, Damien," I said as I shook my head.

He slid his hands into the pockets of his slacks, his silver watch visible around his wrist.

I took a deep breath and let the air escape my lungs. "Damien."

His eyes narrowed like he knew what was coming.

"This is the man I love..."

He cringed like it was painful to hear, disgusting. "No. He gives you good sex. That's it."

I stilled at the crass comment because I'd never heard my brother talk like that.

"You can get good dick anywhere, Catalina. Don't fall for his macho bullshit. Don't fall for the bad boy turned good routine. Because they never turn good. Ever."

"Well, this one has, Damien. He's proved it to you."

"No." He stepped closer to me. "He's only playing nice because I have something he wants—and I won't give it to him."

"Have *something* he wants?" My eyes narrowed. "I better not be that something, Damien. Because you don't *have* me."

"When Dad is gone, I'm the man of this family. So, yes—"

"Fuck you. I'm glad I won't have your last name when I get married."

"You'll never have his last name, that's for damn sure." Now he raised his voice, now he lost his temper, now his green eyes were vicious like mine.

"Damien." I stomped my foot. "This is how bitter you are? This is who you really want to be? Because you're being a fucking asshole."

"I'd rather be an asshole than a murderer."

I sighed at the insult.

Damien dragged his hand down his cheek to his chin, like he was calming himself after screaming at me. He looked away, stared at my kitchen for a few minutes, and then cleared his throat and looked back at me. "I don't want us to be like this. That man has caused enough turmoil in our family. We're just going to have to agree to disagree."

I didn't just want Heath because I couldn't have him. I wanted him because it felt right, because he made me happy. "Damien...please."

"No."

"How would you feel if I told you I would never like Anna? The woman you love? The only woman you've ever loved? What if I said I didn't like the fact that she's already been married twice? What if I said I didn't like the fact that she caused danger to our family because of her ex-husband?"

His eyes narrowed. "Not the same thing at all."

"But what if I felt that way? What if I refused to get along with the woman you're in love with?"

He stared me down.

"It would kill you. So, imagine how I feel right now."

"You know what kills me?" he whispered. "Walking up to you with my fiancée, holding her hand while I look at the man who took her from her hospital room, the man who broke through my window, which resulted in her being shot in the first place. You forced me to stand there, with them just feet apart, and not shoot him in the fucking face."

"Heath would never hurt Anna—"

"But he already did. My job as her husband is to protect her. But I have to stand there like a goddamn joke."

"She's not afraid of him."

"How do you know how she feels?" he snapped.

"Because Anna would want me to be happy."

His wide eyes shone with ferocity. "There are a million guys out there, Catalina. And you're so beautiful that you could have anyone you want. Just find someone else. It's that simple."

"How would you feel if I told you the same thing?"

"Well, I'm marrying her, so there is no one else for me."

I crossed my arms over my chest. "And I might like to marry Heath...someday."

He shook his head slightly, showing how much that irritated him. "You're smarter than this, Catalina. Even if you two are Romeo and Juliet, the infatuation and lust aren't worth your demise."

"Damien, it's not infatuation and lust—"

"It must be because you would never love someone who's hurt your family." He came closer to me, starting to yell again. "I refuse to believe you would be that disloyal, so I'm going to give you the benefit of the doubt and assume this is a really potent hit of lust. You want to fuck him? Fine. Fuck him and move on."

"I told you I loved him—and I meant it."

He stepped back, rubbing the back of his head. "I can't believe you're going to do this. I can't believe you're going to hurt your family like this—for a guy. Come on, look at yourself." He raised both hands at me. "I've never had a poorer opinion of you than I do right now."

That hurt—so fucking bad. My eyes immediately watered. "Don't say that to me..."

"That's how I really feel, Catalina. I've always been proud of you as my sister because you're strong, fierce, independent, and so fucking smart that I'm pretty sure you're smarter than me...and this is who you want to be with? It's like a princess wanting to be with the assassin that tried to murder the king— her father. It's like you're brainwashed or something."

"Look, you don't know what we have. You're seeing it from an outside point of view—"

"I'm seeing it objectively."

"He's not the same man, Damien. He didn't just change because he wants something from you. He's changed because...he's changed." I wanted to tell him what had happened to me, that Heath had rescued me when he could have easily walked away, that the incident more than vindicated him. But if I did…it would hurt Damien beyond repair, to know what had happened to me.

He rolled his eyes.

"You just said how smart I am. Could you please just take a leap of faith for me? Could you please just do this for me? Just try? It would mean—"

"No." He slid his hands back into his pockets. "Heath and I have a long history. He's walked into my office so many times and made me feel like his bitch. This hatred runs deep in my veins for many reasons, not just one. You're asking me to forget all of that."

"No, I'm asking you to forgive all of that. Just try—"

"*No!*." Now his eyes were wide, matching the loud sound of his voice. He ended the conversation when he unleashed his rage.

The words left my throat.

"You have no idea how hard it was for me to drop my vendetta." He lowered his head and stared at the floor for a while before he looked at me again. "How hard it was for me not to avenge my father, the woman I'm marrying…but I did it for you. Because I love you. Because I don't want to hurt you by hurting him. That's the most I can give, so don't ask for more."

SEVEN

HEATH

I sat on the couch for hours, in the dark, staring out the window at the city beyond. My back leaned into the cushions, and I rubbed my fingers across my temple, trying to numb the gentle pulse that would soon become a headache. All I had to do was take a couple pills, but that seemed like too much work right now.

I couldn't stop thinking about the exchange that just happened, the way Damien had ordered me away, treating me like a stray dog no one wanted to adopt.

I was scared.

I was scared of what Damien would say to Catalina.

That he would convince her to leave me.

It'd been hours, and she hadn't called. She hadn't texted me.

She was already on the fence, hardly agreeing to stay until I talked her into it, so if her brother was that furious by my presence in a public place...I could only imagine what he said to her behind closed doors.

That he would never stop hating me.

And then she would leave...and rip my heart out of my chest.

When midnight arrived, I was certain Catalina wasn't with her brother anymore, so I called.

It rang...until the voice mail picked up.

"Fuck."

I texted her. *Baby*.

No response.

Why did I go to her show tonight? Why didn't I pay attention to my surroundings? Why didn't I treat this situation with the delicateness it deserved?

Fuck.

I texted her again. *Answer me. Or I'm coming over*.

The three dots appeared right away.

But then they disappeared and never came back.

This was bad. I already knew what I had to face when I got there.

It almost made me not go at all.

WHEN I WALKED in the door, she was on the couch, her cheeks puffy because she'd been crying. Her eyes were red, her olive skin was flushed and blotchy because the tears must have lasted for a while.

This torture was worse than the beating Damien had given me.

Because this killed my soul.

She didn't look at me, her knees to her chest with a blanket draped over her, her arms wrapped around her legs. She was completely closed off from me before I even walked in the door.

I moved to the couch, watching her not look at me. I sat on the couch beside her, staring at the side of her face, observing her look at the other wall of the living room instead of me.

I'd already lost her.

"Baby." I took a deep breath as I felt her slip away, felt her move further and further into the distance, felt her soul fight against the rope that bound us together months ago.

Nothing.

"Give it time," I whispered to her, wishing she would turn and look at me, that she wouldn't give me the cold shoulder like this when we'd just been a forest fire hours ago. "The wound is still too fresh right now. I will fix this, but you need to give me a chance. Don't pull the plug yet."

When she spoke, her voice was defeated. "He's not going to change his mind…"

"Right now."

"Ever."

My heart was beating so fucking hard right now. "Don't give up on me. Don't give up on us."

Her arms tightened around her legs. "Please don't make this harder for me..."

"It's gotta be hard—but we're worth it."

"Heath—"

"No." My breath came out shaky, because I'd never wanted something so much in my entire fucking life. She was everything to me, my family, my best friend, my woman. "You told me you would give me a chance. You have yet to do that."

She slowly turned to me, finally revealing her entire face, all the damage her sobs had caused. "He said letting you live is the hardest thing he's ever had to do, but he did it for me. That's the most he can give."

"You'd be surprised what a man can give when he loves someone..." I believed Damien could give more, if he had more time to let the past become the past. Everything happened only a month ago. It was practically the present.

"I can't live this way, Heath." She shook her head. "I'm so close to my family. I go over there all the time, play chess with my father, have dinner with everyone all the time... I can't lose that."

"You never will."

"But it's already different."

"I won't come to your shows anymore. We won't go out in public anymore."

"And that's not the relationship I want to have. Don't you see that?"

"It's just temporary." I had to keep my voice controlled even though I wanted to let my emotions out of the cage and burst from my lips. "I know you're upset right now. I'm sure he said things that hurt you—"

"My brother has never spoken to me like that before."

"Because he's upset—and he's entitled to be upset. But I'm telling you, those emotions will fade...in time. You need to give me time."

She turned away again.

No.

"I'm sorry...I am."

"I don't accept that."

"Well, you have to." She got to her feet and let the blanket slide off her legs and back to the floor. "Please don't make this more difficult for me. I told him how I felt about you. I told him I want to be with you...even marry you someday. And it didn't make a difference." She placed her hand over her eyes, like she didn't want me to see her cry. "I don't have the strength to have this conversation with you, to have this argument, especially when I'm not going to change my mind. So please...just go." She walked behind the back of the couch then across the kitchen, moving slowly like her body was broken, and then entered her bedroom. She shut the door behind her. And then it went quiet.

THE GUARDS STOPPED me at the entryway.

"No more money for you."

My emotions were at the surface, a combination of rage, ferocity, and agony. So, I didn't have the patience for this. I yanked the rifle out of one of the guard's hands, smacked him hard in the head, and did the same to the other guard before he could move his finger to the trigger. I dropped the gun and entered the building.

Damien must have known I was coming because the other guards stood down on my way. I took the stairs then crossed the concrete floor as his crew prepared the next shipment to be dispersed across the country.

Some stopped to look at me.

I approached the office door, which was halfway open. He sat at the desk, relaxed in the chair like he was prepared for a long conversation.

I shut the door behind me and approached his desk, staring at his aloof features without saying a word. I hadn't prepared a speech. I hadn't asked my brother for advice. After my conversation with Catalina, I knew that I had to do something now, not later, that I was fighting for the single thing that mattered to me.

He propped his cheek on his closed knuckles, regarding me with indifference.

There was a beast inside my chest, trying to break free so he could crush Damien's skull, cause him pain. I was a fucking volcano of agony, constantly spewing lava packed with my heartbreak. "Please." That was all I could manage to get out, to convey my desperation, to show this man I had no pride when it came to the woman I loved.

He dropped his hand and straightened in his chair, regarding me with the same coldness.

"I love her. Please don't do this to me."

He watched me without blinking, a dead look in his eyes.

"I'll do whatever you want, Damien. Name it. I'll do it."

He cocked his head slightly. "All I want is for you to disappear."

I closed my eyes hard, my hands tightening into fists at the same time. When I opened my eyes again, I could feel the moisture coating them, feel a sensation I hadn't felt in so long I wasn't even sure what was happening.

He continued to stare at me, heartless.

"I love her so fucking much. Please." I locked my gaze with another man, tears in my eyes, so desperate, I didn't even try to hide them, didn't feel any shame for wearing my heart on my sleeve.

"No."

I felt like a knife was stabbing me in the chest.

"You didn't break for me in the cage, but you're breaking now...and I'm not going to pretend that I don't enjoy it."

My lungs expanded to take the breath I needed, to fight the desire to bash in his skull with my thumbs. "I'm not the only one you're hurting, Damien. You don't have to give a shit about me, but what I feel, she feels." I placed my hand over my heart. "You're doing this to her too. You're making her cry to herself at night because she can't be with the man she loves."

"She'll get over it."

I dropped my hand, realizing Catalina was right. He would never change his mind. "I'm sorry for what I did. I'm apologizing to you."

He shrugged. "I don't want an apology. I just want you to leave."

"Damien, come on..."

He shook his head. "You're lucky I agreed to let you go. So instead of whining like a dog, you should be grateful."

"I'd rather be killed than have to live without her."

He chuckled slightly, like my heartfelt words were simply comical to him. "Then take your own life. Nothing would make me happier."

"How can you do this to her?"

"Do this to her?" he asked incredulously. "I'm protecting her. She deserves a lot better than you. Don't deny it."

"Yeah, she does," I said honestly. "But even if she marries another man, that doesn't mean she'll love him...not the way she loves me."

"It's just lust, Heath."

"No, asshole," I snapped. "I know what lust is. I've had a lot of it in my life. That's not what this is."

"Yeah, call me an asshole. That's a good approach to get what you want."

"Looks like you've made up your mind anyway."

He snapped his fingers. "You aren't as stupid as I thought. I guess that means she broke it off with you. Can't think of any other reason why you're standing here."

I took a painful breath. "Yeah, it's the only reason I could cry in front of another man when I never cry at all." I felt two tears drip down my cheeks, and I quickly wiped them away, blinking away the rest of the moisture so the tears would stop.

"Are we done here?" he asked bluntly.

I looked into the eyes of the cruelest man I'd ever met, who had the same eyes as the woman I loved. "You've made me suffer enough. Please…"

"I'm not trying to make you suffer. I just don't want my sister to be with a piece of shit who tried to kill our father."

"If she can forgive me, then you—"

"I'm not getting good dick from you, so I have no reason to forgive you."

I didn't know why I continued to stand there when this man was giving me no hope. "Our relationship is a lot more than that. I would die for her."

"But you won't bow out? Interesting…"

"Because I thought you'd love your sister enough to be the bigger man here."

"Bigger man?" Now, he got to his feet, meeting me head on. "Do I need to remind you of everything you've done? How many times you've walked in here and taunted me? I don't care if she wants to be with a kingpin like me. He doesn't have to be Prince fucking Charming. But he can't be you. My dad won't be around much longer, so it's my job to take care of her—"

"She doesn't need a man to take care of her," I snapped. "She needs a brother to be there for her, to support her, to be her friend. Stop this patriarchal bullshit. She's a grown-ass woman who can make her own decisions—"

"She obviously can't if she thinks this is a good idea."

My nostrils flared because I couldn't keep the anger inside. "You took her to the gypsy in Marrakech."

His posture immediately changed at my words.

"Did she ever tell you what the gypsy said?"

He was still quiet, his eyes focused because he'd clearly never had this conversation with his sister.

"She said Catalina would only love one man—but he would be an enemy to her family."

He took a deep breath, like the statement actually meant something to him.

"So, you would rather she marry a man she doesn't love than be with me?"

His taunts were gone, like he didn't know what to say.

"Come on, Damien." I felt hope again, saw the light at the end of the tunnel. Catalina told me both Hades and Damien had fortunes that came true, so they would believe every word I said. "Are you really going to be the reason Catalina can't be with the only man she'll ever love? Are you really going to stand in her way?"

"Did the gypsy say anything else?"

Now the hope died away again. "That was all she told me."

He bowed his head for a moment, breathing quietly as his mind no doubt raced. His fingertips were pressed to the desk, both of his hands on the wood. When he'd gathered his thoughts, he lifted his chin and looked at me again. "I never told her she couldn't be with you. I just said I didn't want anything to do with you."

"But you know she needs both, Damien."

"I'm not going to change the way I feel about you. That hatred runs too deep—and you know it's completely justified. I told her she could marry you, spend her life with you, but I don't have to be subjected to your company or your presence. Her decision to leave you is entirely her own—I'm not forcing her."

"But that implies you'll never come to our wedding."

"You've known her for a few months. How can you—"

"Because I just know."

He pulled his hands off the desk and slipped them into his pockets. "I've made my decision, Heath. She can love whomever she wants. She can do whatever she wants. But I don't have to change the way I feel about it. If you don't want her to leave you, I suggest you talk to her—not me."

"Damien, she needs your approval—"

"And I'm not going to give it. Not now. Not ever."

"You don't see how that's a problem?"

"If it is, it's because her family is more important to her than you—and that's how it should be. My feelings toward you are completely valid. Our problems don't derive from something inconsequential."

"I never said they weren't valid. I just hoped you loved your sister more than you hated me—"

"I guess I don't." He lowered himself into the chair again. "Get out of my office, Heath. I've already wasted enough time on you."

I stayed rooted to the spot, even though I'd already fired off all my ammunition. I'd already put my heart on the line, let the tears fall down my cheeks, begged for forgiveness. I'd done everything I could—and it didn't matter.

I had no other choice but to leave.

I WALKED into her apartment and came face-to-face with her.

It was well after midnight, so she would normally be asleep, but she stood at the kitchen island with a glass of wine in her hand. When she looked at me, her eyes still had signs of tears, like she'd cried just a few hours ago.

I couldn't believe this was happening.

I stopped at the opposite side of the counter, my hands gripping the edge.

She dropped her gaze and looked into her glass.

"I just talked to Damien."

She lifted her gaze, surprise in her eyes.

"I went to his office. We had words."

She didn't ask how it went, like she already knew.

"I told him about the gypsy... I was surprised you didn't tell him about that."

She was still quiet, her fingers on the rim of her glass.

"He asked if the gypsy said anything else. Did she?"

She ran her fingers through her hair. "No."

I was hoping the gypsy had said something else, something that could help us. "Did you tell him about the basement? When I saw you there..."

She pulled the glass closer to her. "No."

"Why?" I felt like that might give me a chance, because I'd saved her life when I had no obligation at the time.

"Because I know it would kill him...to know what happened to me."

"But maybe it would give us a chance."

She looked into my eyes, just as heartbroken as I was. "Nothing is going to change his mind, Heath. You've witnessed it with your own eyes now."

I bowed my head. "I can't lose you..."

She sighed deeply, like hearing my words caused her heart to break again.

I looked at her again. "He said he never told you to stop being with me. You're free to be with whomever you want. So, let's stick to what we agreed on. We'll be together...and hope his attitude changes in time."

"He's not going to change his mind."

"We can't give up," I whispered. "I refuse to give up on you—"

"Stop." She closed her eyes, her hand going to her face, like she was about to explode into tears. "Please don't do this to me..."

Those were the same words I'd said to Damien, and it hurt to listen to her beg for the same relief.

"I understand why Damien feels the way he does. I understand why his feelings haven't changed—because he's not the one in love with you. You're just a man to him, and there's no reason for him to feel differently about you..."

"Making you happy is reason enough to me."

She dropped her hand, her eyes downcast as she stared at her glass. "I don't think he'll ever feel differently. So I don't want to spend whatever time we have left together and then be crushed when I have to leave. It's already hard enough right now. Imagine doing this years from now."

"Maybe we won't have to because he'll come around."

"And if he doesn't, it'll be devastating."

"That's why we have to take the chance, baby. Come on..."

She still wouldn't look at me, and then she burst into tears. "No." She sniffed loudly and took a deep breath, closing her eyes so she would stop crying, stop showing her weakness in front of me. "I know him... I know he's not going to change."

It killed me to watch her cry. Fucking killed me.

"I'm sorry, but this has to end."

"No."

"Yes..." She turned away.

I took a breath and steadied my own tears, knowing I couldn't give in to the turmoil, let her see my pain...because it would just make it worse for both of us.

Her fingers curled into a fist under her nose as she stifled her sobs, facing the fridge so she wouldn't have to look at me, let me see her break apart.

I gripped the edge of the counter and stared at the stove, listening to her cry, listening to the sound of my heartbreak echo back at me. It was the first time in my life I'd felt complete, that my life had a purpose, that there was more to life than money, violence, and whores. I had something better than all of that.

And now I had to let it go.

"Don't make this harder," she said through her sobs. "For both of us..."

I closed my eyes and felt the tears escape my eyes. I was silent as I felt the tears flow like rivers down my cheeks. I opened my eyes and took a deep breath, feeling the tears reach my lips, drip through the opening of my mouth, and stick to my tongue. I was grateful she couldn't see me, that she had no idea I'd stifled my own pain so she wouldn't have to listen to it.

How did I go on after this? How did I live a life without the one person I loved? I'd done terrible things that deserved punishment, but this was too harsh. It was too fucking cruel.

She was the reason I became a better man, but I didn't get to keep her.

It took all my strength to walk out of that apartment.

It took all my strength to leave her behind.

It took all my strength to turn my back on the love of my life... and leave her.

EIGHT
CATALINA

It was different from the first time we broke up.

Because I had no rage to mask my pain.

Now, I just felt the heartbreak, raw and potent, making my hands shake even when I was lying absolutely still. The winter was bitterly cold without his hand on my heart. My life had been decimated with the loss of him. I didn't know how to move forward even though he'd been in my life for such a short period of time.

But now, everything was different.

The sky looked different.

My heart didn't beat the same. It didn't have a steady rhythm, uneven, racing.

I was lost...like I didn't know who I was anymore.

A week passed, and I didn't leave the house. Damien didn't text me, and neither did Anna. So, my time between the couch and the bed continued uninterrupted. The pain in my chest was difficult to describe, the depression a constant blanket of clouds over my ceiling. There was no sunshine... even on a clear day.

I didn't eat much, but I drank more wine.

I expected texts from Heath, but they never came.

I didn't text him either, because it would just make it worse.

I just would have to feel this way...until I stopped feeling this way.

When the weekend came, I couldn't mope around anymore. I couldn't call in sick either because I'd done that enough over the last few months. If I continued to do it, it would put my job in jeopardy.

I went backstage, got ready, and did my job.

When it was over, the girls wanted to go out, but the last thing I wanted to do was get dressed up to impress men I didn't care about. I just wanted to lie in bed and stare at the ceiling, wait for sleep to pull me under.

But Tracy wouldn't let that happen. "The sooner you get used to living normally, the easier it'll become."

Nothing seemed easy right now. "I don't think it's that simple."

"You gotta start somewhere, Cat." She sat beside me on the bench. "I brought that purple dress you like. It'll look so good on you."

I rolled my eyes. "Not as good as it looks on you. You've got those nice tits."

"Shut up. You have nice tits too."

"But they aren't boobalicious."

She gave me a playful nudge in the side. "Come on, just a few drinks. Then you can go home."

I sighed.

"You gotta get your feet wet."

"I don't want to meet anyone."

"I know. But you can't mope around the house forever."

After we got dressed, we went to the bar with the rest of the girls, but the loud music from the speakers was just obnoxious to me. I missed the silence of my apartment. I missed the solitude. Every time I got a free drink, I wanted to dump it on the floor. Every time someone wanted to make conversation with me, I couldn't even pretend to be polite.

Tracy had a lot of admirers tonight, probably because she was wearing a backless black dress, showing off her amazing figure. She tried to wave them off, but since she was having such an on night, it was an effort to get rid of them.

"Don't worry about it, Tracy. You're fine."

"I'm not going to leave you."

"But these guys are hot." I gave her a squeeze on the arm. "Seriously, I'm fine. I'll finish this drink and head home. We both know I've wanted to leave since the moment I got here."

She gave a slight chuckle. "Alright. Well, thanks for coming out for a bit. I hope it made you feel a little better."

"Yeah," I lied. "A bit."

She left the table and returned to the guy she'd blown off before, and he was clearly enthused she'd had a change of heart.

I swirled my cosmo and took another drink, but I didn't intend to linger to finish it all. I had a stockpile of wine at the apartment that I could enjoy in my pajamas. I'd rather be there—alone—than here.

I rose from the chair and started to walk out, to move past the sea of tables with couples and friends drinking. That was when I noticed Heath sitting alone, in a long-sleeved shirt with an untouched drink in front of him, watching me from a distance with a dead expression in his eyes. His strong shoulders sagged, and his eyes were down like he hoped I wouldn't notice him, like I wouldn't realize he'd come to my show then followed me here just so he could look at me.

I almost walked out—but I couldn't.

I walked over to him, stopping when my thigh nearly touched his chair.

He didn't look at me, as if he was annoyed I'd spotted him.

It was hard to look at his face, see his masculine jawline, the blue color of his eyes. He was the man who'd made love to me every night, the man who loved me with just his look. And now he sat there...unsure what to do with his life now that I wasn't in it.

My arm hooked around his shoulders, and I lowered myself into his lap, my face nestling into his neck because I couldn't resist the chance to feel him, to let the affection comfort me.

His arms immediately wrapped around me, hugging me tightly, his chin resting on the top of my head. He took a deep breath, his broad chest rising against my body and making me shift with the movement. Then he released it, a long deflation of his lungs, his fingers digging into my skin.

Both of my arms were hooked around his neck, holding him close as I took advantage of the effect he had on me, to wash away all my pain, to pause all the agony instantly. I clung to him with no intention of leaving, giving in to the weakness for a little while.

NINE

HEATH

THE ELEVATOR DOORS OPENED, AND I STEPPED OUT ONTO the top floor of the building.

Balto came down the hallway, his phone beeping when the alarm was disabled, and he probably assumed I'd come for a visit in the middle of the night. He flipped on the lights, wearing his sweatpants without a shirt. "What the fuck, Heath? It's two in the morning—" He stopped talking when he saw the look on my face. He paused his stride, his eyes shifting back and forth as he looked into mine, and then he continued to walk.

I stood there, my gaze sinking to the floor because I didn't want to look at him, didn't want to see him look at me.

When he came close to me, he placed his hand on my shoulder, his fingers digging into my flesh to comfort me. He didn't say anything as he stood there with me, silently understanding that my world had crashed down around me.

"She left me," I whispered, the words barely escaping my lips. "And this time, she's not going to come back." I took a deep breath, my face hurting from the tightness in my jaw and cheeks, not hiding anything from him because I didn't have to. I could hit rock bottom, and he wouldn't think less of me.

Balto looked at me for a while before he embraced me, wrapping his arms around me, one palm cupping the back of my neck.

I held my brother, the only person I had in the entire world.

I'd attended her performance because I missed her. I went to the bar because I wanted to see her face. But when I saw how miserable she was, it only hurt me more. Then she came to me...and that embrace was good...but so painful. She sat on my lap for an hour, then silently rose to her feet and walked out.

Leaving me alone again.

Balto held me for a long time, wordlessly embracing me, wordlessly grasping me.

It helped...but not much.

He eventually pulled away and faced me head on. "How can I help?"

I shook my head. "There's nothing you can do."

He moved his hands to his hips, standing in front of me. "Damien won't change his mind?"

"No. I tried talking to him, but that didn't go anywhere."

"What if I talk to him?"

"I don't see what that's going to do."

"He respects me."

It was nice of him to offer, especially when he'd made it clear he wouldn't interfere in anything after he'd walked away from his responsibilities as the Skull King. And he'd already taken my place...already did enough. "I don't know... I think it's a long shot."

"Let me try." He pulled out his phone.

"Now? It's the middle of the night."

"Work never sleeps, right?" He pulled up Damien's name and made the call, pressing the phone to his ear, the rings loud enough that I could hear just fine. "He'll take my call when he sees my name on the screen—even if he knows why I'm calling."

Damien answered on the fourth ring. "I think I know what this is about, but I'm going to give you the benefit of the doubt." He sounded slightly sleepy, like he'd just rolled out of bed and he was now walking out of the room so Anna wouldn't wake up.

"I appreciate the doubt, but your instinct is right."

He sighed into the phone. "I don't have a problem with you, Balto. I'd prefer if we kept it that way."

"Me too. But I care about my brother's sanity more than our friendship."

He sighed again. "I know how I feel about Heath. Whatever you're going to say isn't going to change that, especially with a phone call."

"But you respect me enough to let me try."

He was quiet.

"I'm not going to lie to you to get you to change your mind. So, I'm being honest when I tell you this. Heath is different. He was a heartless tyrant, caring about the profits instead of the people his actions affected. He was such a handful that I threw him in jail for six months to straighten him out. But you know what? He met Catalina—and everything changed. I changed when I met my wife—and he's changed now that he's met his."

Damien stayed quiet.

"Same thing happened with Hades. Same thing happened with you. I know you aren't the same person anymore—in a good way."

"I didn't try to kill an innocent old man…"

"We're all guilty of a lot of shitty things, Damien," he said simply. "But Heath is not that person anymore. You've got a powerful man who would do anything and everything to protect your sister. Maybe you don't like him, but you can't deny there's no better man to keep her safe, to hunt down anyone who even looks at her the wrong way. You want her to be with some average guy? Then she's going to have an average life."

He was still quiet.

"I can personally vouch for him, Damien."

"I know, Balto. I've always liked you, always respected you. You were a good Skull King, listened to reason, understood your subjects. But when I had my argument with Heath about my taxes, he was arrogant, ignorant, and refused to change his mind. So, why should I change mine?"

Balto looked at me as he continued to speak. "He did change his mind, Damien. And he changed it before you even knew about his relationship with your sister. He changed his mind without Catalina even asking him."

He didn't have anything to say to that.

"He's different in every way you can think of, Damien. And if it comes down to it, he'd step down if that's what you wanted." Balto assumed without asking, knowing I would sacrifice anything.

"I'd prefer if he stayed the Skull King so I can continue not to pay my taxes. Once he's replaced, the new king will come after me."

Balto closed his eyes briefly in annoyance. "Bottom line, Heath will do anything for Catalina, for you, for anybody in your family. Don't focus on what he did before. Focus on what he can do for you now."

Damien respected him enough not to snap back like he did with me. "I don't need him to do anything for me, Balto. The only reason I've listened to everything you've had to say is out of respect for our past. But now that you're done, I'm done too. You're having a kid, right?"

Balto seemed slightly confused. "A boy."

"Alright. What if you were having a girl...and that girl wanted to marry someone like Heath. What would you say?"

He blinked as he stared at me. "I would want my daughter to be happy, because I'm not always going to be around to take care of her. Damien, you're going to have your own family someday. Catalina will be someone else's problem. Wouldn't you want that man to be—"

"There're a lot of strong and powerful men out there who could be a suitor for Catalina. There's only one man I don't want for her. She can have her pick of the rest." He hung up.

Balto slowly lowered the phone, sighing in disappointment.

That conversation went as I'd expected it would. "Thanks for trying."

He slipped the phone into his pocket then looked at me. "Want a drink?"

I nodded. "Yeah..."

I'D BEEN SHOT.

Stabbed.

Beaten to within an inch of my life.

But nothing had ever felt as bad as this.

Another week passed, and other than work, I didn't go anywhere.

I lay in bed or watched TV on the couch, my mind usually on the fiery brunette who'd lit my life on fire...then turned it to ice when she left.

I was miserable, worse than miserable.

Balto stopped by often, just to keep me company without actually asking me anything about Catalina. He talked about sports, the baby, Cassini...anything that had nothing to do with Catalina.

But I thought about her, regardless.

I drank a lot because I had nothing else to do. A week had come and gone since the last time I saw her, and I couldn't imagine being with another woman, even if two months had passed. I couldn't even imagine paying for sex, even if it was only physical. How would I ever recover from this? How would I ever enjoy another woman when there was only one I really wanted?

I lay in bed that night, looking at the ceiling as the lights of the city filled my bedroom. I usually closed the electronic drapes, but I hadn't been sleeping much, so it really didn't matter.

My phone lit up on the nightstand.

It was never Catalina, so it was hard to be excited about that subtle vibration. But I grabbed it anyway, knowing it could be about work.

It was a notification on my phone—that the garage had opened.

My pulse started to pound in my ears, my heart began to beat erratically. It could be Balto, but it was unlikely that he would show up in the middle of the night and leave his wife unattended.

So it might be her.

Fuck, I hoped it was her.

The house was silent, so I heard the faint sound of the door. Then there were footsteps, growing louder and louder as they approached my bedroom, the tread light, like a small person with a purpose was headed toward me.

I stopped breathing.

My door was open, so she stepped inside, a shadowy silhouette in the darkness. She crept closer to the bed, the lights from the city rising up her body until she stepped completely into the light—and it illuminated her face.

Her gorgeous fucking face.

I sat up slightly, holding up my torso with my elbow against the bed. My eyes stared at her, unsure what happening, unsure if this was even real.

She was in a sweater and jeans, makeup gone from her face as if she'd had no intention of going out when she decided to come to my place. It was impulsive, like she'd missed me so much she couldn't bear it a moment longer.

I stared, paralyzed, the sheets over my boxers, hiding how hard I was at the sight of her in my bedroom.

She came closer to the bed and grabbed the hem of her sweater. Then she slowly pulled it over her head.

Yes.

Her bra came next and then her jeans, a pile forming on my bedroom floor, her panties on top.

I breathed hard, unable to believe this was happening, that I would be inside the woman I loved in just seconds.

She came to the bed and got on top of me, her hair falling down around my face as she held herself above me.

My hand slid into her hair, and I brought her face to my lips, kissing her hard, kissing her as quickly as I could.

She breathed into my lungs, panting at the cosmic explosion of our touch. Her hand gripped my shoulder, and she clawed me like a wild cat climbing up a tree. Her other hand moved to my chest, planting itself hard against my muscle.

My hand pushed my boxers over my hips, letting my cock come free.

She lowered herself onto my length, rolling her hips back so she could position my head directly over her pussy, straightening it so she could slide down in one fluid motion.

I groaned so loud against her mouth I sounded like a monster.

She moaned against my mouth, her nails digging deep into me.

"Baby..." I wrapped my arm around her waist and flipped her to her back, wanting to make love to her the way I used to, smash her into my mattress as I pinned her down, keep her underneath me so she couldn't get away.

Her legs locked around my waist, and she gripped the back of my shoulders, breathing hard into my mouth, tears escaping the corners of her eyes from emotion, not because I'd made her come. "Heath..."

I thrust into her hard, like I was being timed, like I only had so long to enjoy her. "Baby, I fucking missed you."

———

THE WORLD TURNED QUIET, and the heartache in my chest died away when we were together. With every thrust, I got lost deeper, swept away by the comfort of our connection, my mind turned off completely so I could just feel...feel her.

With my forehead pressed to hers, I moved into her slowly, pushed my cock all the way inside before I pulled it out again, getting coated in her cream and come. It felt so good to be with her, like there'd been no time spent apart, like I'd never lost her.

Like she'd always been mine.

She clung to me just the way she used to, her nails enthusiastic, her hold demanding. Her pussy was soaked, like I could fuck her over and over and she would never run dry.

I thrust into her a final few times, feeling myself reach my threshold once again, making me fill every inch of her with another load. How could I ever be with someone else when this was who I was supposed to be with?

Fuck, I talked like a pussy.

I pulled out of her and rolled over, slick with sweat, satisfied, and so damn happy. I closed my eyes and lay there, feeling the peace settle into my soul, the fear and sadness disappearing like the setting sun.

Then she got out of bed.

She walked to her clothes and started to put them on.

I opened my eyes and looked at her. "What are you doing?"

She clasped her bra then pulled her sweater over her head. "I have to go…"

I was so shocked by what she'd said that all I could do was stare at her.

She pulled on her jeans—and walked out.

What the fuck just happened?

I jumped out of bed and went after her. "Stay until morning." It was the dead of the night. I didn't even know what time it was, but it was sometime between midnight and sunrise.

"I can't…" She reached the stairs and began to descend.

I grabbed her by the elbow and tugged her back. "Why are you treating me like a booty call?"

She turned back to me, her eyes guarded, like she didn't even want to look at me.

My eyes narrowed further.

"I missed you…and I caved. I just wanted to be with you."

Why was I so fucking stupid? "And you didn't consider my feelings at all?" This separation was hard for me too, but I didn't storm into her bedroom in the middle of the night and drop all my clothes.

She lowered her eyes. "I-I won't do it again. I just didn't want to go out and pick up some random guy, not when you're the one I want."

That was the last thing I wanted. "So, you're just going to come by whenever you feel like it?"

"I don't have to."

"No…it's fine." I was too weak to say no. I was too weak to deny the only woman I wanted.

"I can't sleep over. That's just too much."

Straight down to business, then.

"No kiss goodbye…"

Purely physical.

"It's just hard to quit cold turkey, you know?"

I had hoped she'd changed her mind, that she'd realized she couldn't live without me. But now, she just wanted to use me, because I gave her good dick. It didn't make me feel good, but I didn't have the strength to deny her.

"No talking."

I stared at her.

"If that's okay with you..." She watched me hesitantly, like I might say no.

I stared at her like she wasn't mine, instead the ghost of the woman who used to belong to me. She was still gone, and now I had to let go of her slowly...little by little.

"Because it doesn't have to be."

I knew it was a bad idea. It was smarter just to push through it. But I also hoped the cycle would start over again, that we would sleep together, but the sex would turn into something more. I might get everything I wanted...or get hurt even more. "I'd rather have some of you than none of you at all."

TEN

CATALINA

My dad was used to seeing me at least once a week, but since I was too depressed to even leave the house, I never showed my face. I didn't want to go to Damien's at all, didn't want to interact with another human, plaster a smile on my face.

I'd gone to Heath's because I couldn't stand the loneliness anymore. Just wanted the pain to stop—just for a few hours— so I could take a full breath and get some relief. But then I had to leave, and that was hard.

It was hard not to sleep beside him.

Hard not to talk to him.

Hard not to tell him I loved him.

It was a bad idea and I'd expected Heath to throw me out on my ass, but he didn't. He agreed, even though it seemed like he didn't want to. He wanted me to change my mind, to go against the wishes of my family and choose him instead.

I couldn't.

My phone rang beside me on the bed, Damien's name on the screen.

I groaned because I didn't want to talk to him. I'd ended things with Heath so our relationship would be normal again, but now I resented him, labeled him as the cause of my agony.

But I answered anyway. "Hey."

It wasn't Damien. It was my father instead. "Sweetheart, are you alright?"

My dad had an old cell phone he never used, and he'd probably lost it somewhere in his bedroom and Patricia had to search for it. His voice caught me off guard, and I immediately cleared my throat to sound normal. "Yes, Dad. Everything's fine. Why wouldn't it be?"

"Well, I haven't seen you in two weeks." His tone was full of accusation, like I'd seriously betrayed him in some way.

I tried not to roll my eyes. "Just been busy."

"I don't like that. I want to see you. Remember, I won't be around forever..."

He always guilt-tripped me right away.

"I'll have Damien bring me over there—"

"I'll come over for lunch tomorrow, Dad. How about that?"

"Now that's more like it." Then he hung up on me.

I knew exactly where Damien got his asshole tendencies from.

I MADE MYSELF LOOK NICE, wearing a loose sweater, my hair in curls, and wore black leggings underneath with brown boots that reached my knees. Most women loved baggy sweaters with a warm cup of pumpkin spice latte in their hands.

Not me.

God, I missed the heat.

I walked inside, said hello to Patricia, and then headed to the dining room. Damien was probably at work, as was Anna, so I didn't have to worry about seeing them. Obviously, I couldn't avoid them forever, couldn't prevent the inevitable conversation we would eventually have...when I told them I'd left Heath.

My dad was already sitting there, politely refraining from eating his food until I got there. When he saw me walk into the room, his eyes lit up in an indescribable way, as if nothing made him happier than seeing me. There was only one other person who ever looked at me that way—and he wasn't in my life anymore. He got to his feet so he could kiss me on the cheek and embrace me, being affectionate and kind, like he hadn't just snapped at me yesterday. "Sweetheart, you look beautiful as always."

"Thanks, Dad." I kissed him back then took a seat.

Patricia brought the salads first then the soups and sandwiches.

Dad ate right away, telling me about his mediocre life living with Damien, playing chess with him, watching his favorite shows in the evening, and telling me old stories he'd already shared hundreds of times. He rarely left the house unless it was to walk around the block to get some exercise.

It was easier just to listen to him talk because I wasn't in the mood to be talkative.

"What about you?" he asked.

"I've been working a lot. We're finishing our last few shows, and we're preparing for something new. So, lots of rehearsal..."

"That's wonderful. I can't wait to see it. You're the star, I presume?"

I was definitely the best female lead, but I never said that out loud to anyone. "You'll have to see."

He smiled. "I definitely will."

I stirred my spoon into my soup and watched it swirl. It was butternut squash, an autumn soup even though winter was right on our doorstep. It wouldn't be long until Christmas. I couldn't believe how quickly time had passed...how long it'd been since I'd met Heath on that summer night.

"Everything alright, sweetheart?"

"Yes." I lifted my chin and looked at him again, not realizing how long I'd been looking down.

"Come on, Catalina. I'm your father." He pointed his fingertips at his temple. "I know things..."

I smiled slightly. "Did you know your son is an asshole?"

"Yes, I knew that long before you did," he teased. "Now, talk to me."

"Dad, it's nothing..."

"Come on. I'm great at giving advice."

"Well, I don't need advice on this."

"Then I can listen."

I stirred my soup again, my eyes down.

Dad stopped eating, staring at me with his hands clasped together above his soup.

He wasn't going to let this go.

"Alright." I set my spoon down to the side so I wouldn't have to keep stirring my soup and pretend I was hungry. "Well, I was seeing this guy...but it didn't work out. So, I guess I'm a little sad about it." A little? The biggest understatement of the year.

"A man?" he asked, unable to hide his surprise. "Didn't realize you were seeing anybody."

"It wasn't serious. But then it was serious. And then it wasn't serious again..."

"Did he end things?"

"No...I did." I couldn't believe I was talking about a guy to my father, and even more surprisingly, he wasn't being weird about it. Maybe he really saw me as an adult rather than his little girl. Or maybe he just wanted me to be married as soon as possible, to have a man in my life who would take care of me the way Damien took care of Anna.

"Why?"

I tried to think of the best way to phrase it. "When things got serious, I realized he wasn't the right man to be serious with, so I ended it before it could get more complicated."

"So, he wasn't marriage material?"

"I guess."

He nodded like he understood even though there was no way he could. "Does he want to have a family?"

"He said he would do it if it was important to me."

"So, you had that conversation?" he asked in surprise. "Then you must have loved this man."

I shrugged in response, refusing to say the words.

"Then what makes him unfit for you, sweetheart? Because you can have any man you want, and if this is the man you want, he must be something."

He was definitely something, just not the right something. "Damien doesn't like him." I was frank about it. That way, I could cut off all further questions. "And Damien will never like him. I thought it was more important to be with a man who would be accepted by my family."

"Well, Damien doesn't like a lot of people..."

I chuckled slightly. "True."

"You're wise beyond your years to make a hard decision like that. But, as your advocate, I also have to say...you're the one in the relationship. Your brother is not."

Now, I loved my father so much more. My eyes softened, wishing Damien possessed his gentleness. "Well, Damien really hates him, and his reasons are not unfounded."

"Then why would you love a man your brother despises?"

I stared at my soup again. "Because I didn't know the reasons why Damien hated him when we met. If I had, I'm sure it would have changed everything."

"Can you tell me what these reasons are?"

I thought about coming clean right then and there, but I already had to deal with Damien's resentment; I couldn't handle getting it from my father too. "It doesn't matter, Dad. I'm not seeing him anymore, so..." I grabbed my spoon and took a sip, letting the autumn flavors splash into my mouth.

He was quiet for a long time, regarding everything I said with silent concentration. "If you really love this man, like the way I loved your mother, the way Damien loves Anna, I feel like you should try to work it out. Because love is always stronger than hate, sweetheart. Always."

I stirred the contents and kept my face stoic, even though my expression wanted to slacken, my eyes flood with tears. "I tried talking to Damien many times, Dad. He won't change his mind. So, let's just leave it at that..."

I DIDN'T HEAR from Heath for a long time.

Over a week.

I went to his place, got what I needed to survive, but he didn't reciprocate. He seemed to be keeping his distance, because being with me was harder than being without me. I tried not to think about what he did in his spare time, if he was picking up other women, if he was paying for sex again, if he was doing everything people usually did to get over an ex.

Even if they meant nothing to him, the idea still killed me.

I couldn't be with someone else, not for a long time. It would be so awkward, so sad, so forced. There would never be a time when I met a man who was better than Heath, who made the butterflies in my stomach soar, and not just because the gypsy told me so. I already knew how I felt about him, knew it was special, knew it couldn't be replicated with someone else. Our love wasn't ordinary. Extraordinary, instead.

I asked my father not to discuss about our conversation to Damien, and he seemed to keep my secret because Damien never mentioned it to me. And if my father had, I knew Damien would come at me hard, furious I mentioned anything to him.

I sat in bed with a book in my lap, but I couldn't concentrate on anything I read. My eyes kept glancing out the window, seeing the cold frost the corners of the glass. I wasn't sure what time it was, but I was exhausted from rehearsal all week, but I was never calm enough to go to sleep and make it through the night. I was always awakened by my dreams, nightmares, fantasies...

Then I heard the familiar sound of footsteps outside my door.

The turn of the locks.

And then the sound of a big man walking across the hardwood floor.

The book was still open in my lap because I hadn't moved. My heart started to pound inside my chest, vibrate my rib cage, and my sense of hearing heightened, picked up every single movement.

He grabbed the vase from under the sink, turned on the faucet to fill it with water, and then set it on the kitchen island.

He only did that for one reason—because he'd brought me flowers.

Immediately, tears formed in my eyes, and I closed them so they wouldn't grow. I didn't want those tears to streak down my cheeks, to let my emotions break me down all over again. It was hard not to picture him doing that all the time, for the rest of our lives, and our children remembering what their father did for their mother when we were gone.

He stepped into the bedroom, pulling off his shirt as he went. His shoes and jeans came off next, his expressionless eyes on me.

I closed the book and set it aside before I turned off the lamp, so no one could see us together through the open window. My top came off, my bottoms, and then my panties.

He didn't say a word, just like I asked. He moved on top of me and dug his hand into my hair, kissing me softly, cradling my head as we exchanged purposeful kisses, our breaths coming out at the same time, our tongues eager to greet each other.

My arms circled his large torso, moving across his broad back so my nails could anchor in his flesh. My knees parted and squeezed his waist, my ankles locked together against his ass.

He continued to kiss me, his hand slightly shaking, like he couldn't believe my lips were real, that the strands against his fingertips were really mine. Without saying a word, he showed me how much he loved me, how miserable he was every single day we weren't together. He showed me his devastation, his agony.

I combated my tears until they were gone, but when I felt the pain in his soul, felt how much he hurt on a human level, the wetness couldn't be stopped. The drops grew until they leaked past my closed eyelids, dripping down my cheeks to the thumb of his hand that rested against my face.

He pulled his lips away from my mouth and moved to the teardrop that made it to my neck. He kissed it away before he moved to the other, gathering the drops like they were too precious to fall.

When he came back to my mouth, his eyes looked different.

Wet.

Reflective.

Emotional.

My hands cupped his face and I steadied him, so I could look at him, see the same look mirrored back at me. My heart shattered even more, witnessing the strongest man I'd ever known come apart the way I did, show his vulnerability like he didn't care how it made him look.

He positioned our bodies so he could slide inside me, combine our souls so we wouldn't have to feel the anguish anymore. So, we could get lost in each other for a while...and numb the pain.

THE INSTANT WE WERE DONE, he got out of bed and pulled on his clothes, keeping his back to me. He dragged the long-sleeved shirt over his head and pulled his bottoms over his tight ass, purposely not looking at me, like that was the last thing he wanted.

Then he exited my bedroom, not saying a word.

I went after him, naked, unsure what I would say, unsure why I was following him at all.

He moved quickly, like he wanted to avoid me, wanted to get out of my apartment as fast as possible, unable to look at me because it was too damn hard. He stepped into the hallway and pulled the door shut behind him without turning around, his arm moving behind him and locating the knob by touch. Then he left.

I stared at the closed door and listened to his footsteps as they became more and more distant. Even when they were gone, I thought I still heard them, but that was just my mind playing tricks on me, fabricating my desires.

I turned around and saw the sunflowers he'd left for me. He did his best arranging them, but they clearly had the touch of an inexperienced hand, a man trying to impress a woman without knowing how.

I grabbed the stems and moved them around, turning them into a professional arrangement. I stared at the yellow petals, the light to my darkness, the torch on my forgotten path.

Then I started to cry.

SLEEPING TOGETHER WAS a short-term solution that created an even bigger problem.

Maybe we should stop...for both of our sakes.

That was so hard to do, to take away the one that kept me going, that kept me focused on the future.

It was opening night at the ballet for our new production. We'd been training hard for weeks, getting ready to debut our holiday performances. Instead of doing a show we'd already done in the past, we learned new choreography, new versions of old songs, so our loyal audience always had a reason to come back.

Work was one of the few things that got me through the breakup because it kept me busy—and tired. Without it, I probably wouldn't be able to sleep at all, and it also gave me a reason to get out of the house, to focus on something that had nothing to do with my own pain.

During the second act, I had my solo, dancing across the stage alone so the crew would have time to change the set, the dancers would have the opportunity to change into their next round of costumes.

I'd been dancing a long time, so I considered myself a professional, holding my body tight so nothing would slip, nothing would go wrong.

But there was a small piece of paper that had somehow made it on stage, and when I landed after my jump, I slipped on it.

And fell hard.

Anytime we messed up, we just carried on like nothing happened.

But I couldn't carry on.

I tried to stand, but my foot couldn't support me.

That was when I saw the bone pressing against the skin.

The audience started to whisper, their concerns getting louder. The crew came out to help me, figuring out quickly that something was seriously wrong. They hooked their arms underneath mine and lifted me.

The audience clapped like I was an injured player at a sporting event.

But I didn't hear them because all I could hear was my pain.

I knew what had happened without checking.

I'd broken my ankle—and my career was over.

I WAS IN A DAZE, traumatized by what had taken place.

Did this really just happen to me?

With all the other shit I had to deal with?

Now, I'd just lost my job?

"I'll call an ambulance," Tracy said, looking for her phone.

Andre examined my ankle, sighing at the injury. "Yeah, that's definitely broken. I'm sorry, Cat."

Tears streaked down my cheeks, not from pain, but from heartbreak. "No...it's not broken. It's just a strain. I'll be as good as new in a week..."

Andre gave me a look of pity before he turned to my understudy, who'd just changed into her costume. "After this number, you're going to jump in. You ready?"

She nodded, nervous that she was taking my place on such short notice.

But she wouldn't be just taking my place for long. Now, she would have my job.

Tracy returned once she'd found her phone at her station. "I'll call now."

"I'll take her." Heath emerged from behind everyone, looking at me with an expression that mirrored my own pain, like he knew exactly what I was feeling, like he understood that my entire world had just come apart. He kneeled in front of me so he could scoop his arms underneath my body to lift me.

He must have come to the opening night of my show to watch me dance, to hide in the shadows of the theatre just so he could look at me, admire me from afar. So, he'd watched me fall, watched me lose everything in real time. Looking into his eyes, I started to sob, so grateful that the one person who truly understood was there.

"Baby, I got you." He lifted me to his chest and carried me out the back door.

My arms circled his neck, and I cried against his shoulder, sobbed into his t-shirt. "No..." I was so glad I could hide my face from everyone as he carried me away, that I could use his size to cover me, that I had someone who could take care of me when I was too embarrassed to let anyone else do it...except him.

AFTER SOME X-RAYS and an official diagnosis, I went home with pain killers, a cast, and a pair of crutches.

I sat in the bed with a blank look on my face, praying this was a dream, praying I would wake up and find this was just one of my nightmares. Without my job, I had no way to pay my bills. Without my job, I'd lost my only outlet of happiness. Without my job...I wasn't me.

Heath didn't say anything to me, didn't try to make me feel better with meaningless words. He knew I was traumatized, knew I didn't want anything but silence. He also gave me space, like he knew I just needed some time to accept what happened.

Once I was discharged, Heath picked me up again and carried the crutches with his other arm, because both things at once were no problem for him. He got me into the truck then drove me home, carrying me the rest of the way into my apartment.

I was usually too proud to let someone help me like that, but I had no pride inside me anymore. No fire. Nothing.

He carried me to my bed and leaned the crutches in a corner of the room. Then he grabbed a glass of water and put the pills on the nightstand, the next dose of pain killers to get me through the night.

I leaned against the headboard and stared at my foot, wrapped in a cast, the flesh past my knee swollen from the injury. With my arms crossed over my chest, I just sat there, my eyes as swollen as my ankle.

Heath sat on the edge of the bed, wearing a long-sleeved shirt and jeans, his elbows on his knees as he looked the other way, like he knew I didn't want him to stare at me, to watch me hit rock bottom.

If he hadn't been there, I would have had to ride in the back of an ambulance, call my brother and listen to him lose his mind with concern, or just sit there alone...and cry. I was at my weakest point, and Heath was the only person allowed to see me like this, the only person I was completely comfortable with. So, I forced the words from my lips, tears welling up in my eyes again. "Thank you..."

He was quiet.

I was touched that he'd come to watch me dance, that he was always there for me, even when I couldn't see him. It was so romantic—and it killed me that I couldn't have him. "You can go, Heath. I'm just going to go to sleep."

He didn't move, staring at the open doorway.

I'd ended things with him, so it wasn't his responsibility to take care of me. He wasn't obligated whatsoever. I could handle myself. The doctor said it would take six weeks to heal, so I just had to have Damien drop off groceries and maybe help me with laundry...and take me to physical therapy. Now that I'd thought through everything, I realized how much work it was. Damien and Anna had jobs, Tracy had practice and performances, and my dad was too old to do that stuff.

And now I had to figure out how to pay my bills. I had some cash in savings, but not enough. All I had to do was ask Damien for some money, but I was still too proud to do that. I leaned my head against the headboard and sighed loudly.

Then there was the biggest problem of all... Would I ever able to dance again?

It was hard for people to get back into it after an injury because their body was never the same again. They couldn't be as competitive. They couldn't be as strong. They couldn't be the best.

And dance was everything to me.

Heath slowly turned to me, finally looking at me head on for the first time since he'd lifted me from the bench backstage. "I'm not going anywhere, baby. I'll be right here until you're better."

I did my best to steady my tears, but it was so hard to look him in the eye without being overwhelmed by gratitude, over-whelmed by the way he loved me. He didn't owe me anything, not after the way I broke his heart. "You don't have to do that."

He hadn't blinked since he'd looked at me. "You took care of me. I'll do the same for you."

I shook my head. "But that was—"

"And even if you hadn't, I would still be right here." He rose from the bed and started to strip off his clothes, removing everything except his boxers. He turned off the light then came back to the bed. "Let's get you into something more comfortable."

"You don't have to—"

He pressed his forehead to mine. "Let me take care of you." He gave me a fierce look, his blue eyes commanding.

I didn't even know how to get out of my costume without help since everything was so tight. The doctor had to cut off part of the tights to get to my foot. So, I did need Heath's help. Other-wise, I'd have to sleep in this.

He helped me out of it, taking his time to make sure he didn't hurt me, and when everything was gone, he put a pair of pajama shorts and a new top on me, not staring at my tits like he normally would, like he didn't want me to think this was about sex. "Take your pills, and let's go to sleep."

"You're going to stay with me?" I whispered.

He got in beside me, adjusting the covers so they stayed around his waist like he preferred, but they were pulled to my shoulder so I wouldn't get cold. "Yes."

I took the pills and swallowed them with water before I lay down again.

He grabbed a pillow and placed it under my foot to elevate it. Then he lay down again, keeping a few inches between us so he wouldn't crowd me.

I turned my face toward him so I could look at him, just the way he used to look at me when he was injured in his bed.

His hand snaked to mine, and he interlocked our fingers. "It's going to be okay."

Tears formed in my eyes. "I'm afraid I'll never dance again..."

"You will."

"I don't know—"

"I do. You're the strongest person I know. You're going to get there—and I'm gonna push you until you do."

WHEN I WOKE up the next morning, he wasn't beside me in bed. I moved to get out of bed, but then I was painfully reminded of my broken ankle. I stilled once my nerves winced in pain. I had to use the bathroom, and my eyes moved to the crutches in the corner, which seemed to be a world away. Then I heard Heath moving in the kitchen. "Heath?"

He stopped what he was doing and came to me. "I'm here." He rounded the corner and came to the bed, in his boxers, his hair messy from sleeping beside me all night.

"Could you hand me those?" I nodded to the corner.

"You don't need them. You have me."

"Well, I need to use the restroom and—"

He lifted me from the bed and carried me into the bathroom before sitting me on the toilet.

"You don't need to do that every time..."

"I'm a lot stronger than those plastic crutches." He walked out and shut the door behind himself.

I did my business then balanced on one foot to wash my hands. When I was done, I opened the door.

Heath grabbed me again and set me on the couch. "I just finished making breakfast. We'll eat and watch a movie."

I couldn't believe he really wanted to wait on me hand and foot for the next six weeks.

He placed the food onto plates then brought one to me. It was pancakes and tater tots, my favorite. He also brought a mug of coffee before he sat beside me with his breakfast.

I picked at the food, feeling a lot better having him beside me than being alone. I couldn't imagine doing this by myself, not because I needed him to take care of me, but because he made me feel better...a lot better.

THE WEEK PASSED QUICKLY, even though I didn't do anything.

Heath stocked my kitchen with groceries, did my laundry, took care of me, and when the bills were due, he paid them.

I argued, but that argument didn't last long.

He had to work most nights, but since I was asleep anyway, I hardly noticed he was gone. When he came home, he made me breakfast and put me on the couch before he went to sleep in my bedroom.

It became a routine.

We didn't talk a lot We didn't make love either. Even if we'd wanted to, my foot was such a burden in the cast that it wasn't possible.

When Saturday night arrived, I was hit with another dose of depression.

Because the show went on without me.

My understudy had the spotlight, and if Andre and everyone else fell in love with her, I might not be able to get my job back even if I made a full recovery. I might be booted to the B team...and never climb back to the top.

I sat in front of the TV and stared at the screen blankly, caring more about the time showing on the cable box. I waited for the performance to be over so I could stop thinking about the evening, the way the hot lights used to make me sweat, the way I couldn't hear anything over the orchestra when I danced on the stage.

Then it was finally over.

Heath glanced at me from his seat beside me, like he'd noticed something was wrong. He grabbed my hand, interlocked our fingers, and held it on his thigh. He stared at me with his piercing blue gaze, like he could read written words in my eyes. "This isn't forever, baby. I promise."

I loved that he knew exactly what I was thinking without me having to explain it, that he was understanding of my emotions but also firm in his belief that I would get better, that I would make a full recovery and be as strong as ever.

I would never find another man like him.

No one would ever understand me the way he did.

No one would ever love me the way he did. "I love you..." I knew I shouldn't say it, shouldn't put those feelings into the universe when nothing had changed. But I couldn't help it. Couldn't hold back the emotion in my heart.

His eyes softened slightly, his fingers squeezing mine. "I know."

A KNOCK SOUNDED on the door.

Heath's hand was still in mine as we watched the movie. His eyes flicked to the door then to me, silently asking me if I expected anyone.

I shook my head.

He got to his feet and walked to the door, peering through the peephole. When he turned to me, an annoyed expression on his face, it was obvious who it was.

Damien knocked again before he spoke. "Cat, I know you're home. Open the door."

Oh no.

Heath grabbed my crutches and helped me onto them before he walked into the bedroom and shut the door. He knew showing his face would just make things worse with Damien, so it was better to disappear than provoke my brother's wrath. So, he hid his face...like a dirty secret.

That felt so wrong, it made me sick. Heath was the one dropping everything to take care of me, and he had to leave the room when he had every right to stay. I made it to the door and opened it.

Damien stood there in a suit, Anna slightly behind him in a gown.

It took me less than a heartbeat to figure out what had happened.

He'd gone to my show, realized I'd been replaced, and then came to my apartment to confront me about it. He opened his mouth to issue a million questions, but when he saw my foot in a cast, the crutches supporting me, he shut his mouth and sighed.

Anna gasped. "Girl, oh no..."

"What happened?" Damien entered my apartment with Anna, his eyes on the white cast that encompassed my foot and ankle.

"I broke my ankle, so I'll be like this for six weeks."

He released another sigh, sadness filling his eyes. "Cat, I'm so sorry." He leaned into me and hugged me with one arm, careful not to topple me over. He was my brother again, loving, affectionate, and with a heart of gold. He pulled away and looked down at my injury, even though he couldn't distinguish anything underneath.

"Yeah..." I used the crutches to balance on one foot, but I struggled because I had no experience with them. Heath carried me everywhere. "It's been hard."

"Why didn't you tell me?"

I shrugged. "I just...didn't want to talk about it."

He continued to pity me, like he wished he could fix it for me. But no one could. "When did this happen?"

"Last week."

He looked around my apartment, seeing the dirty pans on the stove and the perfectly clean apartment. "Then how have you..." He turned around and noticed that my bedroom door was closed.

Shit.

Anna connected the dots quickly, shooting me an alarmed expression.

Damien slowly turned back to me, his eyes livid, no longer sympathetic whatsoever. "I thought you weren't seeing him anymore." He clenched his jaw tightly, his green eyes hostile. There was nothing that made him angrier than Heath's existence. He turned into a psychopath anytime he was mentioned.

"I wasn't, but—"

"Then why the fuck is he here?" he immediately yelled, going from zero to sixty in a second. "You don't need him to take care of you. You've got me. You've got Annabella. Dad." He marched to the bedroom door.

"Damien!" I couldn't chase after him, not in my state.

Anna covered her eyes. "Oh god..."

Damien pushed the door open.

Heath must have anticipated it because he'd put on jeans and a shirt. He stood there with his arms by his sides, giving Damien an impassive expression, like he didn't feel anything as he looked at him.

"Get the fuck out." Damien shoved him in the chest.

"Damien!" I couldn't believe my brother was acting this way. I moved my crutches as fast as I could to get to him.

"It's fine." Heath held up his hand to me, not wanting me to slip and fall. "I'll go." He moved around Damien and walked past me to the door.

I couldn't let him walk out of there, being treated like shit by Damien, when he was the one who was there for me. "Wait."

Heath kept walking.

"Heath." I raised my voice so he would be forced to listen.

He stared at the door for a few seconds before he turned to me, unable to hide his annoyance.

I turned back to Damien, who was seething. "He's the one who's been taking care of me, Damien. He was there when I broke my ankle. He was in the audience, and I had no idea. He took me to the hospital, and he's been busting his ass around here to take care of me—"

"I don't give a shit—"

"Shut your fucking mouth right now!"

Damien's eyebrow shot up in astonishment.

"You're going to listen to every goddamn word I have to say." I felt weak on the crutches, but my voice was stronger than ever. "I ended things with him after our last conversation, but I've been so fucking miserable, Damien." Tears came to my eyes, bubbled like boiling water, and then streaked down my cheeks. "I can't do this. I can't live without this man. It's not because he's taken care of me, not because he's been submissive to you even though you treat him like shit. It's because I love him."

He shook his head. "I'm not going to change my mind—"

"I don't need you to change your mind, Damien."

His expression hardened.

"Because I'm going to be with him anyway. He's my fucking soul mate, and if you don't love me enough to even try, then that's just sad. I know you love me enough to look past this, but you just choose not to because you're selfish. If you want to ostracize me because you don't accept who I love, that's fine. But I hope you change your mind someday—for your sake."

Damien didn't move or react, as if he couldn't believe I'd just said all of that.

"Don't tell him to leave because he has every right to be here. You're the one who's unwelcome, Damien. So, get the fuck out of my apartment." I breathed hard because of the exertion my speech had caused. It was a catharsis of emotions, both freeing and damning.

When he spoke again, he was calm. "Dad will never—"

"He deserves a lot more credit than you give him. Because I see the way he loves me, and he would put aside whatever reservations he has about Heath if I asked him to, if I told him this was the man I wanted to spend my life with. And that's a hell of a lot more than I can say for you." My body shook because I was so angry, my tears rivers down my cheeks. "Now go, Damien. Take your approval and shove it up your fucking ass."

ELEVEN

HEATH

I stepped out of the way of the door since I was blocking it.

But I could barely think—because I couldn't believe that had just happened.

Anna opened the door first and walked out without looking at me.

Damien stared at his sister, in just as much shock as I was. He breathed hard and fast, like he wanted to make his own speech, but he must have deemed it futile because he didn't. But he was livid.

Catalina turned around and headed back to the couch, moving slowly because the crutches were a brand-new sensation. She leaned the crutches against the couch then slowly lowered herself down, careful not to hurt her foot. Then she looked away, like she refused to watch her brother go.

Damien finally dropped his gaze and moved to the door.

I refused to move because I would seem weak if I did.

He stopped and stared at me, his expression more enraged than I'd ever seen it. It was like he wanted to kill me, wished his first assassination attempt had been successful so he wouldn't have to deal with all the bullshit my survival had caused.

I didn't say a word, but I didn't drop my gaze either. I didn't give a gloating smile or a sarcastic remark.

Then he walked out.

I shut the door behind him, turning all the locks.

When I turned back to Catalina, her body was pivoted away, her uninjured leg hiked up on the couch, her knee pointed to the ceiling. Her fingertips rested across her mouth, like she was trying to hide a trembling lip.

I slowly moved to the couch and lowered myself to the seat beside her.

She didn't look at me, her watery eyes shining so bright.

My hand cupped her cheek, and I forced her gaze on me. I looked at her in a new way, a way I couldn't describe. The feelings inside me were inexplicable. I still couldn't process what had happened, what she'd just done for me. "That's my baby..." My thumb swiped across her cheek and caught the tear that fell. She'd turned back into the fiery woman I'd met in the summer, the woman who had a mouth that could win a war. It was the reason I fell in love with her in the first place, and the reason my love had just doubled in size.

She closed her eyes, more tears escaping from under her closed lids. "I'm sorry I hurt you..."

"You just made up for it—a million times over." I pressed my forehead to hers as I cupped her face. "I want to marry you right now..." I'd told her I loved her barely a month ago, but I could commit to her for the rest of my life right then and there...because I just knew. I knew she was the one. She was my Cassini. "I love you so fucking much."

She opened her eyes and looked at me. "I love you too."

My other hand cupped her cheek, and I held her there, my fingers pushing her hair out of her face.

"I want to marry you too."

Did I just ask her to marry me...and she said yes? I pulled away slightly and looked at her, my breath coming out shaky because I couldn't believe this was reality, like I was in a dream...a dream where I got everything I wanted. It wasn't my intention to propose, but now that I knew her answer, it could be. "Did we just get engaged?" I'd never thought about proposing to a woman, never even imagined how I would do it with Catalina, but I knew it was supposed to be a grand gesture, a fancy dinner with flowers, a beautiful ring in a box. I didn't give her any of that, but it felt perfect...perfect for us.

She looked into my eyes, more tears coming, but a different kind of tear. Her lips rose in a slight smile, and she nodded. "Yes...if you're really asking me."

I wanted to pull her into my lap and hold her so tight, but she was too injured to move like that. I couldn't lay her down and make love to her. All I could do was touch her like this. But it was enough, because I had the rest of my life to do those things. I closed my eyes for a moment, and when I opened them, I felt the moisture that formed on my eyes, felt the emotion break through the ribs that encased my chest. "Yes, baby. I'm asking you."

————

I WANTED to quit my job so I could stay home with her.

The last thing I wanted to do was leave her...to go to work.

But I had responsibilities I couldn't ignore. At least I was in a better mood, no longer miserable over the woman I'd lost... because she'd fought for me. She'd stood up to her asshole brother and picked me.

She picked me.

I stepped into the Underground and headed to my throne. Half of the guys were there. The rest were doing patrols.

Before I even got to my seat, one of the girls brought me a beer and set it beside me.

I fell into the chair and took a deep drink, letting the foam cover my lips before I wiped it away.

Steel came to my side. "Heath, can I talk to you for a second?"

"What is it?" I turned to him, my chin propped on my knuckles, bored because I wished I didn't have to be there.

He glanced at the men before he turned back to me. "In private."

This must be important, so I rose from my chair and headed to my office, a room I hardly ever used.

He shut the door behind him.

"What is it?" I turned around and leaned against the desk, my arms crossed over my chest.

"Are you not charging Damien anymore?"

The question caught me off guard. "Why?"

"Are you?"

"Why are you asking me this?"

"Because Vox said it's true. Is it?"

I didn't like to be questioned about my decisions, so I glared at him.

"You told Damien you were collecting all his profits, but now you're collecting nothing. Why?"

"For reasons you don't need to worry about. We have enough cash to count as it is."

Now, he glared at me. "So, you aren't collecting from him?"

I cocked my head slightly.

"Because the men are talking, and they're wondering if it's true."

"Why are they talking about this? We have a million things to worry about right now."

"I don't know. I don't know how it started."

I believed Steel wouldn't lie to me or betray me, so I didn't suspect it was him. "Is Ian talking?"

He shook his head. "He seemed just as surprised as I was."

"And who told him?"

"Roger."

"Who told you?"

"Clyde. But it seems like everyone knows, and they aren't happy about it. You might want to change that."

That wasn't an option. After everything that had just happened with Damien, I couldn't provoke him at all. And I intended to marry his sister, so I should be gaining his favor, not pushing it further away. "Let it go."

"What are you telling me?"

"I'll find a replacement and give them something new to talk about." I pushed off the desk and walked around him. "Now, if you'll excuse me, I want to finish that beer."

———

IT WAS a little after sunrise when I stepped off the elevator.

Balto was awake, in his workout shorts, sneakers, and no shirt, like he was about to hit the gym after he'd finished his protein shake. He stepped out of the kitchen as he drank from his shake. "You look like you're in a better mood."

I grinned as I walked toward him, seeing the world with a new set of eyes, a new excitement. "Because I am."

"You win over Damien?" He closed the cap of his bottle and shook it to mix the protein powder with the water.

"No. Catalina told him to fuck off."

He abruptly stopped moving, the bottle no longer shaking.

I smiled. "That's my baby...mouthing off."

He dropped the bottle to his side. "What changed her mind?"

I shrugged. "I don't know. She just did."

"Well, I'm glad to hear it. Maybe you and Damien can resolve your problems sometime down the road."

"Maybe." Probably not. But I was grateful my relationship with Catalina was no longer conditional on his approval. She'd fought for me, stuck her neck out for me, and she was loyal to me like one of my own men. "She broke her ankle a couple weeks ago at a performance, and I've been taking care of her. Maybe that had something to do with it."

"Ouch, that sucks. She going to be okay?"

"She'll be fine. She's made of something harder than the rest of us."

Balto didn't smile because he never did, but he gave me an affectionate look with his eyes, like he was happy to see me this way, to see me get what I wanted.

"And I have some news..."

"Yeah?" He started to stir his bottle again, letting the particles break apart.

"I asked her to marry me."

He halted again, this time his expression full of surprise.

"Yeah...kinda just happened."

"You got down on one knee and gave her a ring?"

"No, it just happened. It was in the moment, hard to explain. But she said yes, so I guess I'm engaged."

"Whoa. Last time I saw you, you were dead like a ghost. Now, I've never seen you happier." He gripped my shoulder and gave me a squeeze. "I'm happy for you, man."

I was glad he didn't question me, didn't ask me if it was too soon, if I was certain I wanted to make this kind of commitment to a woman I hadn't known long. But he didn't.

"I'm going to have a sister-in-law."

"Yes. And you'll be there for her if she ever needs to go to the hospital and I'm not there."

The affection in his expression increased. "I hope that never happens, but if it does, I'll be there. I'll even get her some ice cream if she wants it."

"Good." I smiled.

"And I'll die for her." He turned serious. "The way you would die for my wife."

I held his gaze for a while, knowing that was his way of giving his approval, of giving me his blessing. "Thanks, man." I extended my hand.

He shook it before he pulled me in for a hug and a pat on the back. "So, what now?"

"I guess I've got to get her a ring."

"Yeah. Pretty important."

"I could cheap out and give her my diamond." I held up my hand and looked at the flawless skull diamond on my finger, one of the few diamonds on earth that possessed this unparalleled clarity.

"I don't think that's cheap by any means." That what he'd done with his wife.

"I just think she'd want something else. But I've never asked, and I can't ask her."

"Too bad you can't ask Damien."

"I could ask Anna, but Damien might kill me if I go near her."

"Yeah," he said quickly. "Don't do that. Just pick her out something. She'll love whatever you get her."

I shook my head. "My baby is no average woman, so she can't wear an average ring."

He uncapped the bottle and took a drink. "As interesting as this is, I've got a workout to complete." He walked around me. "Let me know how it goes."

I WALKED in the door and set the plastic bag on the kitchen island. "Baby, what are you doing?"

The faucet was running, and she rubbed the sponge over the dirty plate. "Dishes."

"And what did I tell you about doing the dishes?"

She ignored me.

I came around the island, seeing her balance on one foot. I moved my chest into her back and turned off the faucet.

"Ugh," she said under her breath. "Let me do something."

"You can do the dishes all you want when that cast is off." I picked her up and carried her to the couch, where her glass of wine sat along with her blanket. I set her down, ignoring the irritated look on her face. "I picked up dinner. Thought we could take a break from cooking."

She continued to look mad.

"I went to your favorite place…"

She tried to keep up her annoyed expression, but that didn't last long. The corner of her lip upturned slightly, the excitement in her gaze impossible to conceal.

"That's my baby." I walked back into the kitchen and plated everything before I returned.

Her favorite dish was gnocchi with alfredo sauce, a carb-filled meal that she usually denied herself, but once it placed in front of her, she couldn't ignore it. She stabbed the pasta with her fork and dragged it through the sauce before she placed it in her mouth. "Oh man, that's good."

I got a salad because I'd been eating too much lately. I spent most of my time on the couch with her, so I wasn't as active anymore, not like I was when we had sex all the time.

"How was your day?"

She never mentioned her family after the incident with Damien. It was obvious she didn't want to think about it, didn't want to address it at all. She'd made her speech because her emotions were at their peak, but now that a week had passed, she was herself again. But she probably thought about where her relationship with her brother stood.

They hadn't spoken as far as I could tell. "Fine. Saw Balto today."

"How is he?"

"Same. An asshole."

She swatted my arm. "Your brother is not an asshole."

"Oh, that's right. I'm the asshole. We're twins...so it's easy to get confused."

She chuckled slightly. "You aren't an asshole either, babe."

Babe. She hadn't called me that in a long time. It was nice to hear it again, to hear the nickname wrap around me posses- sively. "I told him we were engaged." I hadn't told anyone else, like Steel, because it felt separate from my professional life. I probably wouldn't even tell them if I were married, just to protect Catalina.

"Yeah?" She finished her bite then looked at me. "What did he say?"

"He was happy for me."

"Oh, that's good. I wasn't sure how he'd feel about me."

I rolled my eyes. "You slapped him once, a long time ago. And he probably liked it."

She smacked my arm again. "Heath."

"What?" I asked playfully. "I know I do..."

"Being your woman is one thing. But being your wife...that's different."

"Well, he said he would die for you. So, if you think he doesn't like you, he does."

She stopped eating altogether, more absorbed in the conversation.

"That's the highest blessing you're going to get." I turned back to my food and kept eating.

"Yeah, I guess so."

I wanted to ask her what she intended to do about her family, if she was going to talk to her father or just elope, but that seemed like a difficult question to ask right now. There was no rush to get married right away. She would tell me when it was time. We could go down to the courthouse or wherever she wanted to do it. I wasn't a fan of churches and they weren't a fan of me, but I'd do it there if she wanted.

After we watched TV for a while, we went to bed.

I carried her into the bedroom and set her down on the edge of the bed.

She still had to wear that bulky cast for a few more weeks, and it tended to get in the way when we slept or cuddled on the couch. She didn't have as much pain, but she still had to be careful when putting any pressure on it.

I got ready for bed then lay beside her in my boxers, used to her queen-sized bed and her old sheets. My place was more comfortable and I preferred to stay there, but since she was the one struggling with an injury, I wanted her to be where she felt most comfortable.

And as long as I got to be with her, I didn't really care.

She lay on her back and closed her eyes, her head turned to me so she could look at me with sleepy eyes.

I was reunited with the woman I loved, watched her fight for me like a pissed-off bull, but I couldn't have her the way I wanted. I couldn't get on top of her and make love to her, feel that powerful connection that ruled us both.

I missed it.

My cock was hard under the sheets, wanting to break free of my boxers and bury itself inside her, but he was restrained in the cotton, anxious. The rest of my body was just as anxious. My chest wanted to feel her little tits rub against me as I moved on top of her. My wrists yearned for the soft flesh behind her knee when I pinned her legs apart. My balls wanted to tap against her ass as I pounded into her. My lips wanted to feel her warm breaths sprinkle against my mouth while she moaned uncontrollably.

I couldn't wait for that fucking cast to come off.

When I couldn't stop thinking about it, I got out of bed then pulled the sheets off her.

She raised her body up slightly, watching me with confusion.

I grabbed her shorts and pulled them off her ass, grabbing her panties too. I slowly tugged them down, and when I got to her foot, I took my time getting the fabric off the delicate area.

"Heath, I'm frustrated too, but—"

I pinned her healthy leg back, opening her wide. I moved her other knee slightly out of the way then dropped my body between her legs.

She was still propped up, and she watched me, finally realizing what I wanted to do to her.

My knees and everything below hung off the bed, my feet pressing into the rug while I kept the rest of my body on the bed, my face moving between her legs. Even though she'd been injured, she still groomed herself in the shower, like she wanted to be ready for sex the second she could get it.

That was my baby.

My hands hooked around her thighs, and I pressed my face into her pussy, my nose diving into her slit as I smelled her, as I smelled the pussy I was hopelessly addicted to.

She moaned quietly when she felt me, lying back so her head was on the pillow, her hair all over the place. Her top was still on, but she pulled it up so she could touch her own tits.

I started to kiss her, kiss her pussy the same way I kissed her mouth, with purposeful embraces packed with love and a nice hit of lust. My dick was hard underneath me, uncomfortable under my body weight as it smashed against the mattress. My tongue circled her clit before I dove my tongue deep inside her, tasting her, loving her.

She stopped thinking about her foot, stopped thinking about the fact that I was doing all the work while she just enjoyed it. Her fingers moved to my hair, and she started to grind into me, her moans becoming louder, raspier, sexier.

Even if I didn't get laid, I still wanted to do this, still wanted to enjoy her, get lost in this indescribable physical connection. I would always be there for her, even if she couldn't be there for me, and that told me I would worthy of her spending my life with her, because I would do that in all things...not just sex.

She started to really get into it, arch her back, moan loudly, whisper my name in the darkness.

I pressed my tongue harder into her clit and made her hit home, knowing she liked that best.

Her hands gripped the sheets on either side of her, and she bucked against my mouth, riding the climax I gave her with tears in her throat, her voice breaking, her tone emotional. "Heath..."

I squeezed her ass as I made her finish, went hard on that little nub until her voice completely died away and the area was raw to the touch. Then I gave her gentle kisses, kind swipes of my tongue.

She breathed hard as she came down, her skin covered in sweat even though she just lay there.

I pushed my boxers off then moved between her legs, my body slightly turned to her right so I could keep away from her injured foot. There wasn't much I could do even when I was inside her, but as long as I could be inside her, that was all that mattered to me. I held myself on one arm and slowly descended, carefully slid inside her, groaning as I was reunited with my home.

She moaned too, rigid as if she was afraid to hurt herself if she did anything.

When I was completely inside her, I held myself on top of her, my face pressed to hers. I had to make love to her, even if it was an alternate way, even if we could only move slow, barely move at all.

Her palms cupped my cheeks, and she kissed me, indifferent to the taste of herself on my lips. She just wanted me, wanted all of me, wanted to combine our souls in any way she could.

I started to move inside her, my lips kissing hers. "I love you, baby..."

Her hands slid over my bare chest, and her right hand rested over my heart, feeling it beat. "I love you too."

TWELVE
DAMIEN

I couldn't believe half the shit she'd said to me.

I mean, I could, but I couldn't believe she said it to me.

That motherfucker had robbed me, had tortured me, and had ruined my life the second he ascended to the throne.

Now he had my sister under his thumb.

I'd hoped she would see reason during their breakup, that there were better men out there, but then she broke her ankle and that jackass came to the rescue. She pledged her allegiance to him.

Now what was I going to do?

I didn't want anything to do with that asshole. But I loved my sister...a lot.

I didn't want to lose her because of it.

The one thing that might undo all of this was our father. If he cast his judgment and said that bastard would never be welcomed into this family, that would probably be the rule of law she couldn't defy.

It was inevitable—because I would tell him everything.

I wasn't being a tattletale. He just needed to know about the situation since it was only escalating.

I sat in my office at the bank, getting nothing done at all because all I could think about was that final conversation with my sister.

"Damien?"

I blinked, finally focusing on the man in front of me. "Have you been standing there long?"

"Long enough to know something is on your mind." Hades stood with his hands in the pockets of his suit. It was only noon, so he probably intended to take off early to help Sofia at home.

"Catalina."

"It's interesting. Anna used to be the only thing you ever thought about, but now your sister has taken her place."

"Well, Annabella is safe. Cat is... I don't know."

He rubbed his palm across his five-o'clock shadow. "I thought she left him."

"Yeah, but now they're back together. And she told me it would stay that way, regardless of how I feel about it."

He shrugged. "There's nothing you can do about it, Damien."

"I'm realizing that."

"Unless you kill him."

"I promised I wouldn't."

He looked at the floor for a while. "Then I think you should let it go."

I gave a sarcastic chuckle. "Yeah…so easy to do."

"The guy is trash and doesn't deserve your sister. But outlawing him isn't going to do anything at this point."

"Do I need to remind you why I hate him?"

"No," Hades answered. "I don't like him either. But what are you going to do?"

I was out of ideas. "She deserves so much better. I never worried about who she'd end up with because she's so fucking smart, so confident. I figured she wouldn't settle for anything less than a handsome billionaire who adores her. Then she threw this curve ball."

"Doesn't mean it's forever. And you know what they say? The more you tell her no, the more she'll want to do it."

"My sister isn't that immature."

He shrugged. "But she is a young woman…" He pulled his hand out of his pocket and checked his watch. "Sofia and Demetri have a doctor's appointment. I'm going to leave early so I can take them."

"Alright. Thanks for the pep talk."

"If you can't change the situation, change how you feel about it."

I laughed again, this time harder. "Yeah...that's not gonna happen."

MY SECRETARY SPOKE through the phone. "Damien, you have a drop-in who wants to see you. His name is Vox. Claims it's important."

The second I heard that name, I got chills.

The last time we spoke, we almost killed Heath together.

I'd promised I wouldn't move against Heath, so I couldn't collude with Vox again. But I didn't want to decline the meeting either. "Send him in."

A moment later, his large frame passed through my open doorway. Over six feet with bulky muscle, he had a crazed look in his eye, like he was always ready for a confrontation, wanted conflict to happen. There was a scar along his left eye, like someone sliced him with a thick knife and barely missed the eyeball. He came to my desk and gave me a slight grunt in greeting.

"Sit." I nodded to the chair.

He moved into the chair, slouching with knees wide apart, sitting like a street gangster instead of a respectable criminal. That was one difference between Heath and him. Heath at least had the majesty of a king.

"How can I help you, Vox?" I was surprised he was still alive after our plan failed. He didn't look like he'd just recovered from several broken bones either. He'd somehow survived Heath's wrath.

"Why isn't Heath collecting payment from you?" He cocked his head slightly, his eyes narrowed in fury.

I wouldn't tell any of his men that he was screwing my sister. I was certain Heath would protect her identity from his men, behave like she didn't exist at all, because that was the best way to keep her safe. "Why are you asking?"

"Because I've noticed he stopped collecting. Told the rest of the men. We aren't happy about it."

"So, you come here to threaten me?" I asked incredulously. "That's not going to go over well."

He smiled, dimples in both cheeks, and it was an inappropriate reaction. "No. I just want to know why." He reached into his jeans and pulled out his phone. "Because I'm putting Heath in the ground once and for all." He stared at the screen as he flipped through whatever he was looking at. "I've been following him, because I thought his ban on trafficking was suspicious. I followed him to a bar and found him with this woman." He slid the phone toward me.

Shit. I knew who I was about to see. I grabbed the phone anyway, looked at the picture of Heath and Catalina close together, gave no reaction, and slid the phone back.

"I went back to Petrov and asked him what he knew about the whole thing. He said that Heath went down there to collect payment, noticed a woman in one of the cages, lost his temper, and demanded for her to be released. That was when everything began, when they got shot down, followed by everyone else. And you know what?" He grabbed the phone and held it up. "Petrov confirmed this is the woman from the cage."

Now my heart dropped into my stomach like a stone. I couldn't even breathe when I heard what he said. My lungs were stuck in place, unable to expand or contract, unable to pull any oxygen into my blood.

"And now he's not collecting payment from you. Whether you pay him or not, I don't give a damn. But I'm going to use that against him—and bring him down. Because he's making a lot of terrible business decisions—and it's time for him to resign. We're the Skull Kings, not the Charity Queens."

I didn't hear a word he said. "The woman in the cage... What are you assuming?"

"I'm assuming that he completely changed our policy for one woman."

"So...she was trafficked?" My fucking little sister had been trafficked?

"Petrov said she caused problems with one of his men in the bathroom of a bar. Pissed them off because he got taken by the cops. Broke in to her apartment and took her. Threw her in the cage. Beat the shit out of her—"

Keeping a straight face was the hardest thing I'd ever had to do.

"And when Heath saw her in there, he lost his shit. The woman asked him to save all the other women too, so he did. And then he started this anti-trafficking crusade immediately afterward."

My eyes remained open and my jaw slack, but my hands were in tight fists under the desk. "When did this happen? With the girl?"

He shrugged. "I think beginning of summer."

So, this was a long time ago, when Heath and Catalina hardly knew each other. She told me she'd rejected his advances after he let her go. Why would she want him after he'd put her in a cage? But he must have rescued her when he saw her in that basement...and that changed her mind.

Vox slipped his phone back into his pocket. "So, why did you stop paying him? You defied him, and he just backed down? What happened?"

It was hard to think clearly when I couldn't stop picturing my sister locked in a cage like an animal. I knew the kind of shit that happened to those women. They were stripped naked, beaten, and... I couldn't even finish the thought. I had no idea she'd been captured because I didn't see her on a daily basis. By the time I would have known she was missing, she might have been shipped to another country, and by then...terrible things would have happened to her. If Heath hadn't walked in there when he did, she might have disappeared forever. Then he outlawed the institution altogether, against great resistance, for her.

Maybe he had changed.

Vox waited for an answer.

"I am paying him."

He cocked an eyebrow.

"Business has been bad for the last month because I gave him all my profits the last time he stopped by. It's just taken me a little time to make some money again." I lied to his face, lied like my life depended on it.

Vox stared at me with a hard gaze, like he wasn't convinced that I was telling the truth. But he didn't call me out on it either.

I'd just lied to protect the man I hated—because I knew I owed him.

I owed him everything.

THIRTEEN

HEATH

I sat on the throne with my beer beside me. Steel kept me informed about the accomplishments of the week because there was too much for me to keep track of by myself. There were so many businesses to monitor, so many streets to keep clean, that it was tough even for a big organization such as ourselves.

The rest of the men drank at the tables, stuffed large bills into the shorts the girls wore as a tip for having nice tits.

Ian stepped through the doors and jogged to the bottom of the stairs. "Heath, Damien is here. Wants to see you."

In bewilderment, I stared at him, digesting the words like a swallowed piece of gum. Had he come here to take me out? To bomb the place so the walls collapsed on all of us? "Is he alone?"

"He's got a few men—and lots of bags of money."

What? Now this wasn't making sense. "Scan the bags before you let him in."

Ian turned away.

"And scan them well, Ian."

Ian nodded before he kept going.

After that last conversation with Damien, I knew he was furious. So furious, he might go back on the promise he made to Catalina. Maybe killing me was his only option to protect his sister, because she couldn't hate him forever, even if he did kill the man she loved.

Steel set down the binder. "Want me to get the rifles?"

I shook my head. "We're all strapped."

The doors opened again, and Damien entered first, taking the lead with a bag of cash in each hand. He carried it down the aisles of men and stopped in front of me, dropping them on the floor, a look of rampant rage in his eyes.

What the fuck was happening right now?

The rest of his men did the same, piling up the cash at my feet. Then they turned and left.

Damien lingered behind, his shoulders as stiff as his upper lip. "There's your money, asshole." He said the final word with such rage that spit flew from his mouth and sprinkled the stairs below me. Then he turned around and exited the room.

All the men looked at me with respect, like I was powerful enough to get Damien to hand-deliver payment at my leisure.

I wasn't sure what my expression looked like—because I was confused.

So fucking confused.

WHEN I GOT HOME, Catalina was still asleep, so I went to bed without waking her. I usually slept until noon, and that day was important because we were getting her cast removed at the doctor's office. After a few X-rays, they'd determined she'd healed, and a little quicker than most people.

Because of her fire.

When I woke up, I rolled out of bed and washed my face and brushed my teeth before getting dressed and walking out the door. I wanted to tell Catalina what had happened, but now wasn't the right time. When we got home and were in the privacy of the apartment, I would tell her what happened.

At the office, the doctor cut into her cast and got her foot free.

When she tried to move it, she winced in pain.

"It's going to hurt for a while," the doctor said. "But that's normal. Start physical therapy immediately, and after a few weeks, try to walk more on your own."

I took her home afterward, carrying her so she wouldn't have to deal with the crutches. When I got her into the apartment, she tried to walk on it, wincing as she attempted to get used to moving it normally again.

"The doctor told you to try after a few weeks. Not right away."

"But I've got to get back to work." She clenched her teeth as she forced herself to move. "If I take too long, people might forget about me, and I'll be the understudy..."

"No one is going to forget about you, baby." Not possible.

"And I need to pay bills—"

"I pay your bills."

She gripped the kitchen island for balance, lifting her foot to take a break. "I don't want your money, Heath. I don't need you to take care of me—"

"You agreed to marry me." I came to her side and stared her down. "So, yes, I'm going to be taking care of you. My money is your money. So, don't worry about money ever again." I gave her an authoritative expression, warning her not to question me.

She was quiet.

I moved to the fridge. "What do you want for lunch?"

"Anything...I don't care." She tried to walk again.

I shut the door and turned back to her. "If you rush it, you're just going to hurt yourself more. Listen to the doctor, alright? Now, sit your ass down."

Both of her eyebrows rose in offense. "What did you just say to me?"

"You heard what I said." I pulled out the chair at the dining table for her.

She walked to the chair, gave me a defiant look, then fell into it. But her look was savage, like I'd pay for the bossiness later.

I stepped into the kitchen and made lunch, indifferent to her wrath. I made sandwiches and salads before I carried the plates to the table. I fell into the chair close to her and started to eat right away.

She didn't touch her food as she stared at me, like she demanded an apology before she would touch anything. "You know—"

"Damien came to the Underground last night." I knew I was being short with her, an abrupt change in mood from our previous joy. She needed to understand why. She needed to know what happened with her brother.

Her mouth stayed open for a few seconds in shock before she closed it again. Then her expression completely changed, turning soft, confused. "What happened...? What did he say?"

"He didn't say much. He delivered money then walked out."

"Oh god..." She leaned forward and planted her face in her palms.

"That's why I'm not in the best mood today."

She held her position as she breathed to herself, sighing loudly, before she pulled her hands down again. "I guess I should have expected repercussions from screaming at him."

"Getting money seems like an odd repercussion."

"Yeah, I don't get it either." She propped her chin on her hand and stared across the room.

I stared at my food, starving but with no real appetite.

"Should I talk to him?" she whispered.

"I don't know," I said honestly. I had no idea what it meant. I'd assumed the money was lined with explosives, but it was clean. Unless he'd invented a device that couldn't be detected, it seemed completely legitimate.

"Damien promised me he wouldn't hurt you...and he wouldn't go back on his promise."

I hoped he wouldn't. I didn't want to fight someone with my hands tied behind my back. My phone vibrated in my pocket, so I pulled it out in case it was important. That was when I saw his name on the screen. "He just texted me."

Her head snapped in my direction. "Oh my god, what did he say?"

I read it out loud. "'I want to talk to you.'"

She sighed. "That's it?"

Another message popped up. I read it. "'At my office. Now. Come alone.'"

Catalina didn't touch her food because it didn't seem important anymore. "I guess that's okay. He's not going to shoot you at a bank..."

"I have no idea what he's capable of."

"Well...bring your gun."

I set the phone down and turned to her. "What's the point, baby? Unless you give me permission..."

She looked into my eyes and struggled with the decision. Then she shook her head. "No."

I didn't take offense to it.

"He won't hurt you. He won't go back on his word."

I hoped she knew her brother better than I did, because right now, I couldn't read him. That was my specialty, but I was going into this completely blind, with no insight whatsoever. I grabbed the phone and texted back. *Be there in 10.*

Another message popped up. *I'm unarmed.*

I turned to Catalina. "He just said he's unarmed."

She sighed in relief. "He wouldn't say that unless he meant it... He just wants to talk."

"About what?" I asked.

"I...I have no idea." She shrugged. "I seriously don't."

THE LOBBY WAS EMPTY, as if he cleared his schedule for this. Hades must have been at home because there was no sign of his presence. There was no secretary at the front desk. I helped myself to the hallway lined with windows.

All the doors were shut—except one.

I stopped outside of it, not nervous, just full of dread. I was prepared for the unexpected, always. But this wasn't a normal afternoon for me. Emotions were in the way of my logic. My future wife was on the line, and this was the roadblock in the way.

After a final breath, I turned the corner and stepped inside.

Instead of Damien sitting behind his desk, he sat in the middle of his couch, which faced another sofa. His office was big, with two leather armchairs facing his desk as well as a seating area. There was a decanter of scotch in the center, along with two glasses that were already filled with the liquor. He didn't turn to look at me, his eyes on the other couch.

I moved to the couch across from him and took a seat, directly facing him.

He leaned forward with his elbows on his knees, his palms together, his fingers spread apart.

I stared at him for a few seconds, and when nothing was said, I grabbed the glass and took a drink. Maybe it was poison. Whatever.

That made him snap out of his reverie. He dropped his hands and regarded me in silence, his expression no longer livid like it had been when he'd stepped into the Underground. He was relaxed, indifferent. He reached for the glass in front of him and took a drink too, like he needed the liquor in his blood to focus.

I didn't speak because I didn't know where to begin.

He looked me in the eye, his fingers interlocking so his hands were an enormous pile of white knuckles. "I want you to tell me what happened. I want every detail, even if you think I can't handle it, and I want every person responsible for it."

My eyes remained focused on his, but my mind was completely blank, unsure what he spoke of. "You're going to need to be more specific—"

"I know she was trafficked." His voice broke slightly, like saying those words to me caused him so much pain.

I didn't know how he'd figured it out, especially when it had happened months ago. I'd dissolved that organization and turned it into a brothel. Unless he was visiting as a paying customer, I had no idea how he knew.

He stared at me expectantly. "Talk."

I didn't want to take this trip down memory lane, because whatever pain he thought he felt, mine was worse. Because I loved her in a way he didn't. I'd loved her when I saw her on the floor of that cage, naked and beaten. Why else would I change my entire belief system in a single second? "She was at a bar, had an altercation with a guy in the bathroom. She fought back, kicked his ass, and called the cops. Turned out, he was the guy in charge of the entire sector. Petrov and the other guys were there, so they followed her home and broke in to her apartment that night."

Damien followed my story, his expression controlled.

"I'm not sure how long she was there…maybe a few days. She and I weren't talking at the time. I wanted to be with her, but she turned me down. That was weeks before this happened. I went down to the basement to collect money, like I always did, and that was when she whispered my name." I closed eyes for a second because the memory was just as disturbing now as when it actually happened. "Her face was so beaten, I didn't even recognize her…"

Damien closed his eyes, releasing a painful sigh that made his nostrils flare.

He told me to tell him everything, so I did. "She was naked."

He didn't open his eyes.

"I told them to open the cage. Then I got her out of there. I killed Popov because he was the one who'd beaten her. I let the others go because they hadn't touched her from what I could gather."

He was quiet for a long time, holding his body still as he processed the horrible tale. When he opened his eyes again, they were wet, like the emotion was too powerful to overcome. He couldn't keep it together, not even in front of me, a man he despised. He didn't look directly at me, his gaze focused slightly to the left of me. "Was she raped?" His voice was shaky as he asked the question.

"She never explicitly told me. But, no, I don't think she was."

"Why would she not tell you?" he whispered.

"Because I told her it didn't matter to me..." Regardless of what happened to her, it didn't change the way I felt about her, didn't change her desirability. I didn't see some asshole when I looked at her. I saw a woman as untouched by trauma as before.

He sighed quietly, his hands moving to his eyes so he could wipe away the moisture that built there. "I want them all killed."

I didn't question the order. "Alright."

"Even if they didn't touch her, even if they didn't—"

"I'll take care of it, Damien."

He went quiet again, moving his gaze to the decanter of scotch between us.

Killing those guys would make things complicated with my men, but if that was what he wanted, I wouldn't deny him. Would replace them with someone else who wanted a job.

He grabbed his glass and finished it, leaving only a single drop behind.

"Why did you bring the money last night?" Now it was my turn to ask questions.

"Because I knew your men were doubting your leadership." His hands were together at his lips, his eyes on the table, his words clear even with his knuckles in the way. "When I found out what you did for my sister, I owed you."

If he owed me, I wanted something else, not bags of money. "If you want to pay me back, give me what I really want." I waited for him to look at me, but he never raised his gaze. "And you know what I want, Damien."

He lowered his hands then looked at me head on. "Vox came to my office a few days ago. He was the one who told me everything about Catalina."

My eyes narrowed.

"He's been following you. He pieced together that Catalina is the woman from the basement...and that you changed all your rules for personal reasons. Then he wanted to know why I wasn't paying you, to use that against you too. So, I lied and said I was still paying you...I just didn't have the money last time."

Now I understood how he'd known all of this.

And I knew I had to kill Vox.

Fuck, Balto was right...and I hated it when he was right.

Damien grabbed the decanter and refilled his glass, his eyes suddenly aged by ten years, like the knowledge about Catalina had changed his entire foundation. "You need to kill him, Heath. He'll never stop coming for you."

"I will." I didn't need to be told what to do, but I swallowed my pride because of the situation. "Thank you for telling me about his visit."

"I did it because he knows who my sister is to you. He might use her against you. So, either kill him, or I'll do it."

"I said I'll handle it." Like I would ever let some piece of shit near my woman.

Now, it was quiet—for a long time.

I didn't know if I should leave. Or if I should push him to fold.

He interrupted the silence as he cleared his throat. "Thank you...for what you did for her."

"I'd do anything for her, Damien."

He bowed his head and gave a slight nod.

"If you really want to show your gratitude, you'll put our past behind us."

He wouldn't look at me.

"We both know you wouldn't have been able to save her. By the time you figured out she was gone—"

"Shut up." He raised his head and looked at me, livid and disgusted by the reminder. "I know, Heath. I fucking know."

"Then you owe me."

"I paid you back—"

"I don't want that," I snapped. "I want *her*."

He looked away again, like he was still opposed to the idea.

"Even if I was willing, my father may not be so open-minded."

"Catalina seems to think so."

"Because he's a harmless old man. But when it comes to his children, he's a grizzly bear. If he knew everything you've done to both of us...it might be different. Catalina only knows him as a loving father. I know him as a man."

I wasn't going to let that man say no. If he didn't like me, I would force him to. "Then you can convince him."

He shook his head. "If I am supposed to convince him with facts, I doubt it."

"Damien."

He sighed before he looked at me again. "I need to talk to my sister. I just wanted to know everything before I spoke to her."

"Honestly, the last thing she wants to do is talk about—"

"I don't need your permission, Heath."

I bit my tongue.

He rose to his feet, like the conversation was finished. "Just give me a couple minutes."

"You're going now?"

"Yes. And I'd appreciate the privacy."

I couldn't even give her a warning, and that felt like a betrayal. "Alright."

He moved to his desk and grabbed his things before he walked to the door.

I got to my feet. "Damien?"

He turned back to me, his expression hard.

"I know I did a lot of fucked-up things to you. But I'm not that man anymore." I stared him down with sincerity in my eyes, needing him to understand my soul had been cleansed once Catalina came into my life. She took my hand and pulled me onto the right path, made me into a man I'd never thought I could be. I didn't even remember who I used to be anymore.

He held my stare for a few seconds then walked out.

FOURTEEN
CATALINA

I never ate my lunch because I was too nervous about Heath's conversation with my brother.

He didn't text me.

An hour passed—nothing.

I still sat at the kitchen table, our untouched food in front of us. My foot had been released from the cast so I should be excited this day had come, but now a black cloud blocked all my sunshine, all my triumphs.

Footsteps approached the door.

I turned at the sound, relieved he was home.

The door opened, and he stepped inside.

But it wasn't Heath.

It was my brother.

My mind immediately jumped to a terrible conclusion. "What did you do to him?" I started to rise out of my chair.

He held up his hand and placed it on my shoulder, keeping me down. "Nothing. I just wanted to talk to you in private."

When I sank back into the chair, I released the breath I'd been holding. "So, he's okay?"

"He's fine." He walked back to the entryway to shut the door. Then he returned to me, sitting in the chair Heath had vacated when he'd left. He pushed away the uneaten food and rested his arms on the table.

The anticipation was killing me. "What happened?"

He still didn't say anything, like he didn't know what to say at all.

"Just tell me, Damien."

He finally turned his gaze on me. "I know what happened to you...and I know he's the one who rescued you." His tone of voice was different, unique, unprecedented. He sounded so sad, so depressed, like he would never be happy again.

There was only one thing he could be referring to.

"The man I plotted with last time came to me and told me everything. He's been keeping tabs on Heath, trying to find a way to take him down. When he told me what had happened to you...it was hard to hear."

"I never wanted you to know."

"I assumed. Otherwise, you would have told me so I might actually like him."

"You should like him, Damien. Even if that never happened—"

He sighed loudly.

"If he hadn't walked into that basement...I never would have been the same. I was only in there for a few days, and it broke me. He didn't just save me physically—he saved my spirit. I didn't want to be with him just because of what he did for me. I wanted to be with him...because I wanted to. He just gave me a reason for it to be okay."

He stared at my sink, his expression unreadable.

"I meant what I said the other day. That I'm going to be with him regardless of how you feel about it. But it would make this so much easier if you did feel differently about him."

"You're asking a lot of me, Cat." He turned back to me.

"Nothing is too much when it comes to me."

His eyes softened slightly.

"He saved me when he didn't have to, Damien. I'd already turned him down before that. He didn't owe me anything."

He gave a slight nod.

"I feel that's reason enough."

"Why do you think I'm sitting here?" he asked quietly. "Because it does change things..."

There was finally hope, finally something to latch on to. "So... you give your blessing?"

He sighed deeply, his breath so shaky that it must hurt his lungs. "One right doesn't erase all of his wrongs, Catalina. That's not how life works."

Disappointment filled me. "This is the man I'm going to spend my life with, Damien."

"You haven't known him that long—"

"Doesn't matter," I snapped. "He's the one. I need you to do this—"

"You really think Dad is gonna be okay with this? You don't know him the way I do. You don't know how protective he is of you."

"I do know that," I whispered. "But I have faith he will listen to me. And his feelings about it have nothing to do with yours."

"So even if Dad hates him, you're still going to be with him?" he asked quietly.

It pained me to go against my family's wishes, but I'd tried to live without Heath so many times, and every attempt was so unsuccessful it was laughable. "Yes."

He bowed his head slightly, as if that answer was disappointing.

I placed my hand on his arm and gave him a gentle squeeze.

He took his time before he looked at me, before he forced his gaze to mine.

"Try."

He stared at me in silence.

"I'm not asking you to feel differently about him overnight. All I'm asking is for you to try." I squeezed him harder. "Try to have him be a part of our lives. Try to include him in our get-togethers. Try to look at him the way I do."

Now, he closed his eyes, like the request was physically painful. "I'll try...but that's the most I can do."

DAMIEN JUST LEFT. Where are you?

He texted back immediately. *Sitting in my truck outside.*

Come up.

Alright.

I waited for him to climb up the several flights of stairs and walk through the door. Damien had literally stepped foot outside of my apartment just seconds ago, so depending on where he'd parked, they might cross paths.

A minute later, Heath's heavy footsteps sounded outside the door.

I got out of the chair and pressed my injured foot to the floor, my crutches inaccessible since they were on the other side of the room.

He opened the door and immediately glared at me for trying to get to him on my own. He pushed the door shut behind him then walked to me. "Baby, enough with the walking."

"I didn't have my crutches—"

"But you have me." He picked me up and carried me to the couch in the living room, so we could sit together. He held me across his lap so my legs could rest on the cushions, one arm supporting my back while the other rested on my thighs. He looked at me with his pretty eyes, his expression the same, like Damien hadn't told him anything he wanted to hear. He looked concerned, like he worried how our conversation had affected me. "Are you okay?"

My arms circled his neck, and I held him close, rubbing my nose against his. "I'm fine."

His eyes moved down to my lips, and he gave me a gentle kiss, his mouth parting my lips so he could taste me.

"He asked me about what happened...but didn't ask for details."

His expression didn't change.

"Then I asked him to try, and he said he would."

His eyes narrowed in surprise, like that hadn't been addressed in their conversation. "Really?"

I nodded. "So, I'm happy..."

His hand cupped the back of my neck, and his fingers gently rubbed into me. "I don't know how you managed to pull that off."

"I think it's fair, considering what you did."

His eyes softened. "You don't owe me anything."

"I do—but I already paid you back. He, on the other hand, does. He owes you the chance."

He shook his head slightly. "I disagree, but I'm not going to pass up the opportunity to move forward."

"Me neither."

"So, now what?"

I shrugged. "I guess we'll see how it goes..."

"And your father?"

"I don't know. Haven't thought about it much."

"Well, I'm ready to meet him whenever you think the time is right."

I thought it was sweet that he was brave enough to face him, to tell him what he'd intended to do to him months ago, and still hope he could look past it...because he loved me so much.

"Did you tell him...about our engagement?"

I shook my head. "Did you?"

"No," he answered. "I thought it should come from you."

"I think we should wait..."

He didn't argue.

"It's not that I don't—"

"It's okay." He kissed the corner of my mouth. "We'll get there when we get there."

My hand cupped his cheek, and I kissed him, my thumb feeling the coarse hair along his jawline. In just a few more weeks, I would be able to have him how I wanted, make love to him whenever I felt like it.

He kissed me back, kissing me like my damaged ankle hadn't changed the way he felt about me at all. He wanted me just the same, no matter how broken I was, even if my family hated him.

When I pulled away, I rested my forehead against his. "He mentioned that guy who conspired against you..."

His body stiffened, no longer affectionate. "I'll take care of it."

"It's not going to be a problem—"

"No. I'll kill him." He pulled away, looking me in the eye with seriousness. "Don't worry about that, alright? That's my problem—not yours."

"Well, you are my problem, Heath."

He rubbed his nose against mine. "My stubbornness is your problem. But all that other stuff is not."

FIFTEEN

HEATH

When I went to the Underground that night, I decided to slit Vox's throat on the spot. It was his second betrayal within a few months, and he didn't take advantage of the mercy I'd offered. I'd marked him as a blood traitor, took away any chance he had to sit on the throne, and he still defied me.

He had to go.

Once I was in the room, I searched for him in the sea of faces. He and his comrades usually occupied the same table every time, but that table was empty. I found Steel and walked up to him. "Where's Vox?"

"You didn't hear the news?"

I stilled, knowing this would piss me off.

"He left—took his men with him."

"What the fuck does that mean?"

"They just walked out and said they weren't coming back. They forfeited their cuts for the month."

Was this seriously happening? "He expects to take me down? When I have more men than him?"

"He didn't say anything about that."

"Then what other reason is there to leave?"

He shrugged.

"I just found out he was planning another coup." When he'd spoken to Damien, and then Damien delivered money immediately afterward, he probably found that suspicious, too suspicious to be believed. So, he took off.

"You should have killed him—"

"Shut up. I'm tired of hearing that shit." Now it was unclear if he'd taken off to start over somewhere else, or he was simply regrouping to take me out. I gripped my skull and started to pace, furious with myself for granting mercy, for giving in to my popularity rather than making the best decision.

Steel watched me. "Moving against you is suicide. He probably just found a better way to make money—"

"He's the most spiteful man I've ever met. Finding him is our number one priority. You understand?"

He nodded.

"Shoot him on sight. I don't care who pulls the trigger, doesn't need to be me." I didn't care if I got to witness the light leave his eyes. I just wanted him in the grave—covered with dirt.

I RETURNED to her place right away because I didn't want to leave Catalina alone in the apartment. She had an alarm system, but that wasn't enough when I wasn't around. Instead of waking her up just to scare her, I slept on the couch, close to the front door, my gun on the coffee table.

The most logical guess about Vox's plans was that he intended to leave the country. He could never make money doing anything else under my rule, because once he was found, we would kill them. He was smart enough to figure that out. To stay in the city just to kill me seemed pointless, especially when he would never rise to the throne through assassination, which wasn't the proper channel to take the reins. The rest of the Skull Kings would kill him because the action was a betrayal. If he really wanted to take me on, he had to do it in the ring with a fight to the death. But he could never ask for the opportunity since he was a blood traitor. And if he wanted to take Catalina, that wouldn't accomplish anything either—because he had nothing to gain from it.

Unless torturing me was all he wanted.

I hardly slept that night because I couldn't stop thinking about Vox. If he was still in the city, it wouldn't take long to find him, unless he was locked up somewhere, biding his time. And if he left the country, I definitely wouldn't find him then.

Catalina woke up and used her crutches to get to the bathroom. When she spotted me in the living room, she stopped. "Why are you sleeping on the couch?"

I sat up and rubbed the sleep from my eyes. "Didn't want to wake you."

"I'd rather be woken by you than wake up alone." She used her crutches to move toward me, the rubber bottoms tapping against the hardwood floor with every move she made. When she reached the couch, she balanced on one foot then sat beside me.

I wrapped my arms around her and kissed her everywhere, kissed her on the neck, the collarbone, and then the lips, pushing her hair from her face so I could enjoy her, appreciate the fact that she was really mine, that I would never have to lose her again.

Her arms circled my neck, and she pulled me close, hugging me tight like she'd missed me all night. "Heath?"

"Yes, baby?"

"Why do I feel like there's something wrong?"

I held her against my chest, my face hidden from her because her chin was on my shoulder. My arms squeezed her tight, and I sighed. "I think we should stay at my place for a while." It was much safer there. She would be protected when I wasn't there. The new door I'd gotten her was nothing compared to the security equipment I had there.

She slowly pulled away, reading my eyes like the answer to her question would be in my gaze.

I told her the truth. "Vox took off with his men. I don't know where he is."

"Okay..."

"He probably took off when he figured out I knew what he'd planned. He's probably already out of the country and I'll never see him again."

She waited because she knew there was more.

"But I might be wrong. He might still be here." I didn't tell her the exact details, that he might kill me...or hurt her. It was implied in my silence, in the way I gave her so little information. "My place is better equipped. It's safer—for the both of us."

Instead of getting scared or asking a million questions, she nodded. "Alright. I'll get my things."

"You don't have to stay with me. If you'd rather be with Damien—"

"I go where you go, Heath." The resolution in her eyes told me she was certain, that she understood what she'd signed up for when she agreed to spend her life with me. There would be dangers. There would be uncertainty. But she could handle it.

My hands cupped her face, and I brought our foreheads together, closing my eyes as I held her. She was loyal to me like my men, loyal to me like a soldier on the same battlefield. That was what I needed in a woman—bravery. "You'll be safe. I promise."

———

I MOVED her clothes and essentials to my place and stocked my kitchen with everything she might need when I wasn't home. I hadn't been there much, so I had nothing but unperishable products.

I suspected she wouldn't return to that apartment, not unless it was to remove her things for good. Why would she live there alone when she had me? She would live here with me, whether she was my wife or not.

When I walked into the bedroom, she already had her things in my closet. She moved my clothes to the other side, getting them out of the way so she would have room. Leaning on one of her crutches, she hung up another shirt before she noticed me.

She turned around, looking slightly guilty. "I hope you don't mind..."

"Not at all." She could throw all my clothes on the floor and take up every inch, and it wouldn't make a difference to me. I walked into the closet and wrapped my arms around her waist, holding her and balancing her on one foot. "I was going to make dinner. Any requests?"

"No. I like anything you make." Her hands planted against my neck, her fingers reaching up to my face as she rested her face close to mine, her eyes looking me over like she couldn't believe I was hers, couldn't believe how much she loved me.

I never thought a woman like her would want me, not when she could have any guy she wanted. But she went against her brother's wishes to be with me, accepted the danger my title caused without blinking, chose to be with me even though I led an underground army of criminals.

That kind of love was unconditional.

Unstoppable.

I pulled her closer and kissed her, tugging hard because I wanted to hold her so close that she was practically inside me, her heart beating right directly next to mine, pumping together. I wanted more of her than I could have, wanted the kind of closeness that simply wasn't possible on the planes of our physical existence. Maybe that wouldn't happen until we shed our bodies and traveled as two spirits.

When I pulled away, I pressed my lips to her forehead and kissed her, kissed her in a way I'd never kissed another woman. It wasn't sexual, possessive, or lustful. It was adoration, the best way I could worship her, express the depth of my love in an unquestionable way.

HER FIRST SESSION of physical therapy wasn't easy.

She struggled, grew so frustrated that tears were in her eyes. She pushed herself further than she could handle, wincing in pain because she was trying to force something that just wasn't meant to be—yet.

When we got into the truck, tears dripped down her cheeks.

"Baby—"

"I'm never going to be able to dance again." She closed her eyes and covered her face, like she didn't want me to see her break down.

I kept my voice gentle, reminding myself that I couldn't hammer into her without empathy, that I couldn't give her the tough love I naturally wanted to respond with. "Baby." I grabbed her hand and pulled it from her face.

She twisted out of my grasp and covered her face again.

So, I decided to try to talk to her. "Baby, that's not going to happen—"

"I could barely do anything he told me—"

"It's your first day." It hurt to see her like this, to watch her break down with hopelessness. "You know what my first day was like?"

She stopped sobbing, as if she wanted to listen.

"It was rough, Catalina. Really rough."

She sniffed and dropped her hands.

"I never told you that because it's not me—to complain. But it was really hard. I was scared I would never be me again. But I did it. And if I can do that, you can do this. You think a broken ankle is gonna stop a powerhouse like you?"

She'd stopped sobbing, but leftover tears streaked down her cheeks.

"Nothing is gonna stop you, Catalina. It's gonna take a few weeks, but you're going to get there. And you're going to dominate that stage just like you used to. No one is gonna give a damn about your understudy. She didn't get the part in the first place for a reason—because you're better. Much better."

She wiped her fingers over her cheeks, her mascara running.

"You're gonna get there. I promise."

"How can you promise that?" She finally stopped crying. She sighed and looked out the window.

I grabbed her chin with my fingertips and forced her to look at me. "Because it's you."

I CALLED IN EVERY FAVOR.

No one had seen him.

No one had heard from him.

My men were combing the streets, questioning everyone, doing everything they could to track him down.

Nothing.

I tried to convince myself that he simply took off to save his own ass, that he took his friends so they could start over somewhere else, like in Scotland or Russia. They would start their own business away from my jurisdiction.

But I couldn't lower my guard.

Anytime Catalina went anywhere, I was with her. Even if I was dead tired from working late the night before, I always escorted her. I wouldn't take any chances leaving her alone, even though she was capable of taking care of herself under normal circumstances.

She improved with physical therapy, getting stronger with every session, until she was finally able to walk normally without the crutches. She couldn't move quickly, but she was walking, and that was all that mattered.

And her fire started to come back.

I made dinner in the kitchen, mushroom risotto with grilled chicken on top. Spending so much time with me had taught her how to cook, so she helped me most of the time, and I suspected she would do it on her own eventually.

Not that I minded cooking for her.

I set the table with a bottle of wine, and we sat together, like we did every night.

She cut into her food and took small bites, eating fewer calories than she did before because she was afraid she would gain weight now that she wasn't dancing anymore. Her waistline was bigger, and so was her ass.

But I liked it.

"Have you talked to Damien?" It'd been a few weeks since that conversation with her brother.

She shook her head before she took a bite. "No. I thought I would give him space."

I ate much quicker than her, so I was almost done already. The bottles of wine in my cabinet were all from Barsetti vineyards now, but I'd acquired a taste for it...now that I was too happy to care about shit like that.

"How are things at work?"

"Same." I wanted to tell her I'd caught Vox to give her peace of mind, and I was disappointed with myself every time I couldn't. "He doesn't seem to be anywhere."

She kept eating and didn't ask about it further.

I finished my meal then stared at her, drinking the rest of my wine while I waited for her to finish.

When she was done, she did the same, swirling her glass and drinking from it as she looked at me.

The silence was comfortable, like I was sitting across from Balto, where I didn't feel the need to say something just to fill the silence with words. It was the strongest sense of companionship I'd ever had, to be completely comfortable with another person, to be completely accepted.

She propped her chin on her knuckles as she stared at me. "What?"

I shook my head.

"I can tell you're thinking."

"I'm always thinking," I answered quietly.

"Yeah, but you're thinking about something specific. I can tell by the look in your eyes." She took another drink, adding another faint smudge from her lipstick.

I finished the rest of my wine then looked into the empty glass before I regarded her again. I was silent, looking into her green eyes as I considered exactly what to say.

"I'm waiting..."

I'd never been good with words, so I decided not to say anything at all, because she accepted me exactly as I was, all the good and all the bad. I reached into the pocket of my sweatpants and placed my closed fist in the center of the table.

She watched me.

My fingers lightly released it, letting it land gently on the table before I pulled my hand away.

The diamond ring sat there, shining brilliantly under the lamp hanging above us. It was a white gold band with an enormous diamond, ten carats. The band was also studded with small diamonds, equally flawless.

Her eyes got so wide, it looked like they would pop out of her face.

I'd gone to a couple jewelry stores, trying to figure out what she'd want without asking anyone. A few ideas came to mind, from getting a smaller ring or getting something with an emerald or a unique setting. But then I realized she was the most stunning woman I'd ever met, shining like the sun in every room she stepped into. I wanted her ring to be that way, flawless, brilliant, just like the woman who wore it. It was flashy, just like she was. It was noticeable, just like she was. And there was no way any man wouldn't notice it so they'd stay the fuck away from her.

She continued to stare at it, her eyes not blinking even though it'd been several seconds. "Oh. My. God." She didn't touch it, like she wasn't sure if she was even allowed, and she admired it from a distance. "Jesus, it's fucking beautiful." Her hands covered her mouth like she was swallowing a gasp.

She liked it—I could tell.

She finally grabbed the ring with her fingertips, admired it with excited eyes. She had no idea that the diamond reflected a prism of light across her face, brightening up her eyes more. She turned it side to side, her gaze softening as she immediately formed an emotional attachment to it. "It's exactly what I wanted..." She placed it on her left hand and slid it over the knuckle. Perfect fit. Then she looked at me again, like she didn't know what to say, where to begin.

"So, you'll still marry me?" I whispered.

Her eyes crinkled as they softened further, as if my question was ridiculous. "Without or without a ring, I'd marry you."

SIXTEEN

CATALINA

My knees hugged his hips as my ankles rested against his ass. Every time he rocked into me, I squeezed him harder, trying to hold on as he entered me, giving me all of him, until his balls tapped my ass.

My arms were hooked under his shoulders so my nails could claw his back. My left hand felt different, because of the diamond ring that sat there, so heavy it was like holding a bowling ball.

I loved it.

I'd always known I wanted a flashy ring if I ended up with a rich guy, a big-ass diamond in the middle that was so flawless, it looked like it'd been formed under the earth for millions of years. He'd obviously spared no expense. And he got me a ring that competed with his.

I wasn't going to let my husband have a bigger diamond than me.

I closed my eyes and moaned against his mouth, my fingers digging in deep as I came around him, getting so tight I might break his dick. It was the kind of climax that made me whimper, a strange array of moans escaping my mouth, tears flooding my gaze.

When I finished, he gave his final thrusts, rocking into me while barely pulling out his length like he didn't want to leave. Then he came quietly, his eyes on my lips as he gave me all his seed. A gentle moan escaped his lips, so quiet it was barely audible. His dick was still hard because it was fucking magic, and he kept going. "First one is just a warm-up." He rubbed through my wetness and his own come, our bodies so slick that this would last a long time. "Now, we really begin." One hand moved into my hair, his fingers sliding into the sea of strands that were all over the place. He fisted it then kissed me, giving me a hot embrace with tongue, driving his hard dick inside me over and over.

My hand moved to the center of his shoulder blades, the band from my ring pressing into him. I loved my ring. Picturing myself wearing it while he fucked me turned me on more. This gorgeous man gave it to me; this gorgeous man loved me. It didn't matter that he'd been with whores and any woman who would give it up in the past. He made me feel special, like I was the only one who mattered.

He was the only one who mattered to me.

He suddenly grabbed both of my hands and pinned them above my head, a single one of his large hands enough to hold both of mine. His fingers covered mine, touching the ring he gave me. His eyes looked into mine, focused and possessive, as if he needed to remind me that I was his.

Oh, I knew.

"I love you." He spoke against my lips, whispering his truth with a deep voice, turning me on more than I already was. A man who was vulnerable and open with his feelings was the sexiest thing in the world, especially when he only had those feelings for me. He'd never said the words to another woman, never felt anything close to love. But when he'd met me, he knew exactly how to love me, as if the instinct came to him naturally.

I didn't fight against his hold because I knew I would never win. So, I let him restrain me, looked into his eyes as he kept me down, watching him work his powerful body to please me. "I love you too."

***

CHRISTMAS WAS JUST A WEEK AWAY. I liked the holidays, but I hated the season, and after Christmas, it was January...and I hated January. It was just this long, cold month of nothingness. It sucked.

But Heath kept me warm now, and he would probably keep me warm until spring returned.

I got out of the shower, dried my hair, and put on my face before I looked through my side of the closet to find something to wear. I decided on a long-sleeved dress with thigh-high boots and with my long coat.

I intended to go to Damien's for lunch, so I walked to my nightstand and pulled the diamond ring off my finger. It was the first time I'd taken it off since Heath gave it to me. It was painful to set it down, to part with the diamond ring I'd become so attached to. It was like having a piece of Heath with me everywhere I went, even if he wasn't with me there. It was such a stunning ring. I wanted to show it to Anna, show it to my family.

But that was a really insensitive way to announce my engagement.

Especially since my father didn't even know about Heath.

I sighed as I looked at it, touched my left hand with my fingertips, my hand suddenly so light...and naked.

Then I left the bedroom and entered the living room. "Oh my god...is that a Christmas tree?"

He secured the base of the tree in the corner, a tall pine that was only a few inches lower than the ceiling. On the counter were boxes of ornaments and lights, like we would decorate it together. He straightened and turned to me. "Do you like it?"

"Who doesn't like Christmas trees?" I came close to him, smelling the fresh scent of the needles as they filled the living room. I rubbed a green needle between my fingertips, the smell becoming more potent. "Do you always have a tree?"

"No."

My eyes softened. "So, you did this for me?"

"Baby, you know I do everything for you." His arm hooked around my waist, and he pulled me close. "Let's decorate it tonight. I don't have any personal ornaments—"

"We'll make our own every year."

He gave me a slight smile. "I've never had a tradition before. Every year, I kinda forget it exists until Balto and I get together."

"Well, things are about to change." I turned into him and kissed him as I wrapped my arms around his neck.

His hands immediately went to my ass, underneath my coat and dress. "You look hot, by the way."

"You always say that."

He chuckled against my lips. "Well, you do."

I pulled away, a permanent smile on my face because I was happy, so happy that I forgot there was a possibility that one of Heath's enemies might hurt one of us. It was easy to forget during romantic bliss.

"Going somewhere?"

"Yeah, I'm going to see my father."

His eyes glanced down to my left hand, and he immediately looked disappointed to see the ring absent. He looked at me again, his mood noticeably different. "So, this is gonna be a secret forever—"

"I was going to tell him about you today." I didn't want to deal with his wrath when we were having such a nice moment. "And I think walking in there with a baseball-sized diamond ring is not the right way to do it. My family is very traditional. You need to ask permission first."

"Well, I didn't, and you already said yes."

"And my answer is still yes, but let's just put on the show for them."

He was still irritated. "And if his answer is no?" He'd been hurt by me many times in the past, so now, he was always afraid he might lose me, that something could change and I'd walk out the door for good.

"My answer is yes—no matter what."

He finally relaxed, the irritation in his expression fading away like smoke from a dying fire. "Should I come with you?"

"I think I should just talk to him alone. I don't know what his reaction will be, and if I bring you, it might overwhelm him. He's very intelligent, but he's also over seventy, so he gets worked up sometimes."

"Alright. But I'd like to talk to him—man-to-man."

"You will." I turned to the kitchen counter to grab my purse.

"I'll take you."

"No, it's okay—"

"It wasn't a question." He grabbed his keys and wallet and headed to the stairs.

Caught up in our joy, I'd forgotten about our current situation, that he didn't want me going anywhere alone...just in case.

HE PULLED up to the curb right outside the double doors that led to the three-story mansion Damien called home. "I'll wait out here until you're done."

"It might be a while."

"Then I'll grab lunch and eat it in the truck. Just text me when you're going to leave soon."

"Alright." I leaned over the middle seat and kissed him.

His hand cupped my cheek, and he kissed me hard, like he didn't want me to forget what we had in case my father hated him as much as Damien did. Heath had never been insecure, never been anything but potently confident, but now he wasn't quite himself.

I pulled back and licked my lips. "Heath, you think I'm going to go anywhere after you gave me that gorgeous ring?"

"You could find another guy to buy you one just like it."

I'd meant to make a lighthearted joke, but it didn't land. "Nothing is going to change. I promise."

He struggled to believe me, and he still wore a wary gaze.

"Standing up to my brother doesn't prove my credibility?"

He stared at me with an unreadable gaze, like he was in a poker match and didn't want to reveal his cards. "Your brother is not your father. It's a very different relationship. No daughter wants to marry a man her father doesn't approve of. So...I'm not sure what will happen once you tell him."

My hand moved to his. "We're spending our lives together, Heath. Period." I stared at him with my fiery expression, telling him that I had my mind made up, that my choice was as clear as a message written in black ink on white paper.

He brought my hand to his mouth and placed a gentle kiss on the knuckles. "Go."

I couldn't convince him further. He would just have to wait and see. "Love you." I leaned over and kissed him again before I got out of the truck.

"Love you too." His deep voice followed me before I shut the door.

I walked into the house without looking back, chatting briefly with Patricia before I entered the dining room.

My father was old-fashioned, so he still got dressed up, even for a casual lunch. He wore a sweater-vest over a collared shirt along with a sport coat. All he needed was a pocket watch, and he would look like a historical figure plucked out of the 1920s.

The second he saw me, his eyes lit up, just the way they used to when he looked at my mother. "Sweetheart, you look beautiful." He got to his feet and kissed me on the cheek.

"Thanks, Dad. You look pretty cute in that outfit." I shed my coat and placed it over the back of the chair before I sat down.

He looked down at his sleeves. "Patricia picked it out for me. It's thick and stuffy, can barely move my arms, but she makes my meals so..."

"She has great taste."

Patricia came in a moment later and brought cappuccinos along with our lunch. Then she left us alone to talk.

We made small talk, discussing my ankle, Damien's wedding date, and the weather.

"When do you think you can go back to the ballet?" he asked.

The theatre always took a winter break during January, so it wouldn't be until February, assuming I could perform again. "Sometime around Valentine's Day. I've been continuing physical therapy, and I feel like I'm getting stronger every day. This is the first time I've been able to wear heels."

"I was never worried about you making a full recovery," he said before he sipped his coffee. "You're such a driven person."

"Well...thanks." He sounded like Heath.

"So, Christmas will be exciting this year, with a new member of our family."

"Yeah..." I would love it if there were two new members. "You know, Dad...there's something I wanted to talk to you about."

"You can tell me anything." He waved me forward. "Go ahead. Speak your mind." He slid his spoon into the bowl of soup then dragged the bottom across the edge of the dish before he placed it in his mouth. It was chicken noodle, to make our stomachs warm on this cold day.

I couldn't be as candid as he encouraged me to, as much as I would like to be. It was a delicate situation, and now that the moment was upon us, I was so nervous. My heart was racing like I was on the treadmill...or having sex with Heath. "You remember how I told you I was seeing someone?"

He continued to eat, but he did pause for a second to look at me. "Yes. Damien didn't care for him."

"Yes."

Now, he stirred his soup without eating, interested in what I had to say next.

"Well, Damien has kind of had a change of heart about it. Said he's willing to give him a try."

"Oh, that's good news for you. You know how men are—butt heads a lot because they're stubborn."

I wished it were that simple. "Dad, the thing is...Damien has every right to feel the way he does. He's not overreacting. His feelings aren't unfounded. But...I feel like this man isn't the same person he used to be. He's changed. And I think he deserves a fresh start...because I love him." I'd just told my father I loved a man, and my heart was about to explode with anxiety. I knew I would only have this conversation with him if I were going to get married, because I wasn't going to bring a guy around unless that was the kind of future I pictured for us.

He dropped the spoon, taking the weight of my words with complete seriousness. "You love this man?"

I nodded. "Yeah. I do."

"If you love him despite what he's done, I'm sure you have a good reason. You're a smart woman with impeccable judgment."

My eyes softened so much I thought I might cry.

"I'm sure Damien agrees."

Not in the slightest. "He wants to meet you. But I thought we should talk first..."

"Alright. I'm ready to listen whenever you're ready to speak."

"Well..." There was no way I could phrase any of this to make Heath sound good. He was the villain, no matter how I explained it. "We both know what Damien does. Heath has been an adversary—"

"His name is Heath?"

"Yes."

He nodded.

"Heath basically demanded taxes from Damien because he runs the city, at least underground. When Damien refused... they didn't get along. And then to make Damien pay for his defiance...he took you."

My father slowly understood what I was saying, the light of comprehension coming into his eyes.

"He had his men hold you somewhere until Hades came to rescue you." It pained me to say all of this, to feel disloyal as I spoke.

He didn't say anything, but he dropped his gaze, which wasn't a good sign.

"Then Heath took me and locked me in a cage as part of a ploy to get back at Damien, but he let me go. He said he couldn't go through with it. I didn't see him again for a while, and when we bumped into each other, we just had the right chemistry. I told him I didn't want to be with him, but he wore me down...and never told me what he did. I found out later— and left him. I didn't want to be with a man who moved against my family like that. I tried not to care about him. But then I realized...he's not that man anymore. He would give his life to protect mine, to protect anyone I loved. He's different... and even Damien acknowledges it." I waited for him to look at me.

He didn't.

I was hoping this would go better, but I'd been too optimistic.

"I wanted you to know the truth. I didn't want to lie about any of it."

Nothing.

"But he's not that man anymore. He's saved Damien's life, he's saved mine... He takes care of me."

My dad wasn't a quiet guy. He usually had something to say, lived for the opportunity to have a conversation because he was lonely. But now he was silent, processing everything I'd said. "I've got to be honest, sweetheart. I was expecting you to say something completely different..."

"I know it's a lot to take in..."

He was so disturbed that he pushed his lunch aside and rested his hands on the table, his fingers interlocked. His eyes were still down, deep in thought. "I wasn't expecting this man to be a criminal mastermind."

"That's not all who he is..."

He shook his head slightly, sighing quietly.

Heath and I hadn't gotten this far just to trip over the finish line. "Dad, he's different now. I know what he did was wrong. It took me a long time to look past it. But he's the man I love, the man I want to spend my life with, and it would mean the world to me if you could keep an open mind."

His thumbs gently brushed together, his eyes watching his movements.

"You said I wouldn't love this man unless I had a good reason, that you trust my judgment."

"I know what I said, sweetheart. This is just a lot to take in at once. Honestly, I didn't expect you to want a man like Damien, like the men in his world. I pictured you with a successful man, but someone more ordinary."

"Well...I guess I don't like ordinary." Now that Heath had put the thought in my head, I couldn't imagine spending my life with a mediocre man, one who just went to work in an office or something and was always home by five. I came from a line of criminals. "And Damien lives in that world, but you don't blink an eye over it. You did too—"

"Yes, but we're men—"

"That's sexist," I snapped at my father, the first time I ever had in my life.

He was just as stunned.

"It's unfair for me to be excluded just because I'm a woman, Dad."

"But you can't take care of yourself—"

"Heath can take care of me just fine. Isn't that what you want? A man who can take care of me? Physically, financially, emotionally...he can do it all."

He bowed his head with a sigh. "It doesn't sound like he's similar to Damien, who makes a product and sells it to shady characters. This man is much higher on the food chain, and the more eyes on you, the more enemies you have. I bet this man has a target on his back every single day."

That was true. He did.

"That's my issue, Catalina. He's the Skull King, isn't he?"

All I could do was blink because I couldn't believe he even knew what that was. He'd been out of the game for decades.

He didn't need me to confirm it. "That's a whole different level, Catalina. As long as you're with him, you'll have a target on your back too. Yes, he can protect you, but he's also the reason you need protection. I'm sorry to disappoint you, but I don't want that."

Hope slipped through my fingertips. "If you meet him, you'll feel differently."

"No, I won't."

I sighed loudly, disappointed. I thought Damien would be my biggest hurdle, not my sweet and loving father. "Please try... for me." I pleaded with him with my eyes, needing this to happen, needing his approval to be happy.

He stared at me with a cold gaze, no longer the man I knew.

"Please...I love him."

He sighed just the way Damien had, his nostrils flaring. Their features were never more similar than when my father was angry. The vein thickened on his forehead, and his skin tinted red, just the way his son's did. "I want to talk to him."

I had no idea if that was a good thing or a bad thing. "He's outside."

He leaned back in the chair, crossing his arms over his chest. "Then bring him in." His body was rigid, the muscles flexed through his layers of clothes. The kindness in his eyes had vanished along with all of his affection. He seemed to fall back in time, back to his youth, back to the time when he intimidated people for a living.

I hadn't expected this conversation to go this way, so I felt terrible that Heath would be put on the spot without any time to prepare. But he should be able to handle it. He'd probably done worse things than meet a potential father-in-law. "Alright...I'll be back."

I GOT INTO THE TRUCK.

"Went that bad, huh?" he asked, barely looking at me.

"Why do you say that?"

"You look like snow."

I stared straight ahead before I had the courage to turn to him. "No, it didn't go well..."

His eyes fell with disappointment.

"He said he wants to talk to you."

He gave no reaction.

I kept staring at him.

"Right now?" he asked calmly.

I nodded. "I told him you were outside."

He sighed quietly, his chest rising with the air that filled his lungs.

"I know this is unexpected. We can come back at a later time—"

"No. He challenged me—and I'm not going to decline."

"I don't think he's challenging you—"

"He put me on the spot. That was intentional. Trust me, I know what he's doing. It's a test—to see how much of a coward I am."

"You aren't a coward..."

"Exactly." He opened the door. "Which is why I'm going in there."

SEVENTEEN
HEATH

I was in jeans and a long-sleeved olive-green shirt. It was too casual to make a good impression, but it was all I had. I stepped inside, and Patricia immediately recognized me from the time Damien had marched me inside with my hands tied behind my back. She stilled on the spot, unsure if she should scream or run.

"Richard asked to see me." I kept my distance, kept my voice low so she wouldn't be scared.

She nodded to the large archway past the entryway. "He's in there." She probably wasn't privy to family drama, but the help always knew the intimate details of the people they served. She probably already knew Catalina and I were together.

"Thanks." I moved farther into the house, having been there before. But I'd been marched to the left, and now I was headed in a different direction. I passed through the archway and entered a large dining room, a table that could easily accommodate twenty people. Cathedral-style windows were on the wall, letting in the faint light from the overcast day.

Richard sat there, his hands together on the table, his eyes on me.

I moved farther into the room, holding his gaze with confidence and toning down my naturally intimidating persona. It didn't feel right to try to shake his hand, to be polite when this wasn't a normal meeting between two men on good terms. I dropped into the chair facing him, taking the spot my fiancée had previously occupied.

I hoped she was still my fiancée. I didn't buy her that two-hundred-thousand euro diamond ring for nothing.

Patricia came into the room and cleared the plates, placing a cappuccino in front of me even though I didn't take my coffee with sugar or cream.

Richard stared at me the entire time, not saying a word.

I held his gaze, listening to Patricia's footsteps fade until she returned to the kitchen on the other side of the house.

I didn't know what to say.

Catalina hadn't shared details about their conversation, so I walked straight into the dark. I assumed he didn't like me one bit, and somehow, I was supposed to change his opinion in a simple conversation. I had a tiny bit of hope, because he wouldn't have asked me to otherwise.

When he spoke, he didn't sound like an old man. He sounded confident, as if his youth had returned to his veins like muscle memory. "I don't care that you attempted to have me executed. It was just business. I get it."

That was the last thing I'd expected him to say.

"If Damien can drop his prejudice when he's had to deal with you firsthand, then I don't see why I can't too."

Maybe this wasn't so bad after all.

"I believe men can change. I know I did."

The coffee in front of me released steam that rose to the ceiling, smelling like fresh espresso beans.

"But I don't like you for my daughter."

It was a terrible blow. A bat was in his grip, and he smacked me hard with it, just as Damien did in the basement, spilling blood everywhere.

"I'm going to give you one chance to change that."

Jesus, talk about pressure.

"Don't blow it."

"I don't need more than one chance, sir." I loved her and would do anything for her. That was all that mattered.

He didn't react, but his silence showed that he approved of that response. "What kind of life can you give my daughter?"

"Whatever life she wants." I sounded like a pussy, letting the woman tell me exactly what was about to happen, but that was how it was. I folded for her, took the knee for her, allowed her to take my power because she was the queen I wanted to serve.

"Be more specific."

I didn't see the necessity. "I'm not going to sugarcoat who I was. I was greedy, selfish, egotistical...nothing to be proud of. My life was filled with money, women, and booze. But then I met Catalina, and I think that very night I loved her. Everything changed. I changed. Now, I would do anything for her, make any sacrifice, if it made her smile."

"I want you to put your money where your mouth is."

I had no idea what that meant.

"You want my daughter?" He raised his forefinger. "Here's your one and only chance to prove yourself."

I kept a straight face, but my chest rose with the breath I needed.

"You step down as the Skull King. Now."

Was not expecting that.

"My son is a kingpin in the drug world. But he's not the leader of the underworld. You can't be both. You can't keep her safe if people want you dead. You can have my daughter, have my approval, if you do this."

I wanted to argue that I could keep her safe even as the Skull King, that she was safer with me than anywhere else. But this was a test I couldn't fail, and if I argued, I would lose my only chance. This was his sole demand, my chance to prove that I would sacrifice anything to be with his daughter—and that would make me worthy of her. "Alright."

He couldn't hide his surprise, as if he expected me to argue, expected me to try to have it both ways.

"I want to marry her." A part of me was glad her father was a former criminal, someone who understood my world. If he were some average guy, he would never understand anything. He would be ignorant and scared.

"I'll consider your request—after you step down."

I didn't want to walk away from my position. I expected to continue to be the Skull King for a few more years, until Catalina wanted to start a family. This was short notice. My reign had barely begun. "I need time to prepare." I couldn't just put in my resignation on the spot. I hadn't even decided who would replace me.

"I said now."

"And you know that's a ridiculous demand. I need a successor. I need to wrap up loose ends. I will fulfill my promise. I want to marry Catalina as soon as possible, which I don't want to do without your blessing, so I will take care of it as quickly as I can."

He didn't argue with me, but he didn't look happy either. But he did give a nod in agreement.

I had to make a big sacrifice to keep her—but at least she was my prize. "You don't want to interrogate me?" He hadn't asked me about kidnapping her. He hadn't asked me about my beef with Damien. He hadn't asked me anything personal.

"No."

I sat there, surprised this conversation was so brief.

"My daughter told me she loves you. She wants to spend her life with you. I trust her judgment. All the details about who you are, your past, all that stuff doesn't matter. All that matters is how much you love her. And you just proved that to me by giving me what I asked. For a powerful man, that

wasn't an easy sacrifice to make. I know because I've personally done it."

I didn't ask what he used to do, but I assumed it was signifi-
cant if he left it to be with Catalina's mother, to be a father to
Catalina and Damien. It was probably difficult for him, but a
necessary sacrifice if he wanted to keep his family safe. It was
the biggest test he could give me—and I passed. "I like you."
He didn't need my approval, but I said it anyway.

He didn't react to my words.

"Your personal feelings toward me and my crimes are signif-
icant. All you care about is your daughter's happiness, and I
respect you for that." His reaction was completely different
from Damien's, showing a man who possessed maturity he
had accumulated through both time and experience.

His hands remained linked together. "Make my daughter
happy. And someday...I might like you."

———

CATALINA IMMEDIATELY FIRED off questions when I
got into the truck. "What happened? What did he say?"

I started the engine and drove away. "It's fine."

Her eyes burned into the side of my face from her position on
the other side of the truck. "What? It's *fine*? What the hell
does that mean? What did he say?"

I drove through the streets and headed to my place.

Our place.

"He said he accepts me."

"How did you pull that off?" she yelled. "What did he ask you?"

I kept my eyes on the road. "Said he trusted your judgment."

"That's not what he said to me..."

"So, he asked me to prove myself."

"Okay, what does that mean?"

"Asked me to do something—and I agreed."

"Well, what did he ask you to do?" she asked. "How could a fifteen-minute conversation be enough to resolve all of this?"

I shrugged. "Guys don't say much."

"Heath," she said with a growl. "Why won't you just be straight with me?"

I turned down all the right streets, getting closer to the home where I shared my life with her.

"Heath, what did he ask you to do?"

"I'll tell you when we get home."

She sighed, furious she couldn't get what she wanted on the spot.

I drove in silence the rest of the way, feeling her grow more anxious by the minute. When I pulled into the underground garage, she was on me again.

"We're home."

I hit the clicker, and the garage closed behind us. Then we sat together in the dark, quiet now that the engine was off.

"Why won't you answer me?"

I unfastened my safety belt and turned to her, feeling like I was betraying her father by telling her the truth. But there was no way to hide it from her. "He told me to give him what he wanted—and he would let me marry you."

"And that was...?"

"He told me to step down."

Her expression focused as she heard what I said, taking a few seconds to make the conclusion.

"And until I do it, I can't marry you. I agreed."

She released the breath she was holding. "So, you aren't going to be the Skull King anymore?"

I shook my head. "I just need to find a replacement and tie up loose ends." Vox was my loose end.

"I can't believe he asked you to do that."

It had shocked me at the time, but once the element of surprise had passed, it wasn't that unreasonable. "Those were his terms."

"I just...I know that must be hard for you."

I shrugged. "Living without you is much harder." It was a bit difficult to be forced into retirement when I was young and in my prime, but I didn't need the money. Boredom would be a problem, but I could find something else to do with my time.

Her eyes softened. "He didn't ask you anything else?"

"No," I answered. "He said the past doesn't matter. The only thing that matters is how much I love you—and I proved that to him."

She moved to the center seat so she could hook her arm through mine and rest her chin on my shoulder. Her hair fell down my chest, her perfume mixing with my cologne.

"I like your dad."

"Yeah?" she whispered.

"Now I know where you get it from."

"Get what from?"

I pressed a kiss to her forehead. "Everything."

EIGHTEEN
CATALINA

I sat on the couch alone because Heath wasn't home.

He was at work.

The TV was on, and I twirled my hair, the diamond ring on my left hand still so heavy that it was hard to sleep with it. I wondered if I'd get used to it, but I suspected the weight was such that it was impossible to ever feel normal.

My phone started to ring.

It was Damien.

I answered right away. "Hey." It'd been a few days since the conversation with my father, and that meant Damien knew about it.

"What are you doing?"

"I'm at home watching TV."

"I just went by your apartment, and you weren't home."

I didn't even realize what I'd just said. "Sorry...I meant I'm at Heath's."

Damien didn't respond to what I said. "Wanted to swing by and talk to you. Can I come over?"

"Uh...sure." It was Heath's house, but I didn't think he would mind. I gave Damien the address.

"Be there soon."

I whipped up something to eat in the kitchen, making enough leftovers so Heath would have dinner whenever he came home. The doorbell rang throughout the house when Damien was on the front doorstep.

I walked down the stairs, undid all the locks for the vault door, and then got to the normal ones on the outside.

Damien stared at the two-foot-thick metal doors, his eyebrow raised like he was surprised by what he saw. "He doesn't fuck around, does he?"

I shook my head.

He came inside and watched me pull everything shut before the mechanisms loudly clicked into place. There was a TV on the wall, showing the different camera feeds of the property. Damien looked around and followed me upstairs to the second floor. "Is he home?"

"No. He's at work." I moved to the pan on the stove and plated the food. "Hungry?"

He eyed the pan with interest. "I mean, if you've got it ready..."

I smiled and handed him the plate. "Wine okay?"

"Sure." He carried it to the dining table and sat down.

I opened a bottle of wine then sat across from him.

"Wow, pretty good," he said after his first bite.

"Why the tone of surprise?"

"Last time I checked, all you could make was a frozen pizza."

"Well, Heath has taught me some things." I grabbed the bottle of wine from the center of the table, and that was when I realized the ring was on my finger. Thankfully, Damien's gaze was on his food, so I discreetly put my hand under the table and pulled the ring off my finger, slipping it into my pocket. I hated hiding the ring, like it was a secret to be ashamed of, but Damien was finally in a better place, and I didn't want to provoke his wrath. "So, what brings you here?"

"Do I need a reason?"

"You never stop by without one, so yes."

He kept eating, holding his fork and knife correctly. "Dad told me about his conversation with Heath."

"I figured."

"And that Heath would step down."

"Yes." I lifted my gaze and looked at him.

He chewed as he stared at me. "I'm surprised he agreed."

"Dad didn't give him a choice."

He took another bite and chewed slowly.

"If Dad can get on board, I don't see why—"

"I said I would try. I will." He cut into his food and kept eating. "Actually, I was going to ask if you wanted to come over for Christmas morning."

"Me? Or me and Heath?"

He stared at me for a long time, like he had to think about it. "Both of you."

That was music to my ears, finally allowed to wear the man I loved on my arm. Because if I had to choose, I wasn't going to leave Heath alone on Christmas while I spent time with my family. We were a set. "Thank you."

He shrugged in response. "I know if he's not invited, I won't get to see you."

"And by inviting him, you just made me very happy."

He grabbed his glass and took a drink. "Dad handled the whole thing a lot better than I expected."

"Because he understands what Heath means to me."

"Yeah, I guess."

"And I wouldn't ask him to look past the situation if this wasn't the only man I want to be with."

He swirled his glass and took another drink.

"How have you been?"

"Fine."

"That's it? I figured you'd be really happy."

"I am," he said. "I just... This whole thing with Heath is a lot."

"All you have to do is accept him. I'm not asking you to be his brother."

"I know. It's just weird. I hoped Dad would lay down the law and get rid of him...but guess not."

"I know you don't mean that," I whispered. "Because I would be really devastated..."

A guilty look came into his eyes, like he did feel bad about what he'd said.

"When do you think you guys will get married?" Just as I finished the sentence, the door downstairs closed.

Damien heard it too, because he went rigid.

Heath didn't usually come home until much later, so that was a surprise.

His heavy footfalls became louder as he headed up the stairs. My back was to him so I couldn't see, but Damien's serious expression told me that it was him. Heath opened the cabinet, got a plate, and scooped the food onto it. Then he came to the table, joining us. "Hey, baby."

"Hey." Once he was beside me, I leaned in and gave him a quick kiss on the mouth. It wasn't the way I would usually greet him, but I felt awkward doing anything else with my brother sitting across from me.

Damien kept eating, not looking at him.

Heath didn't say anything either, his eyes focused on his meal.

The men preferred silence to forced conversation.

"Damien." I said his name quietly, giving him a nudge.

He stared at me, his eyes hostile.

I gave him a kick under the table.

He kicked me back and stayed silent.

Heath grabbed the wine bottle and filled his glass. "Damien. What do you think of Catalina's cooking?" When my brother couldn't bring himself to break the ice, Heath stepped up.

Damien took a while to answer, like he wanted to resist. "Good. Surprisingly good."

"I taught her how to make this. And it's better than mine." Heath ate like he was starving, always scooping all of his food into his mouth like he was in a rush.

Damien went quiet again, picking at his food. "I like your front door."

"A tank couldn't get through it," Heath said, his elbows on the table.

"So, are you living with him now?" Damien asked, looking at me.

"Not technically," I answered. "But yeah, I guess. I mean, I like his place a lot more than mine—and not because of the door."

Damien finished his food, so he sat with his elbows on the table, his fingertips at his lips.

"Tell Heath why you came over here." I had to hold both of their hands and get them to talk, like they were boys who didn't get along on the playground.

Damien gave a quiet sigh. "Wanted to invite you to Christmas." He cleared his throat. "Both of you."

Heath raised his gaze and looked at Damien, like he'd just extended a lifeline. "Thank you."

Damien still wouldn't look at him. "I guess I should get going..." He started to rise.

"Sit your ass down," I said as I pointed my fork at him. "It's rude to leave a meal when other people aren't finished."

"I'm a pretty rude guy, so..." He shrugged.

"I'll stab this fork into your eye, alright?" I moved the fork back to the plate.

Damien stayed put and finally looked at Heath for the first time. "When are you going to quit?"

I imagined their conversations went much better when I wasn't there, even if their discussions were hostile. But in peacetime, they had no idea how to behave around each other.

"I just need to take care of a few things." Heath drank from his wine.

"That wasn't what I asked," Damien barked.

"Damien, chill," I said, giving him the eye.

"Baby, it's fine," Heath said. "I told them I would. They have a right to ask." He took another bite and swallowed. "Two weeks, probably. I can't just drop everything right this second. I'm in the middle of something."

Damien seemed satisfied by that answer and looked away.

This was not the kind of relationship I wanted them to have, but at least it was a start. They were in the same room, at the same table, eating together.

"What are you in the middle of?" Damien asked.

"Damien," I snapped, knowing it was none of his business.

Heath answered without an attitude. "I'm hunting down a traitor."

Damien shifted his gaze to him, as if he knew exactly what he was talking about. "Vox?"

"Yes," he said between bites.

"You haven't killed him yet?" Damien asked.

Heath kept the same stoic appearance. "He took off. Your conversation must have tipped him off."

Damien sighed.

"I have to kill him before I leave," Heath said. "I hope it won't take that long."

"Yeah, me neither," Damien said. "So, after you leave, is the next Skull King going to come to my door and demand money?"

"Probably," Heath said bluntly. "And I hope you learned your lesson..."

Damien looked away, visibly annoyed. "I should get going." He rose to his feet and set his plate in the sink. "You've got a nice place, Heath. Let me know where you got your door." He left without giving me a proper goodbye, taking the stairs to the front door.

Heath finished eating like nothing had happened.

"You're home early."

He chewed as he stared straight ahead, his mood suddenly turning sour. He finished the last bite then abruptly left the table and stepped into the kitchen. His shoulders were tight with anger, his entire body fuming.

I got to my feet and joined him at the sink. "I didn't think it would be a problem having him over—"

"Where's your ring?" He stared at the pile of dishes at the bottom of the sink as the water ran. He watched the bits of food and sauce wash away down the drain at the center before he slammed his fist onto the lever, stopping the water.

I tensed at the question, feeling the large ring stuffed in my pocket.

He turned toward me, looking down at me with a potent look of disappointment. "Either wear it, or don't wear it. But stop going back and forth." He pivoted his large body toward me, towering over my small stature. "I didn't drop two hundred grand for you to shove it in your goddamn pocket."

Guilt washed over me when I saw how much I'd hurt him.

"You're either with me, or you aren't. Choose."

"I just didn't want my brother to find out like—"

"Then tell him. Or don't wear it. That fucking simple." He walked past me.

I grabbed him by the arm and pulled him back to me. "Heath, I'm sorry. I'm not embarrassed of you. I'm not unsure if I want to marry you. I just...don't want to announce it that way."

"Isn't that how women announce they're engaged? Walking into a room with a diamond on their hand?" He looked down at me with annoyance, like all he wanted to do was go upstairs to his gym and work out for a few hours. He didn't want to spend his time with me, even though he always wanted to spend his time with me.

"I thought my father said you couldn't marry me until you quit—"

"Yes. Never said I couldn't give you a fat ring and ask you to marry me. I already asked his permission. He said I could have you if I do this—and I'm fucking doing it." He came closer to me and held up his hand. "I don't give a shit whether you want to wear the ring or not. But I do give a shit when you take it off the second someone comes around. It's a commitment. You're either in, or you aren't. Fucking choose." He turned away to head down the hallway.

"Heath?"

He sighed and turned around, like he wanted nothing to do with me.

I walked up to him as I fished the ring out of my pocket. I returned it to my finger—where it belonged. "I'm sorry. It won't happen again."

His eyes burned into mine, as if he was searching for my sincerity. "That means when we go over there on Christmas—"

"Yes, I'll wear it."

Now he didn't look so angry, but he was still in a bad mood, so he walked away.

He'd just gotten home, so he probably wanted to take a shower first, kick back with a drink on the couch, decompress after all the shit he had to deal with all day, so I let him go—and let this go.

AFTER GETTING DRESSED, I went into the kitchen and grabbed my purse from the hook at the top of the stairs. My keys and wallet were inside, and this was my last chance to get this taken care of before Christmas.

Heath emerged down the stairs, in workout shorts and shirt, his skin shiny with sweat. He yanked off his headphones when he spotted me digging through my purse, knowing I was trying to leave if I was dressed up like that. "It looks like you're leaving, but that can't be right..." He reached the bottom stair then walked toward me, the promise of retribution bright in his eyes. "Because I specifically told you to not leave the house without me." He stopped in front of me, calling me out on the spot.

"Look, there's something I wanted to get you for Christmas—"

"I don't need anything for Christmas."

"I know, but I—"

"I'm not a child expecting presents under the tree on Christmas morning. I'm a grown-ass man who only cares about one—my fiancé. So, keep your money and keep your ass home." He turned around and started to walk away.

"Heath?"

He turned back to me, clearly still angry about the fiasco with the ring.

"I really need to do this."

He shook his head slightly. "No."

"Can Damien take me?"

"I don't need another man to protect my woman." His eyes narrowed. "Ever."

I sighed. "Then can Balto take me?"

"I'm sorry, is Balto another man?" he said sarcastically.

I kept my mouth shut.

"Then no."

"Then I guess I need you to take me."

"Doesn't that negate the whole point?"

"I'll drive, and you'll keep your eyes closed."

He didn't look the least bit happy about that.

"I'll place you at the entryway, looking out away from the store so you don't know where you are. And then you'll close your eyes again when I escort you to the truck. Come on, please. I know you'll like it."

"I don't need anything, Catalina."

I stomped my good foot. "Just do what I say. Please."

When I said that final word, he softened, knowing he couldn't deny me even if he was still a bit resentful. "Let me shower."

THE TREE WAS DECORATED with white lights and red and gold ornaments. It brought light into the house, a special sense of merriment that made this place less sterile. Now it really felt like a home rather than a bachelor pad.

I sat with him on the couch, my arm hooked through his. "Want to watch a Christmas movie?"

"Sure."

I grabbed the remote and flipped through the channels until I found a good one. "I love *Home Alone*. The first two are great. The third one is weird...it doesn't even have the same kid in it."

He stared at the TV blankly.

"Have you seen it?"

He shook his head. "Never seen a Christmas movie."

"Ever?" I asked incredulously. "What did you and Balto—" I stopped speaking when I remembered his childhood, that their father had been an abusive drunk and killed their mother. I cringed because I realized how careless I was.

His arm moved behind my shoulders, and he pulled me close. "Baby, it's okay."

"I'm sorry..."

"Really. It's fine."

"Well, we'll watch all the Christmas movies together."

"Really?" he asked, slightly sarcastic. "I think I'd rather just have sex."

"Come on, that's not very Christmassy."

"If sex isn't part of the holiday, then I'm probably not going to be a big fan of it."

I smacked his arm playfully. "Are you and Balto getting together?"

"We don't usually."

"Why don't we invite them over for Christmas dinner?"

"What's Christmas dinner?" he asked blankly.

"Just dinner on Christmas night."

He shrugged. "Sure, if you want."

"I think it'll be nice. The four of us are family now."

He turned to me, watching me with a subtly soft expression. "Yeah...I guess we are."

"And next year, we're going to have a nephew."

When he heard me describe our life together, calling his family my family, his expression changed, like that was a future that got him excited the way Christmas excited everyone else. "Yeah, that will be nice."

"It'll be really nice." I got off the couch and dropped my shorts along with my panties while the movie played on the TV. "And there can be lots of sex at Christmastime."

His eyes ignored the TV altogether, moving straight to the apex of my thighs as he sat up, eager for me like he hadn't just had me this morning. He pushed his sweatpants down so his cock could come free. His entire countenance changed, tightened in a sexy way, like the conversation we'd had never happened at all.

I straddled his hips and moved on top of him, lowering myself until my sex pressed against his.

His hands gripped my hips, and he looked into my face, the Christmas lights reflecting in his eyes, giving him a special glow that was indescribable. It was timeless, like it would stay ingrained in my mind forever as one of those moments that was special to me, even though there was nothing different about it compared to other moments.

His fingers slid up my shirt to my belly, not carrying about the couple pounds I'd put on in the last six weeks. He didn't care that my ass was bigger either. In fact, he seemed to enjoy it more, judging from the way he liked to take me from behind so often. My tits were bigger too—and he definitely liked that. "Now I understand why everyone loves Christmas..."

WHEN I WOKE up Christmas morning, I immediately got into the shower and got ready for breakfast with my family. I did my hair and makeup more extensively than usual and grabbed an outfit I'd bought just for the occasion.

I'd officially blown through my savings, didn't have a euro to my name anymore because I spent everything I had on Heath's gift. So, I had to start using his money to buy things, which didn't bother me as much as I thought it would.

I really had no other choice.

He gave me a debit card he'd ordered at the bank, giving me access to his account even though I wasn't his wife yet. But I took it because I wouldn't return to the ballet until February, and as of right now, I wasn't even sure if I was physically able.

When I finished getting ready, I looked at my appearance in the mirror, wearing a long-sleeved red dress with black tights underneath and thigh-high black boots. My hair was curled, and the rock on my left hand accentuated my outfit in a way I could only have dreamed of.

Heath stepped out of the shower with a towel around his waist. "Damn, Merry Fucking Christmas." He moved to me, bending his neck down to kiss me as he grabbed my ass through the tights.

I smiled into the kiss. "Merry Christmas."

"Lose the tights," he said. "I want to fuck you in this later."

"Romantic…"

His hand moved into my hair until he grabbed me by the back of the neck, turning possessive in just seconds. "I'm romantic in my own way." He gave me a hard kiss on the mouth before he released me, noticing the ring on my left hand. "You're sure about that?"

I cradled my hand with the other, admiring the most beautiful ring I'd ever seen. "Yes."

He didn't give any outward reaction, but there was a slight look of approval in his gaze. "I'll get dressed." He dropped the towel, his dick nice even when it was soft, and stepped into his closet.

I opened my nightstand and grabbed the small box I'd wrapped for Heath and carried it into the living room to place it under the tree.

But when I got there, there was already a present sitting there.

It was wrapped in silver wrapping paper, and instead of a bow, a single sunflower sat on top. It was lush and full, like it had just been plucked in the last day. It was such a stark contrast to the gloomy weather outside, the bitter cold that frosted the windows because Heath kept this place warm like a furnace—for me.

I grabbed the tag and flipped it over.

To: Sunflower

From: Your Man

He'd never called me Sunflower before, just baby, but it fit me so perfectly. I didn't expect him to get me anything because Christmas was a foreign holiday to him. I got him something because I wanted him to have a special Christmas with a special gift. I sat there for a while, staring at the box, having no idea what he could have possibly gotten me.

He came into the room a moment later, looking like a new man in his dark jeans and his deep olive-green sweater, wearing dress shoes that were much fancier than the boots he usually wore. I'd picked everything out for him, and he wore the clothes without complaint, which was great, because he looked so handsome.

I was still on the floor. "You got me something?"

He sat on the couch, leaning forward with his arms on his knees. "Yes."

"You didn't have to do that…"

"You didn't have to get me anything either."

"Well, you didn't need to get me something just because—"

"I got your gift a month ago."

So, he'd already picked it out before I even thought about Christmas. "You want to open them now?"

"Sure."

I grabbed both of them and sat beside him, handing him his small gift.

"You first." He rested it on his thigh.

I grabbed the flower and brought it to my nose, immediately thinking of summer from the smell alone. The petals grazed my cheek, making me think of a meadow in the hot sun. "You should take me to your place is Tuscany sometime."

"How about this summer?" he asked. "We'll have a second honeymoon."

I rested the flower on the couch beside me before I broke through the tape that affixed the wrapping to the box. I ripped it off, revealing a simple black box with a lid. When I took off the lid, the contents were wrapped in tissue paper, like it was a pair of shoes. I pulled everything away until I stared at a pair of pink ballet slippers.

They were beautiful.

I could tell they were well made, and when I looked at the designer imprint on the sole, I released a quiet gasp. Philippa Julio. It was one of the most luxurious brands in the world, something I'd never been able to afford on my own.

And they were pink.

My fingers felt the fabric, felt the wrapping, felt the instant connection that formed in my soul. My whole life was dancing, and looking at the slippers made me realize how much I missed it.

His hand moved to my wrist. "You will dance again, Sunflower."

I turned to him, my eyes wet from his confidence, his belief in me.

"I know you will—and you're going to wear these."

"Heath..." A tear dripped down my cheek. "Oh fuck." I wiped it away. "Not my makeup..."

"Personally, I think you look better that way." He made a joke to lighten the mood, knowing that his gesture was almost too much for me to handle.

I sniffed. "Well...thank you. I love them."

"I know you do."

I placed the lid back on top, hiding the shoes from view.

"I can't wait to see you put them on." He leaned in close to me and pressed a kiss to my hairline. "And then dance in them."

"Yeah...me too." I placed the box on the table, along with the flower. "Now, your turn."

He picked it up and held it between his fingertips, noting how light and small it was. "It's not lingerie, so that's a disappointment." He gave me a gentle smile before he peeled the wrapping away and got to the black box underneath. When he popped off the top, he saw the simple black band inside, the wedding ring made from a fallen meteorite. I didn't just want to give him a random piece of jewelry made of gold or steel. I wanted something special, so I gave up my savings to give him something that didn't even come from this world.

He examined it with narrowed eyes, his fingers sliding across the material as if he recognized its unusual properties.

"It's made out of meteorite. There's this special jeweler that carries it..."

He turned to me, his eyes soft and deep, like he didn't know how to feel about my gift.

"I'd like you to wear that for the rest of your life..."

He slid it onto his left hand, putting it in place on his ring finger. It fit perfectly after a gentle shove over his knuckles. Then he examined it, turning his hand over to see it from different angles.

He was hard to read sometimes, so I wasn't sure how he felt about it. But I hoped he liked it...or at least the thought behind the gesture.

He finally turned to me, leaving the ring on his left hand. "I love it."

"Yeah?"

He pressed his forehead to mine. "I'll never take it off, baby."

I knew that wasn't a jab at me, but a declaration.

"And I'll be buried with it."

"I know it's not as nice as your Skull King—"

"It's better." He took off the skull diamond and tossed it onto the coffee table, like it really meant nothing to him. "I would much rather wear this for the rest of my life than that."

"Why do you have to choose?" I whispered.

"Because your father made me." He glanced at the ring on the table. "It's time to pass that on to someone else." He played with the ring on his left hand, spinning it around his finger. "The new Skull King."

NINETEEN

HEATH

I STEPPED OUT OF THE TRUCK AND GRABBED THE presents from the back seat.

Catalina eyed me from the sidewalk, looking sexy as hell in those boots and with that diamond ring on her finger. "You know, you're handling this very well."

"Your gifts don't weigh much." I joined her on the sidewalk.

"No," she said with a chuckle. "I mean, spending the day with my family. You don't seem nervous at all."

I looked down at her, not understanding the statement. "Why would I be nervous?"

"I don't know...you've never done this before."

"Your father gave me the rundown, and your brother and I have tried to kill each other. Having breakfast together is like taking a nap, baby." I walked up the steps to the front door.

She joined me, giving me a slight smile. "I forget that you aren't scared of anything."

I was scared of only one thing—losing her.

She opened the door and walked inside. "Merry Christmas, Patricia."

"Merry Christmas, dear." She hugged her and kissed her on the cheek. When she saw me, she was rigid, still terrified of me.

Catalina took it in stride. "Patricia, I don't think you've formally met Heath...my fiancé." It was the first time she'd said those words out loud.

It had a nice ring to it. I shifted the boxes to one arm and shook her hand.

She relaxed a little, but she still had her guard up, like getting used to me would take time. "They're in the dining room."

We walked into the dining room where I'd spoken with her father, and there was a large sixteen-foot tree in the corner, fully decorated with lights and ornaments. Red and green centerpieces were along the table, along with covered serving dishes like the food was already ready.

Damien sat next to Anna, while Richard sat across from them, enjoying their cappuccinos as they waited for us. They were a normal family, growing up with the kind of wealth and love I'd never had.

But Catalina had given me all the love I didn't receive all those years ago.

"Merry Christmas," Catalina said as she announced us. She barely made it to the table when Anna screamed.

"Oh my god." She pointed at Catalina's left hand. "What the hell is that?"

I was holding the presents, so I walked to the tree and set them down next to the rest of the piles. Catalina may have been dreading this moment, but I wasn't. I did as her father asked, made a big sacrifice, so I had every right to give her a ring. The least she could do was put it on and not hide it.

She'd made the right choice.

Catalina held out her left hand, letting the diamond sparkle under the chandelier. "Beautiful, isn't it?"

"Shit, it's gorgeous." Anna took her hand and examined it, turning it to watch it sparkle.

I'd known stepping into this room would be tense, so the ring broke the ice and made it less awkward.

Damien stared at the ring, not saying a word.

"I love it," Catalina said proudly.

Richard didn't say anything either, probably caught off guard by the sudden announcement. But he recovered much quicker than his son did, and he did it with a lot more grace. He slowly got to his feet and embraced his daughter with a hug and a kiss on the cheek. "Merry Christmas, sweetheart."

"Merry Christmas, Daddy."

He took her left wrist and examined the ring. "It's stunning— just like you."

I respected her father for being selfless, for being there for his daughter instead of getting sucked into his own feelings—like Damien.

"It's perfect for you," he whispered as he dropped her wrist. "It reminds me of your mother's."

"It does, huh?" she said, looking at it again.

Richard turned to his son. "Damien, get up and congratulate your sister."

I stood at the other side of the table, near the tree, watching the scene as a spectator.

Damien ground his teeth, like he didn't enjoy being bossed around, especially when he really didn't want to do what he was told.

Anna got up first, like that would make it easier for him. She hugged Catalina, squeezing her hard like she was genuinely happy for her friend. "I'm so happy for you. That ring is gorgeous, girl."

"Thank you," Catalina said as she squeezed her back.

Richard stared down his son.

Damien got to his feet but didn't move to his sister. He looked at me instead. "My father said you could marry her *after* you left the Skull Kings, and from where I'm standing, it doesn't look like you—"

"I didn't marry her," I said simply. "I just asked her to marry me."

When he shut his mouth, his teeth clenched together tightly.

"I'll uphold my end of the deal." I made my way around the table, passed behind Damien, and joined Catalina's side.

Damien struggled with this the most, like his hatred for me was so strong that my gestures weren't good enough. He released a heavy sigh, as if he was beyond frustrated with all of this.

His father walked over to him, placed his hand on his shoulder and lowered his voice so no one else could hear. But I made out every word. "You trust your sister?"

He sighed quietly.

"I trust her," Richard whispered. "I trust that she wouldn't ask us to do this unless this man was that important to her. We're a family that sticks together and supports one another. You need to let the past go, Damien."

He said nothing.

"A man doesn't walk away from everything unless it's love, Damien. He agreed to walk away. Focus on that—not the other stuff." He clapped him on the shoulder. "Come on."

My respect for him grew tenfold.

Damien finally cooperated, walking around the table until he was face-to-face with Catalina. He took a deep breath before he dropped all his pride. "Congrats, Cat." He wrapped his arms around her and embraced her.

She clung to him harder than everyone else, as if his approval was the one she needed the most. "Thank you..."

He kissed her hairline before he pulled away. "It is a beautiful ring."

"I know it is," she whispered.

"Exactly what you wanted." He patted her arm and stepped back.

That went better than I expected. I moved to Richard next and extended my hand. "Merry Christmas, sir." I'd never called anyone sir in all my life. I was the fucking Skull King. I didn't say shit like that to anyone. But he deserved my respect.

He took it, giving me a firm shake that belied his age. "Merry Christmas, Heath."

Catalina watched us, her eyes a little wet like that simple handshake was all she wanted for Christmas. She lived for her father's approval, dreamed of having us all together—the people she loved.

I moved to Damien next, not bothering with Anna until I figured out what his response would be. He clearly didn't like having me near his fiancée, not after what I'd done. I extended my hand to shake his, wordlessly greeting him.

He struggled with it, struggled with it just as much as he'd struggled to congratulate his sister. We'd never shaken hands before, and that was the final nail in the coffin for his acceptance. A part of him hoped I would just go away, that I would change my mind about stepping down and I would disappear from his sister's life. But now he knew I was in this forever that I wasn't going anywhere. So, he reciprocated, placing his hand in mine, giving a firm shake with eye contact. "Be good to her."

I spoke before I released his hand. "I'd die for her." That was what a man wanted to hear, complete dedication and loyalty. I would always be faithful to her, always protect her, always provide for her. That didn't even need to be said.

He nodded.

I turned to Anna but didn't touch her. "Merry Christmas."

She glanced at Damien, liked she was waiting for permission to come near me.

Damien slid his hands into his pocket and looked at the floor as he nodded.

She walked up to me with her hand extended. "Welcome to the family."

I smiled slightly. "You too."

"Alright," Richard said. "Food's getting cold, so let's eat." He moved to the table and took a seat.

I turned to Catalina, who stared at me with a look she'd never given me before. It was a mixture of love, gratitude, and a million other things I couldn't identify. I watched her come closer to me, watched her wrap her arms around my waist and kiss me on the mouth, showing affection like there was no one there at all. "I love you..."

My arm circled her waist, and I rested my lips against her forehead. "I love you too."

THE LARGE FIREPLACE against the back wall was lit with high flames, and we gathered around the tree in armchairs, exchanging gifts while we enjoyed slices of pie and coffee. Catalina handed a gift to Damien.

"You didn't have to get me anything," he said as he tugged on the bow.

"You always get me something," she argued.

"But you're my little sister," he said. "I'm supposed to." He continued to rip through the wrapping.

I sat next to her father but didn't try to make small talk with him. He didn't strike me as the kind of guy that needed to fill the silence with words because he was uncomfortable. I watched Damien open his gift, a watch to add to his collection.

"Do you have family?" Richard asked, seeming to understand there was a good chance I didn't.

"Yes. My brother and his wife are coming over to my house tonight for dinner."

He nodded. "How do they like Catalina?"

I almost scoffed. "They love her."

"No surprise there," he said with pride.

"My brother is my twin, actually. A few months ago, Catalina spotted the two of them having dinner. She didn't know I had a twin, so she assumed I was two-timing her. She chased down my brother on the sidewalk, told him off, and punched him in the face."

Richard smiled, like he found the story as funny as I did.

"And that was how they met."

He chuckled. "And they still like her?"

"It made my brother like her more, actually. That's how we are."

"Catalina is a lot like her mother, certainly in appearance. But I don't think she realizes she gets more of her feistiness from me."

"Yeah...I noticed."

"I'm very proud of the woman she's become. I never raised her to choose the right man to take care of her. I raised her to take care of herself. So, when she chooses a man, she doesn't do it because she needs him, it's because she wants him."

I stared at the side of his face, seeing a young man in his still-bright eyes. "It took me a while to convince her to give me a chance."

"She's stubborn," he said immediately. "She also gets that from me."

"You aren't stubborn at all," I said honestly. "Damien is, though."

He chuckled at my joke. "Yeah, he is."

Catalina handed a gift to Anna. "This is for you."

"What did you get her for Christmas?" he asked me, continuing our quiet conversation.

"Ballet slippers...in pink."

He turned his head more toward me, giving me his entire attention. His eyes shifted back and forth as he looked into mine, like he needed further explanation.

"Ever since she got hurt, she's been afraid she'll never dance again. But I know she will...it's just a reminder."

Approval moved into his eyes. "She probably loves that more than the ring." His eyes shifted back to them, seeing Anna pull out a top with a scarf.

I noticed he was different with me than his children. I'd heard him interact with his daughter in her apartment, and he was so kind, gentle, affectionate. He was nothing like he was now, as if there was something about me that brought out this side of him. He wasn't even like that with Damien.

Why?

"I noticed you aren't wearing your ring." He didn't glance down to my right hand where my skull diamond usually sat. "Does that mean you turned it in?"

"Not yet." I absentmindedly rubbed the naked knuckle, feeling slightly off-balance without the weight in place. "Still tying up loose ends. But I have a successor in mind." When I realized what he'd said, I turned back to him. "How did you know about the ring?" The Skull King always wore a piece of jewelry that symbolized his power. My brother and I got our hands on the rings and wore them as representation. But I didn't see how he would know that—unless Damien told him.

He turned his gaze on me completely, his eyes focused. "This stays between us." He lowered his voice further, making sure the other three didn't overhear us.

I nodded in agreement.

He leaned toward me, his elbows against the armrests, the loose skin on his arms covered with old freckles. "Because once upon a time...I was the Skull King."

I DIDN'T SEE Catalina the same way anymore.

Her father's secret changed everything.

After my family went home that night, I left all the dishes in the sink to clean tomorrow, but I didn't care about that right now. As much as I'd enjoyed having Balto and Cassini over, celebrating our first Christmas as a four-member family, my mind had been somewhere else.

Now I had a secret I could never share.

Without having to ask, I knew Damien had no idea.

If he did, he wouldn't hate me so much. It was a secret Richard kept from his family, and he confided in me because he knew I would understand. That was why he was different with me, why he gave me a chance when Damien never would. It was why he spoke to me so easily, connected with me when we seemed to have nothing in common.

It all made sense.

When my family was gone, I was finally alone with her.

She set the glasses in the sink and turned to me, her eyes a little sleepy from the wine she'd drunk throughout the entire day. "Well, I think that was a nice Christmas."

I didn't listen to a word she said. I came closer to her, cornering her against the kitchen counter until my hands gripped the edge on either side, giving her no way out, even though she would never run from me.

She stilled, her back straightening with tension, the words dying in her mouth because she knew now wasn't the time to speak.

I breathed hard as I stared at her, looking at those green eyes like they were buried treasure. She was already the love of my life, the woman who stole my heart on the night she basically quoted Beyoncé and threw me off my game. I couldn't remember the moment I fell in love, but now I understood why. I'd always been in love with her, felt that way before we crossed paths, because those feelings had been programmed at birth. "We're meant to be together." I bored into her gaze with mine, needing her to understand what I was saying, needing her to believe in destiny the way I believed in it—with my own heart.

I loved the daughter of a Skull King—and it all made sense.

She was everything I wanted in a woman. She was hard like steel, feisty like a madwoman, argumentative like a pain in the ass. She didn't put up with shit because she was royalty, a daughter of a king.

She was meant for me.

Fucking made for me.

But I could never tell her why, never betray her father's confidence, and I would carry his secret even when he was in the grave.

She stared at the intense expression on my face, her body still rigid because she could feel the pulsing emotions inside me, the chaos inside my mind. But then her eyes softened at my words, the way I meant them with every piece of my heart. "I know..."

I wanted to believe her, but there was no way she could believe it the way I believed. "I mean it. The universe made you for me. Made me for you." My hands moved to her face, cupping her cheeks, looking at her with such an intense form of arousal that I'd never thought I was physically capable of feeling. All our other nights together seemed tame compared to this.

Both of her hands gripped my wrists, staring at me as her chest rose and fell with deep breaths. "Why are you saying this...?"

I could never tell her, never share that fact with her even though I desperately wanted to. "I just know...and I want you to know." My hands tilted her chin up, and I devoured her mouth, kissing her harder than I ever had, like it was the first time I got to have her, the first time she would be mine. "I fucking love you...with all my goddamn soul."

TWENTY

CATALINA

I had no idea what had gotten into Heath.

He couldn't get enough of me.

He was on top of me, his heavy body pressing me into the mattress, the sweat rubbing against my skin as he moved. He gave it to me slow and deep, his endurance better than it'd ever been. He wanted to be with me all the time these days, didn't bother making dinner sometimes and just ordering a pizza because he'd rather do this, which wasn't like him at all.

Christmas had been days ago, and whenever he wasn't at work, he was doing this.

Making love to me.

He grabbed me hard, kissed me hard, fucked me hard, did everything hard. Sometimes, his body shook when he had me, like the fire in his soul consumed him completely. He sucked my bottom lip into his mouth now, the sweat from his forehead mixing with our kiss. Maybe my family's approval made him realize he would never lose me and that turned him on in a way it never had before. My ring was always on my finger, and I never took it off, even when I showered.

His arm slid underneath my lower back and lifted me, effortlessly holding me while he thrust into me, deepening the angle and making me wince as my tits bounced. He looked into my eyes as he made love to me, as he consumed me, conquered me. We weren't even married yet, and he treated this like a honeymoon.

It hurt to have him that deep, but I came anyway because the look in his eyes was so fierce, like he loved me more than ever before and that the love had risen to new heights, unbelievable heights.

He tugged me into him, releasing at the same time, our slick bodies coming around each other.

He kissed me when he was finished, kissed me like he wasn't satisfied at all. It was a kiss full of desire, the taste of his sweat potent on his tongue. When he pulled out of me and got off, he immediately went into the bathroom to rinse off in the shower, like he intended to go to work.

I lay there, feeling sore now that the hormones were gone.

Jesus, I've never been fucked like that in all my life.

I pulled the sheets up my body even though I was warm and sweaty. But I was ready to sleep hard.

He came out minutes later and headed for his closet. He slipped on his long-sleeved shirt, jeans, and pulled on his heavy boots. His skull ring was never on his hand anymore, so I wasn't sure what he'd done with it. He grabbed his phone and slipped it into his back pocket. "I'll see you in the morning." He leaned over me and kissed me goodbye.

"Bye. Love you."

He kissed my neck before he straightened. "Love you too, baby."

Then he was gone.

I JOLTED wide awake when I heard a sound I'd never heard before in my life.

Like a train had just crashed head on into a building.

The sound was too loud to be something I'd dreamed. My adrenaline spiked, and my heart raced like my life was on the line. It was too extreme to be something I'd just made up.

Then I heard it again.

It was coming from the other side of the house—near the entrance.

I jumped out of bed and pulled on my clothes. I nearly tripped getting into my jeans, and my hair got caught in my sweater when I pushed my head through the neck hole. I snatched my phone and ran down the hallway, getting to the monitor on the wall that showed the camera feed.

"Holy shit." I covered my mouth when I saw the group of men outside the front door, carrying a large metal cylinder that they banged against the front door, trying to break it down like they were the Romans who'd come to conquer.

I didn't know what the hell to do.

I could open the garage and drive away, but that seemed too risky. There were probably men waiting for me to do that. I imagined they were here for Heath, or they knew he was gone...and I was alone.

I called Heath as I ran back down the hallway to the bedroom, where the guns were located.

He picked up right away. "I'm on my way." He was calm even though he knew exactly what was happening on our doorstep. "It's going to take them a long time to get through the door, so don't be scared."

"Don't be scared?" I asked incredulously. "Jesus, there are at least twenty of them—"

"Listen to me." He shut me up because there wasn't time. "Grab an automatic rifle from the closet. They're all loaded."

"I don't know how to use a gun. You never showed me—"

"You can do it, baby. Press it against your shoulder, not your collarbone."

Now I was getting really scared. "Am I really going to have to shoot these guys?"

"It's just in case."

Oh my god, I couldn't believe this was happening. The loud gong sounded again, making me jump and scream.

He didn't react. "I'll be there as soon as I can. I called Balto—"

"I don't want him to risk his life for me." He was going to be a father. If something happened to him...

"I called Damien too."

No, not my brother.

"But I will get there first. I will take care of this. I promise."

"Oh my god...oh my god."

"Baby, come on." He gave me tough love. "Stay in our room, aim that gun, and blow anyone to hell that comes for you."

"Okay..."

"I'll be there soon."

"Okay."

"I love you." He barked it out like he was saying it to one of his men, not his woman.

"I love you too."

Click.

I put my phone in my pocket then grabbed one of the rifles from the drawer.

Shit, it was heavy.

I found the safety and clicked it off then held the rifle with both arms, keeping the butt of the gun against my shoulder. Then I waited, listened to the gong every forty-five seconds like clockwork. This wasn't the same as when Heath snuck up on me at the car. He was just one guy, so I had a chance. Right now, there were twenty men trying to break down a solid steel door to get to me.

To do nothing good.

So, yeah...I was pretty fucking scared.

Then the sound changed, like the two doors had flown open and slammed against the walls.

"Shit, that's not good…"

Shouts from the men came from downstairs, loud grunts like they'd put down the big cylinder they'd used to break down the doors and get inside. Then footsteps sounded as they ran up the stairs.

"Shit…shit…shit." Where the fuck was Heath?

A man spoke into the house, his voice deep, taunting. "Come on out, baby. Give daddy a big kiss."

My finger rested against the trigger, seeing the men reach the top of the stairs and step into the house.

My house.

I stepped out of sight of the doorway so they wouldn't see me right away.

When there was no response from me, the taunts continued. "That's fine. I love hide-and-seek anyway."

Footsteps sounded outside the bedroom as men came down the hallway, heading right toward me like they knew exactly where Heath's bedroom was located—and that's where I'd be hiding.

My heart was beating so fast.

Time slowed down because I knew this could be my last few moments of life.

But I wasn't going to go down easy.

Every minute counted, and Heath could arrive at any second. Or Balto. Or my brother. So, what I did now could really make a difference.

I went full *Scarface* on their asses. "Say hello to my little friend, assholes." I stepped into the doorway, right where six of them stood, peeking into the other doors like I was there. I pulled the trigger and didn't let go.

The power of the gun nearly made me stumble back. But I kept my feet planted hard against the wood and didn't let go of the trigger, the machine gun firing off rounds into the guys, making them drop like flies to the ground.

Smoke rose from the barrel of my gun.

I couldn't believe I'd just done that.

"I'm not gonna lie." The taunting voice returned, without a face. "That was pretty impressive."

I squeezed the trigger, pointing at no one in particular. But I was out of bullets.

"Yeah, that's what I counted on too."

I threw the gun on the floor and returned to the closet to grab another.

His footsteps sounded. "Baby, look at your daddy."

I opened a drawer and found a pistol.

He fired his gun, making the glass on top of the cabinet shatter.

I stilled, breathing hard as I stood there, unable to look my attacker in the face. I felt like I was in the basement again, powerless. My face started to hurt because those old injuries suddenly felt brand-new.

"Look at me."

I refused.

"Look at me—or I'm going to start by shooting you in the foot, then the hand, and then I'm gonna shove this barrel up your ass and pull the trigger."

Why did I blow through all those bullets when I didn't need to?

I slowly turned to him, forcing myself not to react when I saw his face.

His disgusting face.

With dark eyes, a scar down one eye, and maniacal look of victory on his face, he was pure evil.

I'd rather die than let him touch me.

"Get over here." He lowered his gun and nodded.

"No."

His eyes narrowed, accompanied by a smile. "That word has never sounded so sexy until now. I'm gonna enjoy this far more than I should." He stuck his gun into the back of his jeans then came for me.

The glass on the top of the shelving unit was broken, so I grabbed the pistol sitting there then pointed it at his face.

But he was too quick, knocking it from my hand before he grabbed me by the throat and lifted me from the floor.

I gripped his wrists as I struggled to breathe, the pain excruciating as my entire body weight hung from the top of my frame.

"Baby, no one says no to me." He set me on the floor and kept his arm around my neck, dragging me across the floor to the door.

I gasped for air, my windpipe finally open again.

He dragged me forward—like a fucking dog.

"Catalina." Heath's terrified voice echoed through the house, sounding different than he ever had before, sounding like a man with a thousand bullet wounds.

"Bedroom—"

The man shook me hard, making me silent. "The man of the hour. I'm glad you took time from your schedule to show up." He positioned me in the doorway, his arm around my neck as he held me close.

Heath stood with his pistol at his side, breathing hard, like every breath was painful for him. He looked unarmed—but so defeated. His face was tinted with rage, but his eyes were heartbroken, like he'd rather die than have to watch this.

"Step aside, Heath." The man pushed me forward slightly, using my body to protect his.

He raised his pistol.

"Go ahead." He forced my head to block most of his face. "Hope you've got a good aim."

Heath's hand shook as he held the gun, furious that there was nothing he could do. He had all the power in the world, but none at the moment.

"Step aside. I'm taking your girl with me." He forced me forward, squeezing my neck tight so I could barely breathe.

"You know what I'm going to do with her, Heath? I'm a kinky guy, so use your imagination."

Heath was so angry that his eyes started to coat with moisture. "What do you want, Vox? You want me?" He raised his hands in the air. "Take me. She's not the one you want." He tapped his chest with his hand. "I am."

"And I have you, more than I would if I were touching you." He pushed me forward again. "Tell your men to back down. Or I could snap her neck right now. How do you want this to play out?" He kicked my knee from underneath me and forced me down, moving his hand to the roots of my hair, dragging me across the floor.

I tried not to scream, but a chunk of my hair flew out.

Vox stopped again. "Move."

I looked up from the floor, seeing the ceiling, no longer able to see Heath's face. But I noticed the gun in the back of Vox's waistband, his shirt slightly tucked into his jeans because the fabric had caught as he'd shoved it there.

"Let her go," Heath said. "And I'll shoot myself in the head."

Vox was quiet, as if he hadn't expected that kind of offer.

"That's what you want more than her. Let her go, and I'll do it."

"Hmm...that's tempting, but—"

I pushed up and groaned as he tugged on my scalp, but I got the gun in my grasp. I clicked the safety like second nature then pointed it into his body, not even seeing where I was aiming. I pulled the trigger.

He stumbled as the bullet went into his back, his hand releasing my hair.

I shot him again.

He fell to the floor.

I crawled to him and pointed the gun at his face, pulling the trigger over and over, spilling blood, flesh, and brains all over the place. I kept pulling the trigger even when the barrel was empty, the gun clicking because it was out of ammo. "You fucking asshole!" I slammed my hands down onto his chest, slammed the gun into his already destroyed face. "Who the fuck do you think I am?" Tears poured from my eyes because I was so angry, so crazy.

"Baby." Heath came up behind me, his hands gripping my arms to steady me, to pull me into his chest. "Baby, shh…" He pulled me against him, his heartbeat strong against my back. "He's gone."

I collapsed against him, kicking away the corpse at my feet. I sobbed, my arms crossing over my chest as I gave in to the fear, the terror, the relief.

Heath held me, his lips pressed against the top of my head.

Footsteps sounded as someone ran to the top of the stairs. "Is she okay?" His voice was identical to Heath's, so I knew it was Balto.

Heath raised his hand, as if he was silencing his brother.

Another pair of footsteps sounded at a full sprint. "Where is she?" My brother's voice was loud, demanding, terrified.

Balto lowered his voice. "She's okay…"

Heath didn't leave me. "Just give us a minute."

Damien didn't reply, as if seeing me safe in the flesh was enough for him. Then he and Balto walked down the stairs again.

Heath held me there, let me cry against him, let me release the terror I'd been holding in my chest for the last ten minutes. "It's alright, baby...it's alright."

HEATH CUPPED my cheek as he looked at me, unafraid to let tears form in his eyes when he stared at me, knowing I was safe, unharmed, just a little upset. He pressed his forehead to mine before he kissed me. "You alright?"

I nodded.

"You killed half of the men on your own."

I still wasn't entirely sure what had happened. It was a fucking blur.

"And pulling his gun from his jeans...badass."

"I was just trying to save us..."

"I know." His thumbs wiped away my old tears. "I know. Everything is okay now. He's dead. His men are dead. It's over."

I nodded.

"Alright?"

I nodded again.

"I want to keep hogging you, but I can't." He pulled away from me and walked to the top of the stairs. "She's ready now."

My brother took the stairs two at a time to get to me. He jogged across the room until he reached me, his chest hitting mine as he hugged me tight, wrapping his arms around me, squeezing me like he wanted to make sure I was real. "You okay?"

"I'm fine. What about you?"

"Not a scratch." He pulled away and looked into my face, seeing the wet eyes. "They're all gone. I checked three times."

"I know, Damien. It just... It's a lot to take in."

"Heath told me how you held your own... I'm proud of you."

I shook my head. "I had no idea what I was doing—"

"Still kicked ass." He squeezed my arms before he released me.

"Please don't hate Heath..." I finally had him in my life, and then this happened. I didn't want my family to turn against him again. I wanted every day to be like Christmas.

His eyes softened. "I would...but he said today is his last day."

"It is?" I whispered.

He nodded. "Vox was his loose end...and it's over. If Balto and Bones can have a quiet life, I don't see why Heath can't too."

"Who's Bones?"

He shook his head. "Never mind." His eyes searched my face, like he wondered if I was really okay.

"I'll be fine." I answered his unspoken question. "I just need some time."

"Alright." He wrapped his arm around my shoulder and walked with me to the top of the stairs. "You guys can stay with me if you need time to, you know, get this place cleaned up. Or the Tuscan Rose. Hades will give you the best room in the place—free of charge."

"Thanks, Damien."

Heath watched me walk back to him, still staring at me with the same intense love, like his love for me had only deepened after what happened.

"How's your brother?" I asked.

"He's fine," he answered, his unblinking eyes on me. "I have to take care of some things. I want you to stay with Damien tonight."

"What...?" My lips sagged into a frown. "Why? I'm not going to sleep—"

"I want to get this place cleaned up, and I have to do some stuff at the Underground."

"Damien told me today is your last day..."

"It is. And I'm formally resigning. I'll pick you up on my way home."

I didn't want to be without him, not even for a second, not after what happened.

"I want to put this behind us. I want to bring you back here—and start our lives together."

I sighed in frustration, but I didn't argue. "Alright..."

TWENTY-ONE

HEATH

I was fucking tired.

It was sunrise at that point.

I killed my own kind, the men Catalina hadn't already pumped lead into. I was the first one there with my guys, and we took out most of them before Damien arrived next.

It was a quick battle on the street corner.

Any doubts my men had about me were gone after what Vox tried to do. He didn't even come after me personally—he came after the woman I loved.

So, while my place was being cleaned and repaired, I spent my last evening with them, last evening drinking beer and talking about our conquests. I sat on my throne for the last time, looking at the rows of tables filled with the people I was closest to.

Vox's table was empty.

He would be stuffed into an oil drum and dropped somewhere in the Mediterranean.

My tenure as the Skull King had been short-lived. Once I'd
taken over after Balto, I'd expected to have the reins a long
time. I wasn't going to set them down for a woman, pictured
my life as a series of images of booze, money, and whores.

But I didn't even last as long as he did.

I had barely been the Skull King a year before I retired.

A bit pathetic.

But with Catalina at home, I knew I would still feel like a
king.

Because she was the Skull Queen.

She had the same kind of criminality in her veins as I did, but
she was also wrapped in a pretty bow of innocence, having no
idea what kind of history was in her blood, where that feistiness came from, where she got her edge.

So, I had something to look forward to when I got home.

The rest of my life.

Steel sat beside me. "You still seem angry."

I turned to him, my mind somewhere else. "Just a bit
sentimental."

"Sentimental?" he asked. "I'm surprised you even know what
that word means."

I gave him a teasing glare.

"Why are you sentimental?" he asked, turning serious.

I slipped my hand into the front pocket of my jeans and withdrew the ring. I held it up, looking at it one last time, finding it difficult to part with the biggest symbol of my identity. It was a piece of me. But now, I would wear a new ring.

Steel's eyes narrowed.

I extended it to him. "You're in charge now, man."

His hold on his beer loosened until it started to drip over the edge. He quickly corrected himself, brushing off the beer that spilled on his knee. "Heath, what are you talking about?"

"It's time for me to move on. You're my replacement."

"I don't understand." He set down the beer. "You're a great Skull King. Why would you want to leave?"

That was why I loved Steel. He'd always been loyal to me, even when power dangled right in front of him. "It's time for me to move on," I repeated. I placed the ring in his hand. "Wear it well."

He stared at the ring in his palm, watching it shine like a prism, and then he closed his fingers around it before he gave a slight nod.

"I'm just a phone call away." I patted him on the shoulder before I rose to my feet, feeling the weight off my shoulders now that I'd sacrificed the title I thought I would never shed. Walking away from my power was harder than I made it seem. I gave an unequivocal answer when Richard put me on the spot, but that was the price I had to pay to have his daughter, and I paid it.

I walked past the guys, clapped them on the shoulders, shook hands, said a few final words, let time slow down as I stepped away from my reign of power and returned to civilian life. I had enough saved to take care of us for the rest of our lives, but she never asked me about my finances.

Because she didn't care.

I walked out of there for the last time. Closing that chapter of my life.

And opening a new one.

"YOU SEEM TO BE ALRIGHT, all things considered." Balto sat on the opposite couch while the morning light filled the living room. Cassini was still asleep, probably tossing and turning all night while her husband was gone, risking his life...again.

I shrugged. "I thought I would last a lot longer than that."

He shrugged. "So did I."

"Wow, I'm an even bigger pussy than you..."

"Hey, I just risked my neck to save your ass—"

"Catalina's ass. And she has a nice ass."

He rolled his eyes. "In all seriousness, are you alright? Couldn't have been easy to give up your ring."

"It wasn't."

He watched me for a while.

"But Catalina gave me a ring to wear...so that'll be my replacement."

He nodded.

"And she's worth it."

He nodded again. "It's not fast-paced, it's not unpredictable, but...it's somehow the most exhilarating experience ever."

I could picture that with Catalina, a long and happy life, a life full of her feistiness and my stubbornness. "I'm gonna tell you something. It stays between us." I pointed between our chests. "You can't tell Cassini either."

"You know I'm a locked vault full of secrets." He stared into his glass.

"When I was with her family on Christmas, I was talking to her father..."

He raised his head and looked at me.

After a long pause, I finished the statement. "He used to be the Skull King."

Balto had the best poker face in the world, but even he couldn't hide his surprise at the revelation.

"That's why he and I...click."

"When?"

I shook my head. "He didn't say. I didn't ask. It doesn't really matter anyway."

"How old is he?"

"In his seventies."

"So, this must have been like thirty, forty years ago."

"Yeah."

"The Skull Kings have been around for almost a hundred years." Balto swirled his drink before he set it on the table. "It's had a lot of members, a lot of rulers."

"Yeah."

"Catalina doesn't know?"

I shook my head. "He told me to never tell her. Damien doesn't know either."

"But he told you... I think that's the best approval you're going to get."

"Yeah." I'd feared her father in the way that all men feared their fathers-in-law, but once I met him, I felt like I was with a close friend, someone I could talk to, someone who understood me...even though he didn't know me. I thought it was just respect, respect for the way he loved his daughter, but then I realized it was deeper than that.

He was a leader—and so was I.

We were two sides of the same coin.

Balto gave a quiet chuckle. "You're marrying the daughter of a former Skull King... What are the odds of that?"

Zero.

Fucking zero.

PATRICIA LET me in the front door, less timid around me now that I was officially a member of the family. "I'll let Catalina know you're here. I think she's still asleep upstairs..." When she turned to walk away, Richard stood there.

He was in a burgundy sweater and dark jeans, a shiny watch on his wrist. He had a bit of a stomach and gray hair, but he also had the musculature of a man who used to be strong. When I'd kidnapped him, I never saw him in the flesh, just told one of my henchmen to do it. If I'd seen him with my own eyes, I wondered if the outcome would have been different.

"Heath, come with me." He nodded to the dining room before he turned around and walked away.

I followed him, entering the room and watching him move to a smaller table at the side, bathed in sunlight from the cathedral windows. He sat down in front of a chessboard, the pieces lined up and ready for a match. "Play chess?"

I shook my head. "No, sir."

He nodded to the chair across from me. "Sit down. I'll teach you."

I gave a slight smile before I lowered myself into the chair across from him.

Patricia brought coffee and sliced fruit, placing everything beside us so we would be comfortable. "I'll let Catalina know you're here when she wakes up."

"Thank you," I said quietly.

Richard stared at the chessboard with his fingertips under his chin, as if he was considering what to say first. "Tied up your loose ends?"

I nodded. "Yes. I resigned early this morning."

He lifted his gaze and looked at me. "It's done?"

"Yes. It's done."

A slight shine of approval moved into his eyes before he turned to the board. "Alright, now pay attention. Because we're a family of chess players, you're gonna have to learn this."

"I'm pretty quick."

"Yeah?" he asked. "We'll see."

"Where did you learn?"

He picked up the queen, like he was going to explain its significance to me. "The Underground, actually."

The guys had a lot of time to kill sometimes.

"Now, protect your queen at all costs..." It was as if his words had different meaning, as if we were talking about something other than the game. "You lose her, you lose everything."

I nodded. "That's easy to remember."

TWENTY-TWO

CATALINA

I'd just washed my face in the bathroom when Patricia's voice sounded in my temporary bedroom. She knew the second I was awake, like she was standing outside the bedroom door waiting. "Heath is here."

"He is?" I wiped my face with a towel then came back to her.

She nodded. "Yes. He's with your father."

"Alright, I'll be done in a few minutes. Just have to pack my things."

"I'll let him know." She stepped out.

I was so excited to see Heath that I shoved everything into my bag and headed downstairs in a rush. It was hard to sleep without him, even if I slept in a house with my family. It just wasn't the same without his big size beside me, his steady beating heart, the way his stubble brushed against my shoulder when he pulled me close.

I stepped into the dining room with my bag over my shoulder and was stunned by what I saw.

My father was playing chess...with Heath.

He looked at the board with his fingertips against his lips, waiting for Heath to make his move.

Heath considered his decision in silence, staring at the board as he tried to figure out what to do. Then he grabbed his pawn and moved it one square.

My father gave a nod of approval. "Not bad..." He grabbed his queen and quickly moved her.

"I thought you were supposed to protect your queen at all costs?"

"You are. I moved—"

Heath moved his piece and captured her.

My father shut his mouth, turning a venomous stare on him.

Heath smiled, a boyish grin that was completely genuine, not arrogant or sarcastic. "Told you I'm a fast learner."

I set my bag on the dining table and walked over to their match. "Babe, I didn't know you knew how to play."

He turned to me, his smile still on his face but a brighter look in his eyes now that I was in the room, calling him babe. "Your father is teaching me."

"Teaching you too well..." my father grumbled under his breath.

Heath chuckled.

My eyes shifted back and forth as I looked at them, unable to believe this was real, that my father was treating Heath like a son...and I didn't even have to ask him to. He just accepted Heath with open arms. It meant the world to me.

More than the world.

"How'd you sleep, sweetheart?" Dad asked me as he looked at the board.

"Alright." I looked at Heath, silently telling him it was a rough night without him.

His gaze turned serious, picking up on my meaning. "That was the last night I'll be gone. I left."

"Yeah?" I whispered. "Are you alright?"

He turned back to the game when my father moved a piece. "Better than ever." He grabbed his pawn and moved it.

"Well, should we go?" I asked. "You must be tired."

Heath kept looking at the board, as if he actually liked the game. "After this match, baby."

"THAT WAS sweet of him to teach you," I said as we entered the house. "But he hates to lose."

"Yeah," he said with a chuckle. "I noticed."

The second I was in the house, the energy felt different, like last night never happened. The bullet holes had been repaired, the signs of violence removed, even the door replaced. "How did you do all of this so quickly?"

"I had a whole crew out here." He set my bag on the couch. "And if you don't want to stay here, we can move."

This house had a horrific memory, but it also had so many good ones. I wasn't sure if I could ever leave this place. "What about your home in Tuscany? What's that like?"

He stood in front of me, his hands in his pockets. "It's a two-story house on twenty acres of land. I'll take you tomorrow."

"Is that where you grow the sunflowers?"

He nodded.

"Yes, I'd love to see it."

"Alright." He gave me a soft smile as he looked at me, taking in my features as if he was trying to make up for the night we'd lost.

"It makes me happy to see you spend time with my father."

"He's a pretty cool guy."

"Yeah...he's sweet. Just hates to lose."

"I'd throw the game, but he's not that kind of man."

My eyes narrowed at his astute observation. "What do you mean...?"

"He doesn't take his defeats personally, just seriously. He wants to earn his victories."

"I used to let him win until he yelled at me. Told me never to throw a game to make a man feel better."

There was a slight smile in the corner of his mouth. "Damn right." His hand slid into my hair, and he cupped my cheek, holding me close, his lips near enough to kiss me if he wanted to. "Now that I'm retired, what should we do?"

"I guess I'll have to bring home the bacon now."

He chuckled, knowing I was making a joke. "You want to get married?"

"Well...I've always wanted a summer wedding."

He sighed quietly. "I don't think I can wait six months to marry you, baby."

"I know."

He kissed me on the mouth before he pulled away.

"So...your ring is gone?"

He nodded.

I looked at his hand, the thick tan line obvious. It would be there for a while.

"Balto kept his. Why didn't you keep yours?"

"He brought the Skull Rings to the Underground. One of them was given as a gift to the organization—so it had to stay behind."

"I'm sorry..."

"It's alright. I have a new ring to wear." He faced me, looking down at me with affection in his gaze.

"Are you sure you're okay with everything? I know it was your life..."

He stared at me for a long time before he shook his head. "That was my life before you. This is my life with you."

"It might get boring."

"No," he answered immediately. "It definitely won't." His hand moved to my arm, his fingertips dragging to my elbow. "How are you? I'm sorry I had to leave. I just had to take care of all those things."

"No, I understand. And I'm fine."

He stared at me blankly.

"I am fine. I just...needed a few hours to process everything."

"That'll never happen again. No one is coming after me. They have no reason to."

"I know."

"No reason to be scared."

"I know."

He cupped my face before he looked me in the eye. "I'm really proud of how you handled that. You didn't need me."

I shook my head. "No, I did need you."

He smiled slightly. "I loved the way you quoted Beyoncé again."

"I guess that's just what I do when I get really mad."

He chuckled. "Then I'll know when you're really mad at me." He pulled me close and kissed my forehead. "I'm going to shower and get some sleep."

"I'm tired too."

"Then let's make love and then go to sleep." He grabbed my bag off the couch and made his way to the bedroom.

I watched him go, watched his strong frame shift and move as he carried my bag down the hallway. I knew this was the beginning of the blissful life I'd always wanted, to have a husband my family considered their own, and someone I was passionately in love with. I didn't think I'd get it all...but I did.

HE PULLED up the private driveway and approached the cobblestone house in the Tuscan countryside. It was a beautiful two-story home with a gorgeous double front door. He parked and killed the engine. "Holy shit, this place is yours?"

"Ours."

I hopped out of the truck and ran to the entryway. "Oh my god, it's so fucking cute." I tugged on the door handle, anxious to get inside.

He chuckled as he came up behind me, pulling out the keys. "Baby, it's locked."

I stomped my foot like a child.

He got the key in the door and opened it so I could go first.

"This doesn't even look like a house you'd buy."

"I didn't."

I looked at him over my shoulder.

"Won it."

"Won it, how?"

"Poker match."

I didn't ask any details before I walked across the hardwood floors, saw the old staircase that hadn't been touched since it was built, the Italian wallpaper with splashes of blue and white. "It's so beautiful." I moved farther into the house, looked at the enormous kitchen that was made for dinner parties. There was a nice dining room and a gorgeous view of the backside of the property, a pool with a cobblestone back patio, along with grass, trees, ivy on the walls, flower beds everywhere. I practically pressed my nose to the glass.

He came up behind me. "We're moving, aren't we?"

"Why didn't you live here in the first place?" I turned around to face him. "If you'd chained me up here, I never would have left."

He smiled at the comment. "Doesn't have the best security."

"But we don't need security anymore, right?"

He shook his head.

"Can we live here?" I asked, moving into his chest with my hands pressed together. "Please, please, please..."

"It's a bit of a drive to the theatre."

"Sooooo worth it."

He continued to grin down at me. "As much as I love watching you beg, you don't need to do that." He pulled my hands apart. "Whatever you want, baby."

"You really wouldn't mind?"

He shook his head.

"Yes!" I turned back to the window. "It's the perfect place to raise a family, and I love how old it is. Your place in the city is nice, but it's so sleek and modern, and I just love more traditional things."

He pressed his lips to the back of my head. "I have something else to show you." He opened the back door and led the way.

I followed behind him, loving the awning and patio, the old fireplace that would be perfect on a cold night like tonight would be.

He rounded the corner and moved farther away from the house, approaching a small building made entirely of glass.

"The greenhouse..."

He unlocked the door and opened it for me.

Inside were rows and rows of sunflowers, the misters at the top spraying them with water, the lamps giving them heat when those rainy days didn't supply enough sunlight. "Oh my god..." I moved to the first sunflower, which was at my eye level, like I was looking into the sun. "This is amazing, Heath."

He pulled a pocketknife out of his pocket and sliced one flower off the stalk before he handed it to me. "Sunflower."

I took it, brought it to my nose for a sniff, staring at him while I did it. I didn't know what to say, how to respond to the most romantic gesture of all time. I held the flower against my chest, overwhelmed by the way he loved me. "You're so sweet to me."

He grabbed another flower then came closer to me, dragging the petal down my arm, looking at me with those handsome blue eyes. He nodded to the house. "Want to see the master bedroom?"

I smiled when I understood what he was really asking. "I'd love to."

WE LAY in bed together in the bedroom where we would soon live. The two flowers were on the sheets beside us because Heath liked to see them on top of me when he made love to me, the yellow petals complementing my olive skin.

Now he rested beside me, his hand holding mine on his chest.

"I have an idea…"

"There's no food here. Sorry."

"No," I said with a chuckle. "I was thinking…what if we get married here?"

"It's pretty cold to get married outside."

"We could get married in the greenhouse…"

He turned his head toward me, regarding me with his unreadable gaze. "It's pretty small."

"We can fit my family and yours in there."

"I thought you'd want a big wedding."

"Not anymore." I just wanted to get married. I just wanted to be with this man forever. We could have a bigger ceremony in the summer if we wanted to, but being husband and wife, that couldn't wait. "What do you think of my idea?"

"Baby, I'd marry you in the pouring rain."

"Yeah?" I scooted closer to him.

"Yeah." He pressed a kiss to my forehead. "When do you want to do this?"

"I don't know... Saturday?"

"Really?" he asked in surprise. "Don't you need to get a dress or something?"

"I'm gonna wear my mother's."

His eyes softened. "That's sweet. I'm sure you'll look beautiful."

"I will," I said with a smile.

"I'll spend the week moving."

"Moving?" I asked. "Where are you going?"

"Moving our stuff in here. Getting rid of your apartment. Getting this place cleaned up. Putting groceries in the fridge..."

"You think you can do it in a week?"

"If my brother helps. You can stay with Damien while I handle everything."

"Wait, what?" I asked. "What do you mean by that?"

"Stuff is gonna be all over the place."

"Where you sleep, I sleep."

He smiled. "Thought it could be romantic...if we sleep apart until Saturday."

"That's a long way away...five days."

"It's the only time we'll ever have to wait. Besides, I want to get this place fixed up for you. So, on Saturday...it'll be your home."

I wrapped my arm around his waist and moved closer into his side, my face pressed into his neck. "I'm so excited. I've never been so excited in my entire life."

TWENTY-THREE

HEATH

Balto taped the box of my clothes shut with duct tape then wrote on the side with permanent marker. *Asshole's clothes.*

I rolled my eyes. "I'll get you back for that someday."

"We aren't moving." He picked up the box and set it on the table.

"Really? Your son is never gonna play outside?" I picked up my box and set it next to his.

"Let me worry about my family, alright?" He wiped the sweat away from his forehead with the back of his arm. "We've got the clothes and essentials. What about the guns?"

"I'll leave most of them here."

"The furniture?"

"The place is already furnished."

"Alright. So, we just need to do Catalina's place?"

"Yeah."

"And then make a few repairs?"

We'd been working nonstop every day, getting the new place ready. I continued to sleep here—alone. It sucked, but it would be worth it on Saturday. "If you've got things to do, I can ask someone else."

"No. Just wanted to get our ducks in a row." He picked up another box and set it on top. "So, you're getting married on Saturday. Getting cold feet?"

I looked him in the eye after I straightened. "No."

"Everything's changing. You're moving, saying goodbye to this place, agreeing to have a woman at your side day in and day out..."

"Yes. I understood all of that when I asked her to marry me."

"It's a big commitment." He seemed to be testing me. "And we need to have a bachelor party."

"My whole life has been a fucking bachelor party."

He chuckled.

"So, did I pass?"

He grabbed his beer and took a drink, sweat stains on his t-shirt. "Yeah...looks like you did."

"I thought Damien was supposed to grill me?"

"It's my job too. Catalina is my little sister now." He leaned against the table, holding the bottle by the neck. "And I want to make sure you aren't making a mistake. You haven't known her long."

"Doesn't matter. I'm ready."

He gave me a grin. "Good. That's all I wanted to know."

BALTO WAS on his hands and knees, ripping up loose pieces of the floorboards to repair them in the entryway.

I removed the ancient paintings and hung the ones I'd asked Cassini to pick out, images of sunflowers on a beautiful landscape.

Cassini made us sandwiches and set them on the table. "She's going to love it when she sees it."

"I know." I was proud of the work I'd done all week, working around the clock to make this house suitable for her. When she saw it, her eyes lit up like Christmas morning. It made me proud, proud that I could give this to her after all the shitty things I'd done.

Cassini kneeled and placed his plate beside him. "Anything I can do to help?"

"No," he barked. "Just sit."

"I'm pregnant, not disabled," she argued.

"Sit," I said in agreement.

She rolled her eyes and took a seat at the dining table, eating the sandwich she'd made.

Balto took a bite but kept working.

Cassini stared at him. "I mean...it's pretty hot just watching you work."

He straightened to his knees and pulled his shirt over his head. Then he tossed it at her and kept working.

"Ooh...much better."

I tried to ignore their foreplay.

A knock sounded on the door.

"Expecting anyone?" Balto asked. "Catalina better not be peeking. We've still got shit to do."

I opened the door and came face-to-face with Damien. "Hey, what brings you here?" I hadn't spoken to him all week, not since the battle at my place. Things were better with him since Christmas, but after all that shit happened at my house, he might have had a change of heart. He'd been on the fence already.

He stepped inside the house, revealing his father behind him. "Wanted to see the place."

"Hello, sir." I extended my hand to shake his. "Come in."

He shook my hand but brushed off that comment. "Call me Richard."

"Alright." I dropped my hand and opened the door wider so they could come inside. "How is she?"

"Excited," Damien answered. "She's wearing my mother's dress, just made a few changes. She and Anna are having a good time together." He spoke normally, looking me in the eye without an underlying tone.

"I'm sure she'll be beautiful."

Richard walked inside and took a look around. "I see my daughter written all over these walls." He stopped at the picture on the wall, an image of sunflowers. He nodded in approval before he kept going.

Balto got to his feet and quickly pulled on his shirt. "Richard, I'm Balto." He shook his hand, being on his best behavior for her father.

Damien stood with his hands in his pockets, taking a look around, admiring the wooden staircase. "It's nice."

"Thanks. You want a tour?"

"Sure." I took him through the house, ending at the backyard where the greenhouse was.

He looked through the window then turned back to me. "She told me about this."

"It's a little small, but she—"

"It's perfect." He was in jeans and a jacket, his hands still in his pockets as he surveyed the yard. "She told me about the flowers..."

I didn't say anything.

"That's some pretty romantic shit."

I shrugged.

He went quiet, like he had nothing else to say.

Catalina would marry me in a few days, so I didn't feel obligated to kiss his ass or prove anything to him. He could take me as I was—or not. "Come here for that brother talk? You know, where you threaten to kill me if I ever do anything to hurt her?"

"No."

I raised an eyebrow.

"I've never seen Catalina so happy." He looked away for a while before he turned his gaze on me. "We've got a rough past, but...it's in the past. A motherfucker who grow flowers in a greenhouse just for her...can't be that bad."

My chest tightened, like that meant the world to me.

"And my father is really fond of you. Not exactly sure why. He's a hard man to impress."

He would never know the truth. "Because I kicked his ass at my first chess match."

He smiled slightly as he ran his fingers along his jawline. "Yeah, maybe that's it."

I crossed my arms over my chest.

"I think my mother would have liked you." The words came out of nowhere, and they carried so much weight, the weight of her spirit.

"Yeah?"

He nodded.

"And I think I like you too."

I dropped my gaze.

"I know you don't need my approval, but you have it...if you want it."

It'd been a long journey with Damien, a lot of shit-talking between two men who didn't put up with shit from anyone.

His blinding hatred had finally settled down, inexplicably. "What changed your mind?"

He stared at the ground below his feet for a few seconds before he answered. "Seeing how much she misses you when you aren't around."

TWENTY-FOUR

CATALINA

IT WAS THE NIGHT BEFORE MY WEDDING.

I sat across from my father, playing a competitive game of chess.

He watched me, his eyes burning into my face as he waited for me to make my move.

I let my fingers rest against my lips, considering the move, before I grabbed another piece and made a diagonal move.

He released a quiet sigh, as if he'd hoped I wouldn't have figured out the perfect opening. He grabbed his piece and moved it.

"So, Heath is a good player?"

He nodded. "Caught on quickly."

"He's a smart man."

"But you can still beat him, sweetheart. Don't let him win just because he's your husband."

Husband. Tomorrow, he would be my husband. "He wouldn't want me to let him win."

"Good. He seems that way."

"Is that why you like him?"

He shrugged. "Doesn't seem like a man who's easily intimidated—especially by a woman."

"He's not. What did you think of the house?"

"Beautiful. He's putting a lot of work into it."

My eyes softened. "I can imagine."

"It's nice to see a man use his bare hands instead of paying someone to do the hard work."

I moved my piece. "See the greenhouse?"

"Yes. It's perfect." He moved his piece.

I made the final blow. "Sorry, Dad. That's checkmate."

He sighed in annoyance. "I'll get you next time, sweetheart."

Damien came to our side. "Can I play the winner?"

"Yes." Dad finished the rest of his wine before he got to his feet. "I'm going to bed. See you in the morning." He patted his son on the back then kissed me on the cheek before he left.

We reset the board and started a new match.

Damien poured himself a glass of wine and drank it while I made my move. "I got engaged before you, but you're tying the knot before me."

"It's not a race, Damien."

He drank from his glass. "I know. Just saying…" He moved his piece. "I loved the house. It suits you perfectly."

"I know. He took me over there one day, and I couldn't believe he'd had it the whole time."

"Maybe he bought it for you."

"No, he said he won it in a poker match."

He chuckled. "Talk about a high-stakes game."

"How is he?" I hadn't talked to Heath much because he seemed busy. But I also suspected he wasn't contacting me frequently on purpose, because he wanted to make our day even more special.

"Fine." He moved his piece.

"I miss him…"

His eyes lifted to mine, a little soft. "Just one more day."

"Yeah, but it's already been five. It's torture."

"It'll make tomorrow worth it."

"Yeah…"

He made his next move. "Heath and I had a conversation."

I rolled my eyes. "If you're trying to scare off my husband, it's not gonna work."

"No," he said quietly. "I told him I approved of him."

I lifted my gaze. "Yeah?"

He nodded. "And I mean it."

"Damien…" My eyes softened.

"You know I'm stubborn, it's hard for me to let things go...but I've let it go. I think Mom would have liked him."

"Yes. And Dad loves him."

"He does. He wouldn't have taught his chess otherwise."

"Well, I'm glad you're on board... That makes me really happy." Now we forgot about the game altogether.

"I want you to be happy, and I can tell he really loves you."

"He does," I said with a smile. "He loves me as much as you do."

He smiled. "Probably more."

MY MOTHER'S dress was elegant, with long sleeves and a bow around the waist. It wasn't exactly my style, so I had the seamstress alter it until it was exactly what I would have wanted if I'd gone to a dress shop.

It didn't look exactly the same—but it was still my mother's dress.

Damien was in the driver's seat of his SUV, my father in the front seat. Anna sat beside me in the back.

We pulled up to the house. It was a sunny day, looking like summer even though it was just a clear day in January.

Heath stood out front, wearing a black suit, his hands in his pockets.

I'd only seen him in a suit one other time—and he looked just as yummy as he did now.

His eyes were on the car, looking at the tinted windows as he waited for me to get out. We'd agreed to meet at the greenhouse, but he obviously couldn't wait that long. His eyes were slightly squinted because the sun was in his face, and his brooding expression showed the emotion that penetrated his heart.

Balto and Cassini were near the door, his arm around her waist. He wore jeans and a long-sleeved shirt. Their eyes were on the car too.

Damien turned off the car. "I think he's waiting for you, sis."

I smiled and pushed the door open, slowly sliding to my feet until my mother's heels hit the driveway. The train of my white dress slid off the seat and to the ground. It had thin sleeves covering my shoulder, a deep neckline that showed the tops of my breasts like it was lingerie, and then it trailed to my feet, the slit high in the front so he could see my legs from the thighs down. It was a much sluttier version of my mother's dress.

When he inhaled a deep breath, it was obvious he liked it.

I took my time crossing the gravel so I wouldn't trip. When I reached the front walk, I steadied myself before I kept going.

Without blinking, he stared at me, his face so hard, he had no expression at all. But the emotion in his eyes caught a subtle glare because of the sun, because of the moisture that built up in his gaze.

I'd only seen him cry once—and that was when he'd lost me.

I couldn't take the long walk to him, couldn't stand the eternity that would take. So, I gathered my dress and ran to him, ran up the pathway right into his chest.

He pulled his hands out of his pockets as he came toward me, moving quickly like he couldn't wait either.

By the time I got to him, I was crying, ruining my makeup, ruining my hair. I jumped into his arms.

He caught me, his powerful arms sliding me to the ground so his hand could move into my hair, cup the back of my neck. He inhaled a deep breath as he kissed me, his other arm squeezing my waist as if he might break me in half like a twig. He didn't care about my family in the car. He kissed me like no one was there at all.

When he pulled away, he looked into my face with wet eyes, like he wanted to take a moment to study exactly how I looked, memorize the fire in my eyes, the emotion in the tremble of my lips.

I cupped his face, my thumbs brushing the two tears that streaked down his cheeks.

He brought his forehead to mine, bringing us closer together. He closed his eyes as he held me, closed his eyes as he breathed with me, held me like it was just the two of us. There didn't need to be a priest to read our vows, to make us husband and wife. Because we were husband and wife now... the second we touched.

AFTER DINNER, everyone left, like they knew they should leave us alone.

Balto hugged me before he stepped out with Cassini. "Welcome to the family, sis."

"Thanks, Balto."

He squeezed my hand before he walked out.

Damien embraced Heath with a hug instead of a handshake. "See you later."

"Thanks." Heath smiled as he clapped him on the back.

My dad kissed me on the cheek. "Your mother is so happy right now." He hugged me tightly, longer than he had in recent memory. "You're so beautiful, more beautiful than she was on our wedding day."

"I find that hard to believe...but thank you."

He turned to Heath next and hugged him the way he hugged my brother. "Come over whenever you get a chance. I want a rematch."

Heath chuckled. "You got it."

He gripped Heath by the shoulder before he walked out.

We watched them from the door, watched them get into their cars and drive away.

Heath shut the door, turning and pressing his back into it, like he wasn't going to let anyone else back through there. His hand moved to the lock, and he flipped it, the bolt clicking into place.

I smiled at him, watching the way he looked at me, like he couldn't wait to get this dress off me.

His eyes roamed over my body. "That dress...Jesus Christ." He pushed off the door and scooped me into his arms, cradling me to his chest as he walked to the stairs.

My arms moved around his neck, and I kissed him as he carried me, not wanting to wait until we were in the bedroom before we got started. I couldn't wait for this dress to slide to the floor, for my husband to look at me for the first time.

He carried me to the bedroom then set me on the bed.

I felt something against my ass, and that was when I noticed the sunflowers he'd placed there, like rose petals on a bed in the honeymoon suite. I grabbed one by the stem, brought it to my nose to smell it as I looked up at him.

He stripped off his jacket as he watched me, yanked off his tie, and destroyed his clothes in his haste like he had no intention of wearing them again. Then he lowered to his knees, his eyes level with mine. His hand moved to one foot, his fingers working the strap to get the heel off. With his eyes locked with mine, he did the other, his hands squeezing my bare feet when they were freed from the shoes.

My hands moved to his collared shirt, getting every button loose until I pushed it over his powerful shoulders, revealing the strong muscles and sexy ink underneath.

His left hand had my ring, the dark material matching the color of his tattoos. That was why I picked it, because I thought it would complement him so well.

"I want to take that dress off you." He pressed his forehead to mine, whispering to me. "But you look so beautiful...that I never want to take it off."

My fingers cupped his face, falling deeper in love with the most incredible man in the world. When I was in his cage, I'd never imagined anything like this would happen, that my captor was the man I would someday marry. "Then don't."

His hands reached under my dress and grabbed my white thong. He pulled it down once I lifted myself, getting it down my thighs and to my bare ankles. Then he looked down at my body, his eyes on my chest. "I just want to stay like this for a while...because I never want to forget this moment."

My fingers moved into his hair as our foreheads touched, my wedding ring glittering in the darkness. "Neither do I."

He stayed still, holding me on the bed, loving me with his touch, blanketing me with the kind of love no one else ever would. On his knees with his heart on his sleeve, he worshiped me, counted his blessings for having me, made me feel more beautiful than I'd ever had. "You're my soul mate..."

"I know..." I cradled the back of his head as we held each other.

The minutes ticked by.

There was no rush—because we had the rest of our lives.

EPILOGUE

The curtains closed.

Everyone rose to their feet and clapped.

Clint sat on my lap, his feet dangling over my knees.

I grabbed his hands and smacked them together. "Clap for Mommy." I pulled my hands away, and he did it on his own.

Marie sat on Grandpa's lap, and she threw her arms into the air. "Yay, Mommy!"

Richard smiled as he clapped.

The lights came on, the music over the speakers started, and I held Clint's hand as we walked down the aisle toward the entrance to the backstage area.

"I'm going to be a ballerina like Mom when I grow up," Marie said.

"Me too," Clint said.

I guided him backstage, weaving through the other dancers and cast members until I saw Catalina sitting at her vanity, her hair already down and her outfit changed. She spoke to Tracy, sharing a few laughs about something that had happened backstage that the audience had no idea about.

When Clint saw her, he dropped my hand and ran forward. "Mommy!" With his hands in the air, he ignored all the people around him and just did what he wanted.

I'd give him shit for taking off, but Catalina looked so happy to see him that I didn't think twice about it.

She turned around on the bench and picked up our son, pulling him close and smothering him with kisses. "Honey, I didn't know you were coming."

"We asked Daddy, and he said yes."

"Aww, how sweet." She kissed him on the cheek then hugged him tightly before putting him on the ground.

Marie came next. "When are you going to teach me how to dance?" She hopped into her lap to hug her.

"Let's get you some slippers tomorrow, and we'll start," she said. "How about that?"

"Okay," Marie said, her dark hair and green eyes making her the spitting image of her mother.

I was the last one she addressed because her love always went to the kids first. They were always the priority, and I was pushed to the bottom of the barrel. But at night when they were asleep, I was at the top of the list.

She got to her feet and embraced her father. "I'm so glad you came. The kids love you."

"Of course they do," he said. "I'm the best grandpa." He saw Marie grab her mother's makeup and start to plaster it on her face. "Marie, put that down." He walked to the vanity and pulled the things from her hands.

Now my wife finally came to me. "What a nice surprise." She moved into me, her arms circling my waist, and she rose on her tiptoes to kiss me.

"I missed you." My hand slid into her hair, and I spoke against her lips.

She closed her eyes and gave a gentle moan. "I missed you too..."

"Clint." Richard grabbed the lipstick out of his hand. "These are not crayons."

Clint had already permanently marked her vanity, because when Richard tried to wipe it off, it was stuck in the wood.

I ignored it because I was used to it by now. "Want to go out to dinner?"

"If my father will take the kids home..."

I kissed the corner of her mouth then looked into her face. "I wish he would take them out to dinner so we could go home..."

"Well, I'm sure there's a dark alleyway somewhere."

I smiled as I looked at her. "That's my baby."

ALSO BY PENELOPE SKY

I hoped you enjoyed the Betrothed Series as much as I enjoyed writing. Heath and Catalina are so close to my heart, the love and intensity they have for one another. If you're anxious for another read, I have something else in the pipeline...and I think you'll be excited about it.

I wrote this story BEFORE Buttons and Lace and came across it recently. It has a closer resemblance to Buttons than my other novels, and my main man is more similar to Crow than my other anti-heros. I rewrote a few things, but it really is an exceptional story. Very dark like Buttons, but even darker than that. It's a thrilling adventure, and the way these two characters come together is complicated, defiant, and unique. I'm very proud of it.

You can order it now!

I've been taking care of my little sister for a long time. When Mom was gone, she suddenly became my responsibility. The best years of my life were spent being a caretaker to someone else...with no one to take care of me.

So I moved to Paris for my study-abroad program and ended up staying, getting a French Literature degree, studying the classics while sipping the best wine I'd ever had.

My sister never makes the best decisions, always makes messes to clean up, and it's finally time for me to have my own life.

But when she comes to Paris for a visit...she brings trouble with her.

She gets herself into a bad situation, and of course, I come to her rescue...like I always do.

Now we're in a labor camp in the middle of nowhere, surrounded by endless snow and mountains, processing drugs for a group of men that never show their faces. There's no chance of escape in this wilderness.

Except for my guard.

He's not a saint, but he's the only man that's kind to me. He knows I want to escape, but he never reports me. When I've had a hard day, he brings me extra things to make my life easier. He tells me not to run because I'll never make it...but he brings me little hidden tools...as if he's giving me the means.

Like he wants me to be free.

<u>Order Now</u>

Printed in Great Britain
by Amazon

29850339R00193